THE ODOR
OF VIOLETS

BAYNARD KENDRICK (1894-1977) was one of the founders of the Mystery Writers of America, later named a Grand Master by the organization. After returning from military service in World War I, Kendrick wrote for pulp magazines such as *Black Mask* and *Dime Detective* under various pseudonyms before creating the Duncan Maclain character for which he is now known. The blind detective appeared in twelve novels, several short stories, and three films.

OTTO PENZLER, the creator of American Mystery Classics, is also the founder of the Mysterious Press (1975); Mysterious-Press.com (2011), an electronic-book publishing company; and New York City's Mysterious Bookshop (1979). He has won a Raven, the Ellery Queen Award, two Edgars (for the *Encyclopedia of Mystery and Detection*, 1977, and *The Lineup*, 2010), and lifetime achievement awards from NoirCon and *The Strand Magazine*. He has edited more than 70 anthologies and written extensively about mystery fiction.

THE ODOR
OF VIOLETS

BAYNARD
KENDRICK

Introduction by
OTTO
PENZLER

AMERICAN
MYSTERY
CLASSICS

Penzler Publishers
New York

Published in 2021 by Penzler Publishers
58 Warren Street, New York, NY 10007
penzlerpublishers.com

Distributed by W. W. Norton

Cover image: Andy Ross
Cover design: Mauricio Diaz

Paperback ISBN 978-1-61316-204-0
Hardcover ISBN 978-1-61316-203-3
eBook ISBN 978-1-61316-205-7

Library of Congress Control Number: 2021901082

Printed in the United States of America

9 8 7 6 5 4 3 2

INTRODUCTION

ONE OF the most beloved characters from the Golden Age of detective fiction and beyond was Duncan Maclain, a tall, dark, strikingly handsome, and immaculately dressed and groomed former intelligence officer who moves with astonishing ease and self-assurance in spite of his total blindness.

Although injured while serving in World War I, Mclain has been able, through ceaseless effort, to master his handicap by developing his other senses. He turned to the profession of private detective—and has found that his resources have been challenged to their utmost but his tenacity has brought him success.

Maclain lives in a penthouse apartment twenty-six stories above 72nd Street and Riverside Drive on Manhattan's Upper West Side. His hobbies are reading (in Braille), listening to music on his phonograph records, and assembling jigsaw puzzles, which he does by fingering a piece and then searching for its companion. He has taught himself to shoot, guided only by sound. He is assisted at the detective agency by his best friend and partner, Spud Savage, his secretary Rena, who is married to

Spud, and his two seeing-eye dogs, the gentle Schnucke and the not so gentle Dreist.

Captain Mclain is the creation of Baynard Kendrick, one of the giants of the American Golden Age of detective fiction. Choosing a blind detective was no mere whim but the nearly inevitable result of his military service.

In World War I, Kendrick was the first American to enlist in the Canadian Army—exactly one hour after that country declared war—and served in the Canadian Expeditionary Forces. When he visited a hospitalized fellow Philadelphian who had been blinded in battle, he met a blind British soldier who had the remarkable ability to tell Kendrick things about himself that exceeded what a sighted person might have known. The experience impressed him and eventually enabled him to create a believable, if somewhat idealized, blind character.

During World War II, Kendrick was a consultant to the staff of the Old Farms Convalescent Hospital for Blinded Veterans (for a dollar a year).

Long interested in the problems of the blind, Kendrick was an acknowledged expert on the subject. He once served as the only sighted advisor to the Blinded Veterans Association and was its organizer and chairman of its board of directors. He held honorary life membership card number one and received a plaque for this work from General Omar Bradley in July 1940.

Kendrick's experiences provided him with the source material for his series hero, Captain Duncan Mclain, and for a non-mystery novel, *Lights Out* (1945), which was filmed as *Bright Victory* (1951), a romantic drama set during World Warr II about a soldier blinded by a German sniper; it was directed by Mark Robson and starred Arthur Kennedy, who was nominated for an Academy Award, and Peggy Dow.

One of the founding members of the Mystery Writers of America, Kendrick carried membership card number one. He served as the organization's first president and was named a Grand Master in 1967.

Kendrick was born in Philadelphia in 1894 and educated at the Tom School, Port Deposit, Maryland, and the Episcopal Academy, Philadelphia. He married Edythe Stevens in 1919 and, following her death, married Jean Morris in 1971. He traveled extensively in Europe and the Middle East and lived in almost every part of the United States. A lawyer and certified public accountant, he had several jobs in the business world before becoming a full-time writer in 1932. His first mystery novel, *Blood on Lake Louisa*, was published in 1934 and the majority of his subsequent fiction was in the same genre.

That first novel was a stand-alone mystery that was followed by a couple of novels featuring Kendrick's first series character, Miles Standish Rice, *The Iron Spiders* (1936) and *The Eleven of Diamonds* (1936), who also was the hero of fourteen stories that appeared in *Black Mask*, the most prestigious pulp magazine in the detective fiction world, between 1937 and 1942. Rice, generally known as Stan, worked as a private detective who, uncharacteristically for P.I.s in this era, had a close relationship with the police. Earlier, he had been a deputy sheriff in Florida, where all the stories are set. The third and final novel in which Rice appears is *Death Beyond the Go-Thru* (1938), but by then Kendrick had created Captain Duncan Maclain, who became a more popular crimefighter.

The first novels in which Maclain and his service dogs, Schnucke and Dreist, appear are *The Last Express* (1937), *The Whistling Hangman* (1938), and *The Odor of Violets* (1941), which is regarded by many as his finest book. It was reissued several times under the title *Eyes in the Night*, the title of the 1942 film that featured Edward Arnold as Maclain, Ann Harding as Norma Lawry, and Donna Reed as Barbara Lawry. Schnucke was renamed Friday for the film, which was directed by Fred Zinneman.

Intended to be a long-running series of detective movies following the success of *Eyes in the Night*, M-G-M made a sequel, *The Hidden Eye* (1945), also starring Arnold, but it did not do well at the box office and the series idea was abandoned.

The tone of Kendrick's novel was darker than most of his work, no doubt due to the fact that the world was at the brink of war and the book combined the pulp-inspired tropes of the hard-boiled private eye story with a spy story, which are seldom light-hearted—and certainly not with the reality of war in the air. Maclain's career as a licensed private investigator make him an ideal choice to work in United States Intelligence when the threat of Nazi spies and their plots of sabotage are suspected.

Although *The Odor of Violets* is a genuine whodunit, its plotting has its roots in the pulp fiction magazines of the time, with a protagonist who has many of the characteristics of such pulp heroes as Doc Savage. Not only is Maclain highly intelligent, but his other faculties have been so profoundly enriched that they appear other-worldly. Add to that his highly attractive physical appearance and his ability to easily dispatch adversaries in fights, and he becomes as close to a super-hero as the Golden Age detective can be.

In all, Kendrick wrote twelve novels about Duncan Maclain but they have been largely forgotten and out of print for many decades. The television series *Longstreet*, which ran for twenty-four episodes in 1971-1972, was created by Stirling Silliphant and starred James Franciscus as Mike Longstreet (an identical twin to Maclain), and Marlyn Mason as Nikki Bell, his secretary. Kendrick is given acknowledgment for his work as the inspiration for the Longstreet character, but some difficulties in the negotiations did not permit Paramount Television or ABC to use the Maclain name as the title.

—OTTO PENZLER

FOREWORD

THE FIRST short story ever written about my blind detective character, Captain Duncan Maclain, appeared in *Ellery Queen's Mystery Magazine* in January 1953 (there has only been one other, which also appeared in *Ellery Queen's*). That was more than fifteen years after the first full-length mystery, *The Last Express*, about Captain Maclain, who was a fictional U.S. Army officer blinded at Messines in World War I. It was published by the Crime Club in 1937. Following is the introduction to this short story, written by Frederic Dannay, co-writer with his cousin, Manfred B. Lee, under the pseudonym "Ellery Queen," who, like this writer, is one of the Grand Masters of the Mystery Writers of America, Inc.:

> Ernest Bramah is generally credited with having invented the first modern blind detective, Max Carrados, but the most famous exponent in the contemporary field of blind detection is, without doubt, Captain Duncan Maclain, created by Baynard Kendrick. Mr. Kendrick acknowledges that it was the earlier blind detective who started him writing about Maclain—but for curious reasons . . . in Mr. Kendrick's opinion, Max Carrados had very strange powers that went far beyond the limits of credibility. For

example, Carrados could run his fingertips along the surface of a newspaper, feel the infinitesimal height of the printer's ink over the paper itself, and "read" any type larger than long primer. Mr. Kendrick questions that feat, and we must say we are inclined to side with Mr. Kendrick....

Indeed, Mr. Kendrick found it so difficult to swallow Max Carrados's supersensory accomplishments that he determined to create a blind detective of his own—a completely believable sleuth who could deduce by touch, hearing, taste, and smell, with no reliance whatever either on sight or sixth sense. And the simple truth of the matter is that while Baynard Kendrick has spent fifteen years of his life unearthing extraordinary things done by the totally blind, he has never had his blind detective do anything which he, Kendrick, had not actually seen done by a living blind man, or had fully authenticated.

When it came to developing the character of Duncan Maclain, Mr. Kendrick again went to the highest authority—real life. He patterned the character of Maclain on that of a real person—a young blind soldier in St. Dunstan's Home in London, who by touching the emblems on Kendrick's own uniform, accurately traced four years of Kendrick's Army career.

Canada declared war on Germany on August 8, 1914, four days after Great Britain. I was living in a boardinghouse in Windsor, Ontario, across the river from Detroit, and left a lunch table to go downtown to the Armory and enlist. So far as can be ascertained I was the first American to join up with the Canadian forces in World War I. After a few weeks' training at Valcartier, Quebec, I became No. 6468, Private Kendrick, B.H., 1st Battalion, 1st Brigade, No. 1 company in No. 1 Section. Since even then I was six feet two inches, I was the tallest man in my company and became flank man on the line. This was a hair-raising experience inasmuch as I was forced to pace 33,000 men in a review before Sir Sam Hughes, of whom the Canadians gleefully sang, to the tune of "John Peel": "Do you ken Sam Hughes, the enemy of booze. The first champeen of the dry canteen. And the camp so dead you have to go to bed, but you won't have a head in the morning."

The first expeditionary force sailed from Gaspe Bay on the twenty-first of September and the 1st Battalion of 1,200 men was on board the White Star liner *Laurentic*. Thirty-three ocean liners crossed in that convoy in three rows of eleven each—the largest convoy to that date that the world had ever dreamed of or seen. There was certainly no tinge of patriotic fervor in my enlistment. I was twenty years old and the idea of putting an ocean between me and Detroit, where I had once been arrested for vagrancy for sleeping out in Grand Circuit Park, and drawing $1.10 a day plus food and clothes and medical expenses looked like paradise.

If this autobiographical prologue seems prolix and redundant I will have to plead guilty as I put it here for just one purpose— to make the point that not until 1917 when I was twenty-three and blindness confronted me face to face, had I ever given it a passing thought. By that time I had served in France, Egypt, and Salonica and had spent over two years in army hospitals. Subconsciously, I believe, like ninety-nine percent of the people in the world, I blotted the condition from my mind beyond relegating it to the shadowy realm of the tin cup, pencil, and street-corner school.

In the winter of 1917, when I had been marked "C-3" by a medical board (light duty), I was stationed in London working as a pay sergeant in the Canadian Pay Office at 7 Millbank. There, quite by accident, I learned that a boy with whom I had gone to school in Philadelphia had joined up with the Canadians a year after I did. I'll call him Paul Henderson, which was not his name. He had been blinded at Vimy Ridge several months before and at that moment was in St. Dunstan's Lodge, the hospital for blinded soldiers in London.

I took to visiting St. Dunstan's in Regents Park regularly on Saturday afternoons to have tea and play the piano. Once having overcome my initial ingrained fear of the blind, I continued these visits for many months after Paul Henderson had been invalided back to Canada and resumed his U.S. citizenship—as I did later, in December 1918. It was on one such visit that Captain Duncan Maclain was born, although I had no inkling of it at the moment and it was twenty years later—in 1937—before he came to life in print in *The Last Express*. The conditions at St. Dunstan's for the training and welfare of the blind—while modern for World War I—seemed antiquated when compared to Valley Forge, Dibble, or Avon Old Farms. Mobility was given little thought and the grounds of St. Regents Park were festooned with strings for the blinded veterans to follow, and knots marked the benches. When I was visiting there the lodge was so overcrowded with veterans and personnel that it had been necessary to move the piano out in the hall. There was little amusement since radio and talking books were unheard of—the big moments came when some noted entertainer, such as Sir Harry Lauder, Sir George Robey, or Alfred Lester, dropped in for an evening from one of the music halls.

It was on a blustery, freezing December afternoon in 1917 when I first became conscious of the fact that while a blind man might have lost his sight, he hadn't necessarily lost his mind. I had seated myself at the piano and given my usual introduction by leading off with "Tipperary" and the coterie of blinded British Tommies quickly gathered around me. There was just one straightback chair to the right of the piano next to double doors in the vestibule (always closed since a rear entrance was used) that led out onto the grounds. I had shed my cap and greatcoat and put them on that chair.

The Tommies were packed in almost solidly around me and one British Tommy was standing with his hands lightly on my shoulders while I went through half a dozen pieces. When I had finished and some requests were made, he moved around to the right of the piano, picked up my cap and greatcoat from the chair, sat down and laid them across his knees. I noticed while I was playing that he was giving them a thorough going-over with his fingertips ("brailling," although it turns a noun into a verb, has become the common term today).

A bell rang and I was suddenly deserted by my captive audience as they poured into an adjoining lounge for afternoon tea. Only the Tommy to the right of the piano remained. He stood up, replacing my cap and greatcoat on the chair, and started in with a preamble, as though something had been burned into his brain.

Then he said: "You certainly have been around in the Canadian army, haven't you? You've been in nearly every bleeding outfit in it. You came over here in nineteen fourteen with the First Battalion, went out to France with them, were invalided back here to England and then joined up with the Fourth General Hospital from Toronto and went out to Salonica with them. You were invalided back from Salonica through Egypt and landed back here at Netley Fever Hospital at Southampton—that big pile of bricks with the corridors a quarter of a mile long.

"When you were discharged from Netley you went to 134 Shorncliffe to the C.C.A.C. [Canadian Casualty Assembly Center]. There you faced another medical board which marked you

'C-3' and transferred you to the Canadian Army Service Corps on light duty instead of sending you back to Canada as you had hoped. When they found out that you couldn't even lift a Ford motor, let alone carry one around on each shoulder, the sergeant in charge of the machine shop kicked to the C.O. that he was tired of being sent walking corpses marked 'C-3.' So they sent you up to this cushy job with the Canadian Army Pay Corps here in London where you will stay for the duration of the war."

I stood with my mouth hanging open, staring at him intently until I was positive that I had never seen him before. Then I blurted out, "I suppose you got all this dope from Paul Henderson who was invalided back to Canada from here a couple of months ago."

"Never heard of him," he said smugly. "He was before my time. I have only been in here just over a couple of weeks. I was blinded in the big tank push at Cambrai."

"Then where the hell did you know me and get all my army history? You sound like you had taken it from a sheet in the Canadian Record Office."

"I don't know you, never saw you, and never will," he grinned delightedly. "Sir Arthur Pearson spoke to us here last week about how much a blind man can really see. I decided to try it out on you. Your army history that I just gave you is written all over your uniform."

I took a closer look at his heavily bandaged eyes and decided that even if he had some vision left, it was obvious that he couldn't see. "Okay," I said. "Start at the beginning and spell it out. I'm certainly listening."

"Well, first," he said, "you have blue shoulder straps sewed on the khaki ones on your tunic."

"Blue?"

"Sure, you're wearing brass C-1's—that is a 'C' with a bar under it and a '1' attached underneath. That was your original unit, the First Battalion of Infantry, and all the infantry in the first contingent in nineteen fourteen wears those blue shoulder straps. The Medical Corps wears red. You were invalided back from France because you have a gold perpendicular wound stripe on your sleeve. Right?"

"Right! Go on."

"Well, the metal bars on each of those blue shoulder straps just read Canada in raised letters so the infantry was your original unit. Now, take your greatcoat. It has just the regular khaki shoulder straps but the bars on each shoulder are cut out CAMC, running from back to front, and easy to feel. Over them you have 'four' with a small bar over a 'G' in brass. That shows you were overseas with the Fourth General Hospital. It came from Toronto and was the only unit from the Canadian Army which was out in Salonica. I'm no wizard but I happened to have had a cousin who was with the same outfit, the Fourth General Hospital, and most of the men from Salonica were invalided back with fever through Egypt. So I took a guess that the same thing happened to you. All the men invalided back to England from anywhere with fevers end up in Netley and then at the C.C.A.C. at Shorncliffe. But the badge on the front of your cap is Canadian Army Service Corps, indicating that was the last unit you were transferred to here in England. My cousin went through that light duty routine, only they sent him out to France again driving a lorry. Now, I know you're stationed up here in London with a permanent pass since you are up here nearly every Saturday afternoon, playing the piano. You have sergeant's stripes on your greatcoat so I imagine you're working as a pay sergeant in the Canadian Pay Office. They have no emblem of their own."

Just then, an orderly stopped in from somewhere to collect him for tea, leaving me too dumbfounded even to inquire his name. He left me with a happy smile and a wave of his hand saying, "I'll be seeing you." He never did, of course, and I never saw him again. It was after New Year's of 1918 the next time I went up to St. Dunstan's and my blind detective had gone.

It was ten years later (1927) before I came in contact with Paul Henderson again.

My father died in Philadelphia in January 1927. Banks had already closed in Florida and our family savings were going fast while I fiddled around without much success at writing. But I had tasted blood because *Field and Stream* had bought my first short story, "The Captain's Lost Lake," in 1926 for $60. I hastened up to Philadelphia from Florida to see what could be salvaged from my father's business and the day after his funeral, Mrs. Henderson, Paul's mother, phoned me to say that she had seen the notice of my father's death in the newspapers. She told me her own husband had died five years before. She and Paul were still living in the old family house on Queen Lane in Germantown, and could I come to dinner. I sensed desperation in her voice and went out to see them the following evening—a filthy snowy night.

The house was a mausoleum, housing a frail invalid already feeling the effects of a cancer which killed her in 1930, and her blind, thirty-one-year-old son, who hadn't been out of the house since his father's death, five years before. The dinner was meager but by the time it was served none of us much cared—the bootlegger had made a delivery earlier and the orange blossom cocktails had flowed freely.

Paul's mother, through ignorance, fear, and too much love, did practically everything for him except take him to the toilet. It helped turn Paul into an alcohol-soaked cabbage with nothing to do but sit and look at the back of his eyes and curse at the fictional Max Carrados and his fictional supernatural powers. Paul was too frightened to move from the house that had become the only world he knew—and his mother, through misdirected love, encouraged his indolence.

I sold out the Trades Publish Company that belonged to my father and went to New York, where I obtained a job as general manager of Bing & Bing Hotels. Within three months after his mother died in 1930, Paul Henderson sold the heavily mortgaged house in Germantown and sobered up long enough to catch a train to New York—purely because I was there. He hoped that I could get him a job—at anything, even making brooms. God knows I tried! But I soon realized that Paul had lost all interest in life, and I dreaded the tenth of every month when his small pension check would arrive. He'd disappear from the room I had gotten for him on Bank Street in Greenwich Village and make the rounds of speakeasies where kindly but misguided customers would buy him drinks when his money ran out. I started to think it might be better for him if he were a troublemaker and created a disturbance so the police could pick him up and tuck him safely away long enough to get off the booze. It took me more than a year to enlist the aid of enough friendly bartenders who would call me as soon as he came in.

The Depression caught me full in 1932 and I was laid off with twenty other administrative office workers a week before Christmas—facing a world that seemed utterly jobless. I determined at that moment that I'd never work for a corporation again and I'd succeed at writing or starve to death trying. I rented an apartment for $25 a month in a basement in Astoria and started my first full-length book—a Florida mystery called *Blood on Lake Louisa*. Paul moved in with me two months later and on and off for a year we existed on what short unsigned pieces I could sell to *The New Yorker* and *Liberty*. I established a moderate credit rating at a nearby friendly Italian grocery and ate so much spaghetti that I finally broke out with a wheat rash. During this time, I sought out a great deal of material regarding famous blind people and read about them to Paul. I hoped that some of their accomplishments would inspire him, but I eventually realized that Paul had slipped into his own private paranoiac world—identifying with Max Carrados, using liquor to bolster confidence that he could duplicate the impossible feats of Ernest Bramah's overdrawn character. Paul would also challenge the accomplishments of blind persons with a negative approach that defied argument, such as claiming that John Milton "was educated at Cambridge, besides being an established poet before he went blind at forty-four."

By 1932 I had reached the point of utter desperation with Paul and made an attempt to convince him that someone with even more severe handicaps than his could do something productive. I finally succeeded, through my agent, in getting in touch with Mr. John A. Macy, whose wife was the famous Anne Mansfield Sullivan who had trained Helen Keller. Mr. Macy was quite ill and died several months later, in August 1932, but the lengthy letter I wrote his wife interested her enough to furnish me with a list of famous blind people—and in reply to my complaints about Max Carrados, she wrote me: "You're a mystery writer . . . so why not draw on the knowledge that you've accumulated and create a blind detective of your own—one who would be the antithesis of Max Carrados, who would never perform any feat in his detection or deduction that couldn't be duplicated by someone totally blind—presuming they had the necessary brains and willpower to train themselves to try it."

Thus the idea of Captain Duncan Maclain was born. It was in 1937 that the Crime Club published the first of the books about him, *The Last Express*. For forty years he has served me well—in serialization, syndication, movies, and foreign editions. He's responsible for the organization of the Mystery Writers of America, Inc., and for the Blinded Veterans Association—formed at Avon Old Farms Army Schools of the Blind at Avon, Connecticut, in 1945, in which I hold honorary life membership Card No. 1. Even today, if you sit up late enough and watch the third repeat of *Longstreet* on ABC, you can see that the series is based on "Characters Created by Baynard Kendrick."

Speaking to the B.V.A. on the occasion of their twenty-first annual convention at the Deauville Hotel, Miami Beach, Florida, on August 20, 1966, I was asked by one of the members if I happened to remember the name of that young blind soldier in St. Dunstan's Home in London who through his perspicacity had quite unwittingly been the progenitor of the B.V.A. I was forced to say no—I hadn't forgotten his name for I never knew it; he was merely one of a number of blinded British Tommies ensconced for the time being in St. Dunstan's.

I intended to call this piece "The Birth of a Blind Detective" because, to me, Captain Duncan Maclain was really born—and I hope will live forever—showing to sighted people that although the blind of the world may have lost their eyes, their brains and their work live on.

—BAYNARD KENDRICK

THE ODOR
OF VIOLETS

CHAPTER I

The Crags was built high up on an eminence above the little town of Tredwill Village, west of Hartford, in the Connecticut hills. Ordinarily, the tall buildings of the city could be seen from the Tredwill home. Now, even the few scattered houses in the village below were hidden from view.

Norma Tredwill (Mrs. Thaddeus Tredwill, number four) sat down at the top of the stairs on a broad window seat and looked out through the mullioned panes. Her warm red lips, always ready to part in humor or sympathy, were pensively set. She stared through the frost-marked glass at the swirling snow, oblivious of the storm.

She was thinking of Paul Gerente. Ten years before, she had put him out of her life completely, determined to forget a year of marriage to him which had been nothing more than a short, unhappy episode in her career.

A step sounded down the hall. Norma stood up just as her stepdaughter, Barbara, came out of her room. Babs was wearing a trim tailor-made suit and carrying a mink coat over her arm. She was the only one of the Tredwill family who had never quite accepted Norma into the Tredwill home. For three years, Norma had vainly tried to break down the barrier between them, a barrier which was never apparent on the surface, but which Babs, in a thousand small ways, managed to make smartingly real.

"You're up early, darling," Babs said with a smile.

The politeness was always there, deference even, but it came through too readily to be genuine. Babs's tenderness was as apt as some adroit line of an author's spotted in a play.

Norma said: —

"You're up early yourself, Babs."

"The weather, probably. Are you coming down? It's a filthy day."

"I certainly agree." Norma looked at the coat on Babs's arm. "Don't tell me you're planning on going out! The wind will blow you away."

"New York," said Babs. "It's Stacy's idea. Christmas is on Monday. If we don't get in today, there'll be no presents for our darling father and you."

Norma refused to be piqued by Babs's tone. "Why not Hartford, if you simply must? It's not so far away."

"Stacy has something special picked out for Thad—and Cheli Scott too, I suppose. Leave it to my fifteen-year-old brother." Babs spoke with all the languid disparagement of an eighteen-year-old for one three years her junior. "It's New York, I'm afraid." She started down the stairs.

Inwardly, Norma sighed. Another conversation with Babs was ending in the usual way, bright and friendly up to a point. Beyond that they never seemed to go.

"Run along if you've a train to catch," said Norma. "Are you taking the coupé?"

Babs turned on the stairs and nodded absently. "Stacy's driving us into Hartford. We'll leave it at a garage near the station.

We're going to spend the night in New York with the Ritters and be back tomorrow. I don't think this snow can last another day."

Norma watched Babs descend the stairs. The girl's youthful beauty was almost too perfect, like a picture done in tints too bright,—gold and white, rose and blue,—which time might fade. Such coloring needed vivacity behind it, but Babs smoldered almost sulkily.

"The Tredwill men have all the temperament," Norma thought. Thad's two sons, Gilbert, twenty-eight, and Stacy, fifteen, though separated widely in years, were much alike. They were quick to laugh, constantly enthusiastic about something, although their cause might change in a day. Thaddeus himself had all the ingrained egoism of a genius. He ruled his house and his family capriciously, and sometimes noisily, but back of his heated displays of temper he looked at life with a humorous glint in his eye.

Norma heard Cheli Scott greet Babs downstairs. Cheli was a playwright, and Thad's protégée. She was working on a new play which Thad wanted to try out in his own small theater, an integral part of The Crags. The house always seemed more pleasant and alive when Cheli was a visitor. Norma liked gaiety and laughter, and Cheli was friendly and amusing—a delightful, considerate girl.

For a moment Norma listened, then she left her post at the head of the stairs and started slowly toward her own apartment at the end of the hall. In front of Babs's open door, she paused and stood indecisively looking in upon the disordered scene.

Babs depended on servants to keep the material articles of living in their proper places. Fastidious about her own appearance, she left behind her a limp trail of dresses, underwear, and stockings. The three-mirror dressing table was a jumble of make-up jars and glittering crystal bottles. Norma stepped inside and closed the door with a feeling of guilty intrusion.

At the back of the dressing table was a crystal bottle of unusual design. It was larger than the rest, and obviously new. The stopper of black, cunningly wrought glass was so skillfully made that it gave an illusion of an exotic black flower, slightly evil, thrust into the bottle by its stem. Colored cellophane had been rolled down to encircle the base of the bottle. The slim *flacon* rose out of it with an appearance of naked beauty, as though it were some tiny woman of glass who had dropped her dress to the floor.

Norma felt a slight touch of faintness, and sat down on the rose-cushioned bench in front of the dressing table. The triple mirror showed her piquant face pale above the blue satin of her house coat. The tiny freckle over the dimple in her left cheek glowed brightly, as it always did when she was perturbed.

Automatically she took her vanity case from the pocket of her house coat and touched her cheeks with rouge. She snapped the jeweled case shut and returned it to her pocket. The perfume bottle was possessed with magnetism of memories. Twice she reached out to touch it, but forced herself to keep her hands away.

She suddenly knew what had brought Paul Gerente back to mind. Ten minutes earlier, on her interrupted trip to breakfast, she had glimpsed that seventy-five-dollar bottle of Black Orchid through Babs's partly opened door.

That single glimpse had swept ten years away. The gift of a similar bottle had begun Paul's courtship. Norma smiled a trifle bitterly. A bottle of the same Black Orchid had ended her marriage to Paul. She had seen it in the bedroom of another woman, and there had been others, too. Paul Gerente had distributed his Black Orchid tokens of affection as liberally as his charm.

Norma made a slight *moue* of distaste at her reflection in the mirror, then stood up and left the room. She did not intend to allow a fantastically incredible idea to run away with her natural good judgment. Paul Gerente, once a famous stage name, had dropped out of sight after she divorced him. There had been various unsubstantiated rumors that he had lost his money in the market and taken to drink. Past association was flimsy evidence on which to base an assumption; just because Babs had an unusual bottle of expensive perfume was no indication that she was seeing Paul.

The house was very silent. Norma stopped again at the top of the stairway. From below she heard Cheli Scott say goodbye. Cheli's words were followed by the opening and closing of the front door and the whine of the starter as Stacy started the coupé. Norma waited until the clank of chains in gravel and snow told her that the car was gone before she went downstairs.

Cheli, brilliant in a suit of red velvet pajamas, was curled up in the depths of a great armchair in front of the blazing log fire in the living room. She looked up from the pages of a manuscript, brushed back thick brown curls to disclose a smile in her blue-gray eyes, and said, "Cheerio, sleepy-head! How do you like the snow?"

"I think it makes me hungry," Norma told her. "Have you and the rest raided the larder completely, or is there anything left for me?"

"Sausage and scrambled eggs in the hot plate," said Cheli. "Coffee in the Silex, and cornbread and rolls in the warmer."

"It's probably far too much." Norma walked in toward the silver-laden sideboard visible through the open folding doors and added from the adjoining room, "At my age, I have to keep a checkrein on my waistline. Thad has a producer's eye for bulges in the wrong place. I want to keep that 'You ought to be on the stage, my dear!' expression on his face when he looks at me."

"At your age!" Cheli laughed softly and rustled a page of her manuscript. "The sight of that skin of yours and your figure simply infuriates me. You're the irritating type that makes aging debutantes sore. You'll never look more than twenty-two."

Norma served herself, poured a cup of coffee, and carried her breakfast into the living room, where she settled herself at Cheli's feet on a bearskin rug. "Christmas compliments!" she told Cheli. "They always crop up around the theater about the twentieth of December, but they're still good, I suppose. You make me feel ready to buy you a new fur coat or a Buick sedan."

She sipped her coffee. "Have you seen Gil this morning?"

The blazing fire touched spots of color on the cheeks of the girl in the chair. "He had to go into New York," said Cheli, reading intently. "He took an early train. Helena and Thaddeus went with him. How come they didn't take you?"

Norma placed her cup and saucer and plate on the hearth. "Maybe my ears are deceiving me," she exclaimed lightly. "I knew Gil and Helena were going—but Thad! Big things must be brewing when my late-sleeping husband hauls himself out into the early morning snow." She tried the sausage and eggs and found them good. "I'm glad he didn't want me to go. He's a bear before eleven. I'm afraid the combination of an early train trip with Thad and Helena—" She ended on a vague note, feeling that she might have said too much already.

Pierce, the butler, gray in Thaddeus's service, came in and said apologetically, "Good morning, madam. I didn't know you had come down. Mr. Tredwill left a note for you."

He stepped soft-footed into the hall and returned with the note on a silver tray. Norma smiled. Under Thaddeus's training,

Pierce could have fitted unchanged into any butler's role in movie or play.

"I'm a bad hostess, Pierce." She opened the note and read it as the butler cleared her breakfast things away.

"Late sleeping is to be excused on such a day," said Pierce with his slow, half-quizzical smile. "More coffee, madam?"

Norma shook her head. Thad's typical note had left her with a glow. *"I love you, my dear! You are life to me and all its possessions— yet today I must go! Forgive me if I do not return until tomorrow. You can reach me at the Waldorf-Astoria. Thad."*

Cheli resumed the conversation as Pierce went into the dining room. Sometimes her frankness was disconcerting. "You don't like Gilbert's wife, do you?"

"Helena?" Norma gave an embarrassed laugh. "Perhaps it would be nearer the truth if you said she doesn't like me."

"I wonder if she likes anyone except herself." Cheli spread the manuscript over the arm of her chair. "That includes Gil. What nationality is she, Norma? She's a mystery to me."

"French, I believe. It's hard to say. She speaks so many languages fluently. The only thing I know is that Gil met her in Washington at the French Embassy."

Norma left her place on the rug and picked up a morning paper from the settee. The conversation was becoming difficult. She disliked discussing the members of Thad's family. Quick to take a hint, Cheli turned to her manuscript again.

The paper was opened to the theatrical page, telling her that Thad had read it over his early morning coffee. She glanced idly at a syndicated column headed, "Rialto Rumors." For a brief instant the room became unbearably warm. She sat down on the settee and smoothed the paper out over her knees.

"A familiar figure, too long absent from Broadway, was seen

at Ronni's 41 Club," the column stated. "He was accompanied by an exquisite creature whom your correspondent identified as the daughter of a grand old master of productions. It would be interesting if Paul Gerente resumed his interrupted stage career by marrying into his ex-wife's family."

Norma sat quietly for a long time staring into the flames. Finally she said, "I hate to leave you alone here today, but I think I'll go into Hartford, Cheli."

"Don't mind me. I'm up to my ears in work."

Norma stood up. There was a train to New York from Hartford at three-thirty. She could catch another one back during the evening. It would give her a few hours in New York—all she needed.

"I may have dinner with friends in Hartford," she said. A cold lump was pressing her throat inside, making it difficult to speak or breathe. If Thad had seen that item—! "He can't have seen it," she assured herself silently. "He'd have spoken about it to me." She dismissed as foolish a quick idea that she might talk with Babs. The girl was too young, too self-centered, to see anything but Paul's charm—to know what such gossip would do to Thad. There was only one course open. It was dangerous to a point where it might wreck her marriage, but she had to take it. She must talk with Paul Gerente.

CHAPTER II

THE NEW YORK train was twenty-five minutes late. Norma purchased her ticket with a feeling of apprehension which finally drove her from the warmth of the waiting room to pace the platform upstairs. There, she kept gazing searchingly up the track as though she might hasten the approach of the train through the snow.

The apprehension stayed with her even when she was settled in the parlor car. At New Haven she thought she saw a familiar face on the platform. She hurriedly picked up her coat and handbag and quit her comfortable seat for the steamy confines of the crowded day coach. Hiding herself behind the unmeaning pages of an open magazine, she had time to reflect on the impulse which had started her on such an arduous trip through the storm.

It was anger, she knew; consuming, almost unreasonable resentment against the smooth suave technique which made amorous conquests so easy for Paul. Her first thought had been that he had deliberately sought out Babs Tredwill to show Norma that his attractiveness still held sway. It was the sort of thing which might amuse Paul Gerente, make him narrow his slightly slanting eyes and lift his thin-line eyebrows in an expression of unholy joy.

That crooked mocking smile had made him famous on the stage. Norma found she was clenching the magazine between her hands and put it down. She had lived close to that smile for a year. She knew the hopelessness of trying to convince Babs Tredwill that across a breakfast table it might become most unpleasant to see.

"Why can't I win Babs over? Why won't she be friends?" Norma wondered unhappily, and suddenly felt very much alone. Babs would see nothing but unwarranted interference if she ever learned that Norma had called on Paul.

There was an even deeper problem to be faced with Thaddeus, whose love for her was blindly unreasoning. He had despised Paul Gerente for years. His methods with Barbara would be harsh and uncompromising. He would flatly forbid the girl to see Paul again or mention his name. Neither Norma nor anyone else could ever point out to Thad that such a course would play right into Paul's clever hands. Whatever Paul Gerente wanted of Babs he would get quickly enough once Babs's father knew. Babs would dutifully listen to Thad's heated orders, then calmly and more determinedly go her own way.

Norma needed weapons to fight Paul. He was a man of force and violence; not physical, but mental force and violence, which made it still more difficult. Nothing but pressure brought to bear would turn him out of his way; yet when she tried to recollect some weakness she might use against him, to find some vulnerable spot for her attack, she was forced to conclude that Paul Gerente had lived his life with a calculating prudence which left him in the clear. Open-handed and begging, she would have to go to him and ask for an understanding he had never shown. Her own good sense told her that her plea would be met with cynical laughter, but there was nothing else to do.

Above the clacking of the train wheels she could almost hear him saying, "You're jealous, Norma—and fading slightly, too. Or perhaps I'm the one who's aging. I've heard that as men get older they prefer their women younger and more unsophisticated—even a trifle dumb." He would pause there, and pull one corner of his mouth back into a deep indentation before he concluded, "Haven't you?"

Weary with battling her unseen foe, she finally dozed uncomfortably away. It was nearly seven when she arrived at Grand Central Station. Struck by a pang of hunger, she realized that she had eaten scarcely anything all day. Downstairs, perched on a stool at the Oyster Bar, she ordered a Manhattan cocktail, but it failed to bring her cheer. She ordered an oyster stew and found with the arrival of the food that her appetite had gone. She left her meal half finished and went upstairs to a row of phone booths where she searched through the book for Paul Gerente. He was back in an apartment in Greenwich Village on West Twelfth Street, where he had lived prior to their marriage ten years before.

Afterwards, when she looked back on that evening, her verdict was that a sense of furtiveness governed her acts all the way. Instead of going to the taxi exit and getting a cab, which she normally would have done, she walked through the press of homeward-bound, package-laden commuters and dipped down into the East Side subway. She caught an express to Fourteenth Street, and stood uneasily on the short ride downtown, conscious that the tired faces of women were eyeing her enviously, estimating the value of her furs.

When she came up into the neon-lighted garishness of Fourteenth Street she discovered that the snow had mixed slushily with rain. Reckless of the fact that the wet muddy streets were splashing her sheer stockings ruinously, she hurried along head down until she turned by Hearn's department store into the comparative quiet of Fifth Avenue.

She stopped by the churchyard on the corner of Twelfth Street and gazed up at Paul's windows a short distance away. A light shone under drawn blinds. Sleet struck sharply against the back of her neck, bringing with it a sobering touch of cold reality. It was followed by a moment of indecision. After an entire day of inner turmoil she was facing the ordeal of meeting Paul Gerente again without an intelligent word to say.

She forced herself to go on. Paul lived in a walk-up. A taxi, with its windshield wipers working busily, swerved into the curb and stopped in front of Paul's apartment house when Norma was two doors away. Still motivated by a sense of doing something foolhardy and wrong, she stepped into the lighted vestibule of the house next to Paul's. Ostensibly reading names on the polished-brass letter boxes, she watched the taxi through the slanting rain and snow.

It may have been the familiar staccato click of high heels which told her that it was Babs descending the brownstone steps of the house next door. Possibly her overwrought senses were super-keen, and in the back of her mind she had expected all along to find Babs there. She huddled back as far as possible into a corner of the vestibule. She couldn't catch the words, but the cadence of Babs's voice was unmistakable as she hurriedly directed the driver where to go.

Norma suffered a bad moment as the taxi went into gear and pulled on by. She had but a flash of the girl as the gleam of a nearby street light passed like a bright shadow across Babs's golden hair. It stayed with Norma for years—that one brief glimpse of Barbara with her face buried in her slim white hands.

There was retributive rage in her heart when she ascended the brownstone steps and rang Paul Gerente's bell.

The automatic opener on the door buzzed loudly, twice, startling her with its vibrant sound. She pushed open the door and stepped inside of the once-familiar hall. It was little changed except that during the years it had been done over in blue. She had ascended four stairs when a voice called down from the second floor: —

"Did you want Cameron?"

"No," said Norma weakly.

"Sorry," said the voice, and she heard the closing of a door.

She went on up, tiring in the middle of the third flight as she'd done so many times before. On the top landing, she stopped to regain her breath. A line of light showed along the edge of Paul's slightly open door. She walked hesitantly toward it, and with something approaching an effort raised the face of the tiny brass gargoyle which served as a knocker and let it fall.

From inside the apartment, the same detestable clock which had startled her years before wound itself up with a whir and cuckooed eight times lustily.

She pushed the door open and forced herself to laugh. "What's the matter, Paul? Aren't you receiving visitors tonight?"

A man in a cherry-red dressing gown was stretched out face down in front of the fireplace. Burning logs crackled as though the fire might have been freshly tended. The light from the flames jumped erratically, endowing with unnatural life the polished-brass poker lying close to the man on the floor.

The scene held her with the powerful magic of horror. From loudly ticking clock to embroidered Chinese robe, which covered the grand piano, nothing had changed in the room. She absorbed all that unconsciously, vaguely sensing that the familiar objects, books, pictures, and furniture, were keeping her from screaming. She fought a mad impulse to seat herself at the piano and play. The wild whirl of Tausig's gypsy dances might do what humans could never do—bring the corpse with the battered head to life; force him to rise in a dance macabre. Anything was preferable to stillness. Madness lay in such finality. Already she was feeling it freeze her, press her back against the wall. She must move before she grew as rigid as the man before the fire; before she toppled down beside him, stretched inertly in that darkened place on the carpet where his blood had ebbed away.

She began to play a frightful game. The man with the battered head was dead, but she had to pretend not to know. It was a game of deceptions and the stake was life, with an opponent she couldn't see. She must keep her eyes away from the curtained doors which led to another room; must give no sign that her mind was strong, that she knew when she had rung downstairs—someone had answered Paul Gerente's bell!

Beyond the curtains to Paul's bedroom, soft as the fall of a playing card, something fluttered to the floor. The sound brought Norma to life again, gave her the strength to flee. She never knew how she got away, or what stopped her flight downstairs long enough for her to pick up Babs's fur-topped galoshes, which were dripping water in the hall outside Paul's door.

Once outside she wandered blindly down street after winding street, holding the galoshes in her hand, bucking against the storm. Deep in the maze of Greenwich Village she became aware that people were watching her. She was standing laughing hysterically into the plate-glass window of an Italian *pâtisserie*.

CHAPTER III

THERE WAS menace in the voice of the news commentator. It lurked behind his vivid descriptions of marching feet and rolling caissons, made doubly strong by words he couldn't say. Subtly, with sharp, clean-cutting phrases, he pictured the forces of a nation on the move; told of women and children waiting for death in huddled groups; hinted at the terror which gripped the world when a country was wiped from the map of Europe in a day.

Captain Duncan Maclain pressed the control button at the side of his desk. The voice from the Capehart radio stopped abruptly. The Captain touched sensitive fingers to his sightless eyes and sat very still. At his feet under the desk, Schnucke, his Seeing-Eye dog, was caught by the darkness of the usually bright penthouse office and the solemnity of her master's mood. She whimpered slightly and comforted herself by resting her warm chin on the toe of the Captain's shoe.

"War, Schnucke!" said Duncan Maclain. "You're lucky to be a dog in days like these. You're living in a world gone mad with senseless slaughter—a world that's blind. Blind, as the last war blinded me!"

Schnucke answered the sound of her name by moving her

head companionably. Maclain's fine mobile mouth smiled into the gloom. It was satisfying to philosophize with Schnucke. She lived a life of such delightful fundamentals with never a word to say. He reached down and felt the wetness of her nose against his palm. Affectionately her tongue touched the back of his hand as he drew it away.

The room seemed uncomfortably warm. Maclain left the chair, back of his wide, flat-topped desk, and walked with quick sure steps to the terrace door. He moved with ease in the familiar surroundings, confident that each piece of furniture was in its accustomed place, firmly fixed to the floor.

For an instant after he opened the latch, he stood holding the French door ajar against the push of the late December storm. Twenty-six stories above Seventy-second Street and Riverside Drive the wind had full sway. Stinging snow beat in through the two-inch crack, tearing smartingly at his face and hands. He shivered under the blast and closed the door. The wind moaned defeat and further wet the dripping diamond panes with a defiant splash of mingled rain and snow.

A thermostat heat regulator was on the wall at the end of the bookcase filled with Braille. The Captain brushed the heavy volumes lightly in passing, located the small arrow at the base of the thermometer, and turned the heating lower. He selected a volume from the bookcase,—Van Loon's *Ships and How They Sailed the Seven Seas*,—sat down at the desk, and began finger reading.

Smoking and reading failed to quiet a feeling of restlessness. He was glad to be interrupted by the buzz of his private phone.

There were two telephones on his desk. One was a unit of the regular apartment-house system connecting with the lobby switchboard twenty-six floors below; the other was smaller and operated by push buttons. It formed a link of seven phones in his apartment which gave communication from room to room. The Captain ignored both phones on the desk and turned to his left-hand top drawer. He opened it and took out a regular French type of dial phone. Not more than a dozen people knew the number. He mentally reviewed the short list before he lifted the receiver from its cradle and said, "Hello!"

"Has your man arrived?" The crisp voice of Spud Savage, the Captain's partner and closest friend, crackled over the wire.

"He's late," said Maclain. "I'll spend the night in town, Spud. He'll certainly be here soon."

"That's what I wanted to know." There were a few seconds of silence at the other end. "Look, Dunc. I'll be in within an hour and a half to spend the night there with you."

"Has it occurred to you that we're guests at a Long Island house party for Christmas?" Maclain asked brightly. No one but Spud Savage and his wife Rena, who had been Maclain's secretary for years, could have detected the underlying annoyance in the Captain's tone.

"Yes, it's occurred to me," Spud mimicked. "And it's occurred to Rena, too. She's worried about Schnucke. Schnucke's sensitive. We don't like to have her staying in a closed-up apartment alone."

"Kindly go to hell, both of you," suggested Maclain. "I'm certainly able to take care of myself for a night in my own home. You're insane if you try to come in town through this storm."

"I'll be there within two hours," said Spud. "Anybody who's been associated with you for twenty years is bound to be slightly fey."

"Perhaps you've affected me!" The Captain hung up the phone. The conversation with his partner left him with a comfortable feeling of well-being. Samuel Savage, whom Maclain called "Spud," was the only person who could be solicitous about the Captain's blindness in an open and aboveboard way. They had served together in the army. During the trying period when the Captain was driving himself to a point of collapse to perfect the senses of hearing, touch, and smell, Spud Savage had scarcely left his side for a day.

Watching Maclain's naturally keen faculties sharpen under rigorous dicipline, Spud had conceived a wild idea. Duncan Maclain was a wealthy man and inordinately proud. Slowly, and with infinite tact, Spud convinced Maclain that he could utilize the foundation of intelligence work mastered in the army. Together they would open a private detective agency. Captain Duncan Maclain would become unique. Blind, he would become the master of them all, greater than any detective who could see.

It was Spud who had engaged Rena as Maclain's secretary, and, as Rena put it, "married her so she would stay." It was Spud who had taught the Captain to shoot at sound—a patient matter of six years' practice, for two long hours each day. It was Spud who had arranged for Schnucke and Maclain's training at the Seeing-Eye school. Happily, with the advent of Schnucke, Maclain found he was free.

The fear of blindness was lifted, and held him enthralled no more. He was no longer a burden on Spud and Rena. Schnucke's warm body was ever close to his side. She was only a German shepherd dog skillfully trained, but she was life to Duncan Maclain, for her deep dark eyes had sight. Sight was all that he needed to be as good as a man could be.

Schnucke stood up and rubbed her back gently against the Captain's knee. The musical triple chime of an electric tocsin announced a visitor in the anteroom of the penthouse office. Maclain touched a button under his desk and clicked a latch which opened the office door.

The visitor paused on the threshold. "Captain Maclain?"

"I'm dreadfully sorry," said Maclain. "You'll find the light switch to your left just inside the door. I was reading with my fingers and for the moment I forgot it was dark in this room."

The man in the doorway laughed softly. "It is black." The light switch clicked. "I'll admit I expected to walk into a lighted office. The darkness rather startled me."

Maclain listened to the rich, cultured tones and said, "Take the chair in front of my desk, if you don't mind." When the man was seated, the Captain continued, "You keep yourself in good trim. Your step is light and quick for such a big man. You must weigh better than two hundred, and you're taller than six foot two."

"I've been told you were blind, Captain. Frankly, I was skeptical that you could ever be of help in the city's defense plans. You're already proving my stupidity to me!"

"Thanks," said Maclain a trifle drily. "After many years I'm able to estimate the approximate height of strangers by the number of steps they take to my desk from the door. My blindness necessarily makes me a bit of a mountebank. I let you enter a darkened room to stop you at the door. It makes counting your footsteps easier." He pushed forward a carved cigarette box. "Smoke? I understand you were to bring some Braille instructions to me."

"They're here. The Naval Intelligence requests that you memorize and destroy them as soon as possible, Captain Maclain. There are five vital points in here where an organized crew might sabotage the light, power, water, and sewage of this city. You're an ex-Army Intelligence officer. I don't need to tell you those would be dangerous papers for certain people to see."

Maclain reached out one hand and papers rustled crisply. He spread the Braille embossed sheets flat on his desk and began to move his fingers over the lines, reading skillfully. He heard the scratch of a match. Tobacco smoke reached his nostrils. The room was silent until he turned the last of the sheets.

"I think I have it," he said. "The instructions are perfectly clear. In the improbable event that New York is plunged into darkness and communication cut off, I know exactly where I'm to go, what I'm to do, and the men I'm to contact."

"Good!" said the other. "Colonel Gray, the head of our defense plans, believes your ability to get around with your dog invaluable. Even under war conditions, a blind man could pass unquestioned where others might be suspected and stopped immediately. The vulnerable spots mentioned in there are in code. Before I leave would you care to name their locations for me as given you personally by Colonel Gray? I'd like to be sure you know."

The Captain leaned back in his chair and locked his hands behind his head. "Let's say I know them and leave it there." He smiled slowly. "Did part of your mission here tonight consist of testing me?"

"You're a cautious man, Captain," the other said quickly. "It's a trait we like to see!"

The Captain felt along a row of buttons beside his desk and pressed one. From a loud-speaker concealed behind a panel in the wall a voice announced: "When you hear the signal the time will be exactly ten twenty-three."

"That's a neat device, Captain. A hook-up with the time bureau, hey? Meridian 7-1212."

"A direct wire," Maclain explained. "I have to hear what I can't see."

"I regret I was late in arriving. I won't detain you any longer." Maclain heard the other rise. "The Army and Navy Intelligence both appreciate your co-operation. Colonel Gray suggested that I make myself known to you in case you might want further information after studying our instructions. I'm a lieutenant in the Naval Reserve, Captain Maclain, but you may have heard of me in my profession. I was on the stage for years—"

"Colonel Gray told me who you are," said Maclain. "You underestimate your own fame. Anyone who ever attended a show has heard of Paul Gerente."

CHAPTER IV

OLIVE-SKINNED GIRLS with dark laughing eyes came into the Italian Café. They were accompanied by quick-moving, sober-faced boys dressed in store clothes of foreign lines. They ate pizza and drank beer or black coffee, eyed Norma Tredwill curiously, and went away.

Babs's galoshes had grown monstrously large. Norma kept glancing at them surreptitiously, wondering how many of the café's customers had noticed them beside her on the floor. Since she had fled from Paul Gerente's apartment more than an hour before, her normal power of reasoning had become dulled. She felt trapped in a situation demanding extreme acuteness, with nothing to help her but a nonfunctioning brain.

Her body was lethargic, too. She had been sitting too long in a straight-backed booth, her spine rigid, her slender feet pressed tightly flat against the floor. Restlessly she shifted her position. Tiny living needles pricked at her legs and arms as circulation was resumed once more.

"Madame does not like the *pizza?*"

A heavy-set Italian was bent over the table. She looked at him uncomprehendingly. His long white apron hid his clothes.

At each corner of his wide mouth the wispy end of a horse-shoe-shaped mustache drooped dolefully. He wiped his eyes slowly with the corner of his apron as though Norma's attitude grieved him.

"Madame does not like the *pizza?*" he asked again, and pointed to the table in front of her. She understood then that he was referring to a large, untouched Italian tomato pie.

The sight of it made her ill, but she forced herself to smile. "I thought I was hungry when I came in," she said lamely. "I guess I was just cold from the storm."

"*Si,*" he said. "The storm she mak' you cold. I get some coffee ver' hot. She heat you up again." He shuffled away before Norma could say no.

Two couples a few booths away were laughing softly and chattering in the liquid syllables of their mother tongue. Norma drew back into the seclusion of her own small cubicle and lifted Babs's galoshes from the floor. Tugging with a quick frenzy, she tried to pull one of them on over her thin overshoe. A single try convinced her that it was much too small. When she tried to remove it, it stuck halfway.

The piece of expensive fur-trimmed footwear seemed malignantly stubborn. By exerting all her strength she finally managed to pull it free. When she looked up, the white-aproned proprietor was standing at the end of the table, coffee in hand, gazing unconcernedly at her silk-clad knee.

Norma uncrossed her legs and smoothed her skirt down carefully. Apparently her blind flight from Paul's had led her unwittingly to the worst place she could have found. Seeking a quiet spot where she might gather her wits into line, she had blundered into a small *pizzeria* where her clothes and actions were objects of curiosity to patrons and proprietor. Once let her picture appear in the papers as Paul's ex-wife, and a dozen Italians would remember her visit to the local café.

As she reflected on the events of the past two hours it was brought crushingly home to her that she was fleeing from something unknown; acting as though she or Babs had felled Paul Gerente with that horrible bloodstained poker. A false calmness took possession of her—the calmness of an actress who has been through many bad first nights. She nodded her thanks, and handed the proprietor a dollar from her purse as he set the coffee down.

"Give me a piece of wrapping paper, please," she said. "I bought these galoshes hurriedly and they're too small. Tomorrow I'll take them back to the store."

She wasn't sure that he understood her, although he nodded solemn agreement. He took the dollar and shuffled stolidly away.

Norma forced herself to drink the hot, bitter draft, although she detested coffee loaded with chicory. It revived her faculties. While she waited for the proprietor's return, questions began to parade themselves dancingly before her. She reviewed them with a sharpened mental astuteness. The answers were vitally important. One by one they capered by her—problems and incidents she should have calmly considered before.

Had Babs killed Paul Gerente?

Another question flashed through her mind before she could formulate a sensible answer. Was Paul Gerente the man in the cherry-colored dressing gown she had seen lying on the floor? Brutally she forced herself to conjure back a picture of the room. The man was about Paul's size and build. Why, in the name of heaven, had she run away like a panicky child? It would have taken but a moment for her to walk closer to the murdered man to see.

Babs might have killed him, if the man was really Paul. Once he was passionately aroused, his methods with women were never tactful. Babs was nervous, high-strung, and strong. Frightened and desperate, the girl might easily have seized the nearest weapon and battled for escape from the apartment too successfully. It was a hideous thought, and Norma promptly put it away, yet she knew it was what she had dreaded from the instant she had picked up Babs's galoshes in the hall.

Eagerly she seized upon the stronger terror which had overcome her in Paul's apartment, that weakening premonition that somebody else had been there. Why hadn't she looked into Paul's bedroom, or spoken, particularly when she knew that someone had answered the ring of Paul's bell?

She remembered the voice which called from the second floor, "Do you want Cameron?" Perhaps in her haste and excitement she had pushed the Camerons' button in the foyer and never rung Paul's bell at all. Babs might have blundered in onto a murdered Paul Gerente as Norma had done. But how? Norma struggled vainly for an answer. If Paul was murdered, surely a killer would not answer the door. There was another possibility which was sordidly depressing: Babs might have had a key.

A throbbing started over her right eye, rhythmic and painful. She pressed it with her finger tips and told herself silently, "A key might explain how Babs got in, but it doesn't explain who opened that door for me."

It was inconceivable that she had erroneously pressed the Camerons' button; she even knew the location of Paul's—the bottom one in the row.

Or was it? Her remembrance of the lighted vestibule on West Twelfth Street became indistinct and cloudy. Perhaps Cameron's button was the bottom one on the row. Perhaps in ten years the bells had been changed. She found herself battling a dragging urge to go back to the Twelfth Street house and see. It was mad, she knew, but somehow before she faced Babs again she had to have some inkling of the truth. A simpler course presented itself—one which apparently could do no harm and which might work, with a little subtlety.

Norma left the table and walked to a phone booth in the corner. Leafing through the directory, she found an A. C. Cameron listed at the Twelfth Street address. Her heart was thumping uncomfortably when she dialed the number. A man's voice answered pleasantly after a few rings.

Somewhat reassured, Norma said hurriedly, "I'm sorry to disturb you, Mr. Cameron, because you don't know me, but I was wondering about the name plates on the bells downstairs. Apparently I rang your bell when I called on some friends a little while ago. If you remember, you called downstairs to me as I came into the hall."

Cameron gave a friendly laugh and said, "Who is this speaking?"

Norma was silent a few seconds before she said, "Do you mind if I don't say?"

"No, not at all, but you're worrying yourself needlessly. I was expecting a friend and had my apartment door open. I heard a bell ring upstairs and called down, thinking it might be for me."

"Oh!" said Norma faintly. "Then you didn't push the buzzer and open the downstairs door?"

"Yes," said Cameron, "I did. And whoever you rang answered too. That's why I called down to you. My friend was coming from a cocktail party. Occasionally he gets mixed up on bells. There's no harm done, though."

"I'm sorry I troubled you." Norma hung up. Cameron's statement, "Whoever you rang answered too," was running through her head liltingly. There was a train back to Hartford at eleven-fifty. She would take it and say nothing to anyone. Someone else *had* been in Paul's room. She needed time to think things out. She could talk to Babs the following day.

CHAPTER V

ARNOLD C. CAMERON put the telephone back in its cradle and walked slowly halfway across the room. He stopped for a moment in front of a pier-glass mirror set in a closet door.

From the depths of an easy chair in the corner an attractive brunette watched him from under languorous lids as he brushed imaginary dust from the shoulders of his well-tailored sharkskin suit and pushed back a lock of his graying hair.

"It sounded like a woman." The girl crossed slender legs and looked at her toe.

Arnold Cameron studied her reflection in the mirror before him and smiled. He was a man in his late thirties and was always reminding people who met him of someone they knew.

"It was," he said.

"Who?"

He left his place at the mirror and stood for a few seconds looking down at the girl before he settled himself in another chair.

"You're the jealous type, Hilda, my dear." He took a cigarette from a jar on the table beside him and rolled it between his palms. Small yellow specks of tobacco fell to the floor.

The girl swished the remains of a highball around in the bottom of her glass and finished it. "Do I know her?"

"No," said Cameron. "Neither do I. I'm trying to figure out what the hell she telephoned me for."

"When you get mysterious," said Hilda, "you're an awful bore."

She held the glass out toward him. "Make another one, will you, darling? I'm dry."

"You're saturated," said Cameron, "and I think you'd better go."

Hilda's soft, full lips curled in a smile. "Afraid of me?"

"Yes." He got up quickly, bent over her, and kissed her on the mouth. When he straightened up again, his strong hands slipped under her elbows and lifted her to her feet.

"Do I really have to go?"

"Yes," he said. "I have some work to do."

"Something to do with the call?"

He opened the mirrored door and took her heavy plaid ulster from the closet, holding it out before him to help her put it on. She thrust her arms angrily into the sleeves, snatched her small stylish hat from the shelf of the closet, and arranged it on her head with trembling fingers.

"This is the last time you'll ever put me out of here!"

"I'm sorry, Hilda, really." His gray eyes were expressionless. "After all, I've only done it once before."

"Twice is too much. I'm afraid I like men who aren't always subject to the interruption of mysterious phone calls." She stopped with her hand on the door. "I went down to your office the other day."

"You did?" he inquired politely. "It's too bad I missed you."

"You'd have missed anybody who came," said Hilda. "The door was locked and there wasn't anyone there at all."

She set her chin firmly and faced him challengingly. "Just what do you import, Arnold? I'd like to know."

"Eggs," he said soberly. "From Australia. The business has been badly affected by the war."

He kissed her again before she could answer and adroitly eased her out through the door. He watched her down the single flight of stairs and called, "I hope you'll change your mind and come back again. I'm really fond of you, and sorry if I've been a bore."

He was answered by the slam of the front door.

Back again in the apartment, he picked up the phone and dialed a number. "Jack," he said when the answer came, "is it true that there's no way of tracing a dial call?"

"None," a voice replied from the other end. "It's a washout when the call's once through. What's on your mind?"

"Nothing particularly," Cameron replied a bit testily. "I'm tired of having my evenings spoiled, that's all."

He hung up and went back to look at himself in the mirror again, brushing more imaginary dust from his shoulder. After staring at himself irresolutely for a few seconds, he turned with the quick decisiveness of a man who has made up his mind, crossed the room swiftly, and took a heavy Luger automatic pistol from the table drawer. He half opened the breech with an expert hand and glanced at the loading.

The gun was sagging in his side coat pocket when he stepped out into the hall, closed the apartment door behind him, and went down into the vestibule to ring Paul Gerente's bell.

He waited for a short interval, staring out at the driving sleet and snow, but no answer came. He let himself back in with a latchkey and climbed the five flights of stairs to the top floor, where he knocked lightly on Paul Gerente's door.

Not a sound came from inside. Cameron took a leather-bound key container from his pocket and selected a key. It fitted the lock perfectly. With the assured confidence of a man entering his own home, he stepped in. The door clicked shut behind him.

The lights were on, and in the fireplace embers burned low. Seconds ticked away on the busy pendulum of the cuckoo clock before he knelt beside the dead man in the cherry-colored dressing gown. A shadow which might have been pity touched his face, and faded into a mirthless smile.

He picked the blood-marked poker up, holding it in the center with a folded handkerchief. A couple of minutes later he was back downstairs in his apartment on the second floor.

Shut in, he went to work with precision. Concealed from casual view behind the many suits in the spacious closet, a small safe stood on the floor. Cameron shoved the impeding clothes to one side and opened the safe door. He took out a small metal box and a tiny camel's-hair brush.

Back in the living room he placed the brass poker on a newspaper spread out on the table. He was humming tunelessly when he opened the metal box, dipped the tiny brush into the contents of light aluminum powder, and brushed the shining poker handle daintily.

The dust adhered in a light unbroken film.

Cameron took a lens from the table drawer and frowningly studied his work. "Damn waste of time!" he muttered, and went into the kitchen to mix himself a highball.

He came back carrying a glass in one hand and a square of paper towel torn from a roll in the other. He took an appreciative drink, set the glass on the table, and using the paper towel wiped the handle of the poker clean.

For the space of two cigarettes he sat in a chair sipping his drink and staring at the poker reflectively. When his highball was finished he picked up the poker again and took it back upstairs.

The fire was almost out.

Cameron replaced the weapon on the floor beside the dead man and began to search the room. He went over it skillfully and swiftly, making sure that he left no signs of disorder. Fifteen minutes satisfied him, and he transferred his search to the adjoining room.

A table lamp glowed softly as he pushed the switch. It disclosed a bedroom furnished in simple masculine fashion with a double bed, a combination bookcase and desk, and two comfortable chairs.

Without hesitation Cameron opened the desk. The front swung down to make a writing table. He reached inside and opened the right-hand drawer, pulling it out entirely. Groping inside the cavity, he located a niche large enough to receive the end of his finger. A slight tug swung out the center of the desk, disclosing a hidden drawer.

The shallow compartment was empty. He closed it slowly, tried it once to make sure it was fastened, and replaced the desk drawer. Answering promptly, as though shutting the desk had released some controlling spring, the cuckoo clock struck half-past eleven.

Cameron's gray eyes turned toward the curtains separating the two rooms. He sucked in his lower lip and bit it lightly, then slid his right hand into his coat pocket and closed it about the butt of the Luger 7.65. Following close on the noisy strike of the cuckoo clock someone had knocked demandingly on the apartment door.

He stood motionless, breathing easily, his thumb pressed

against the safety catch of the gun. The knock sounded again, more insistent. Cameron's eyes widened and his serious face was lightened by a perversely mischievous smile.

Moving effortlessly, and with the quiet ease of muscles kept in perfect trim, he brushed the curtains aside, stepped into the living room, and bent over the still form on the floor. Quickly he seized the poker, and with a rolling motion pressed the shiny brass handle against the fingers of the body's stiffening right hand. When that was done, he grasped the brass handle with his own right hand and for a split second brandished the weapon threateningly in the air.

From the hall, a voice called "Mr. Gerente!" The summons was followed by another knock. Cameron replaced the poker beside the body, strode across the room, and opened the door.

A dark, strikingly handsome man in a sleet-spattered tan mackintosh stood across the threshold. He gave a friendly grin which brought the whole of his rugged face to life, except his eyes. They gave Cameron an uneasy illusion that the newcomer was looking through him, concentrating on some indefinite spot on the opposite wall.

"It's beastly of me to disturb you again tonight." The man stepped inside. "I'm overcautious, I guess—" He stopped just inside the door.

"Come in, Captain Maclain." Cameron fell back precipitately. Two German shepherd dogs had preceded Maclain from the hall. The one on the Captain's left stared about the room with kindly inquisitiveness. Maclain's left hand rested lightly upon a U-shaped brace attached to her harness. It was the dog to the Captain's right which kept Cameron's feet leadenly still.

There was danger in the set of the white teeth, strength in the broad jaws and forechest, unflinching courage in the stance of the full, erect tail. Menacing almond eyes turned their unwavering gaze from Cameron to the corpse on the hearth. The heavy leather leash tightened around the Captain's hand as the dog stepped forward with a threatening growl.

"Stand, Dreist!" Maclain snapped out. The affability of his voice was gone. "This dog is extremely dangerous," he continued in a flat warning tone. "I won't be able to control him and he'll tear you to pieces if you try to pull a gun. Move very cautiously, please, and seat yourself in a chair."

Cameron obeyed without answering. His forehead was damp and a muscle showed tight along the length of his jaw. When he was seated, he said, "Perhaps you don't mind explaining your reasons for coming here, Captain Maclain."

"Not at all. Lie down, Schnucke!" the dog in the Seeing-Eye harness obeyed. The Captain tightened his hold on Dreist's leash and walked toward the sound of Cameron's voice. "Sit quietly, please, and keep your arms out from your sides." An instant later he produced Cameron's gun, and quickly stowed it away in his mackintosh.

"You're very efficient," Cameron remarked sarcastically.

"I've been told so," said Maclain. "My chauffeur, Cappo, is waiting for me downstairs in my car. Either you're not Paul Gerente, or your voice has changed since you were in my office an hour ago."

"How did you get in here without ringing?" Cameron carefully changed his position in the chair.

"My chauffeur found the superintendent. If you're not Paul Gerente, I think you'd better tell me who you are."

"I'll tell you even more," said Cameron. "Arnold Cameron's my name. I was a good friend of Gerente's. I live in the back apartment on the second floor."

" 'Was' a good friend?" repeated Maclain.

"That's right," said Cameron levelly. "He wasn't in your office an hour ago, either. He's very much dead behind you on the floor. Your dog was growling at his body when you came in the door."

"Schnucke!" Maclain called.

The Seeing-Eye dog came up and placed herself at the Captain's side. "Guard, Dreist!" he ordered the other dog, and dropped the leash from his hand. "If you don't move," he said coldly to Cameron, "Dreist won't molest you."

"Then he won't molest me," said Cameron. "That's okay by me."

Under Schnucke's guidance the Captain stopped close by the body. Down on one knee, he ran his agile fingers over the features and lightly touched the clotted blood in the hair.

"He's been dead for some time," he announced thoughtfully, rising from the floor.

"Since seven forty-five," said Cameron.

"You place it with great exactness." Maclain stood holding his chin between thumb and finger. "How do you know?"

"I looked at the clock right after I hit him with the poker," Cameron declared with a nervous laugh. "He came at me with it and I wrested it away. It was self-defense."

"I'll have to phone the police."

"Go ahead," said Cameron. "I can't stop you with this dog slavering over me. I have a witness who can clear me."

"That's probably lucky for you. Who is it?"

"The girl we were quarreling over," said Cameron. "Hilda Lestrade's her name. She's a good-looking baby, too!"

CHAPTER VI

1

SOMEWHERE ALONG the coast of California twelve great bombing planes sat white and impressive, lined up in a geometrical row. Far down the flat cleared surface of the landing field a group of men in khaki stood watching. One of the men placed a pair of binoculars to his eyes, adjusted the focus, then stepped from the group and signaled. A flight commander leaned from one of the flying fortresses and waved his hand.

The dozen giant planes came to life with a roar. Moving with the slow stateliness of imaginative birds from the *Arabian Nights*, they wheeled across the field, seemed to pause even as they gathered speed, and suddenly left the ground for the air.

There they were more at home. Traveling with the dizzy speed of a hurricane, they fell into the arrow formation of herons in flight. Looking down, the flight commander saw ten acres of parked automobiles blur white with upturned faces watching the bombers grow small against the sky.

On the edge of the parked cars bordering the landing field a man and a girl sat in a sixteen-cylinder convertible Cadillac coupé. The top was down, although the afternoon was unseasonably cool. Perched on the back of the seat, the girl watched the vanishing planes through a pair of dark sun glasses.

"What do they do now, Francis? You know all about such things." The girl spoke with the delectable trill of an enthusiastic debutante.

The man behind the wheel of the car sat silent, using his hand to shield his eyes from the glare. His lack of attention displeased his companion. She drew her fur coat closer about her in a gesture which raised her silken skirt a few inches higher, and repeated her question. "What do they do now, Francis?"

The man lowered his hand and turned toward her when she pressed against his shoulder with the round smoothness of her knee.

"Why don't you watch them, Tina darling?"

"They're getting so far away that I can't see."

"They'll come back again." He pointed to the left. "That's their target over there. They're going to bomb that house on the top of the hill." His eyes caught the warmth of flesh above the tops of her stockings. "You're lovely, Tina," he said, and turned away.

From the west the bombers zoomed in like fleeting black spots out of the setting sun. A sigh went up from the crowd as the arrow formation broke and straightened into a single line. Silence followed, gripping the earth. The wings of the leader had turned at an angle. Tons of man-made metal were plummeting earthward. When it seemed that nothing could save it, the great mass flattened out and became an airship again, raining death from the sky.

Noise beat in from the hills as one by one the twelve planes played their game of follow-the-leader. The ground erupted beneath them, shattering the day with the burst of high explosives, the rending of wood which had been a dwelling, the tossing of timbers on high. When the last of the bombs had found its mark the quiet was so great that the noise of whirring propellers seemed lost in the turbid air. Slowly the smoke on the hilltop drifted away, but the eyes of the people kept watching, searching for a house forever gone.

"I'm glad those planes are ours," said the man in the Cadillac coupé. "Every hit a direct one! I'd hate like the devil to have them flying over me in a war—unless they were on my side."

Beside him, the girl shivered slightly. "How do they do it, Francis—hit such a small mark every time from way up in the air?"

"Bombing sights," he told her, patronizingly proud of his knowledge. "They're the best in the world—and going to be even better, I'm told. Gilbert Tredwill, the Hartford engineer who invented them, is working on a new one now. We have to watch our step with everybody else in the world at war."

"Don't talk about it." She took off her sun glasses and her dark eyes looked troubled. "I just can't bear to think that if we get dragged in you'll be one of the first to go."

He laughed and patted her ankle affectionately, "You're sweet, Tina. Going to war is a chance that all of us take in the Flying Corps." He raised himself half up in the seat, and for an instant buried his nose in the large bunch of violets pinned to her breast. "You know," he continued seriously, "if I ever do have to go to war, whenever I smell violets I'll think of you."

The twelve bombers were wheeling down to earth in the light of the setting sun. The whiteness of their wings suddenly turned scarlet with a strange unearthly glow.

"Look, Francis." Tina's voice was husky. "Look at those planes. They're covered with blood right now!"

2

Somewhere off the coast of New England seventeen men were bravely awaiting death on the bottom of the sea.

"How long now, Skipper?" asked the second in command. His question reverberated from the metal shell which formed their prison, but his voice was calm and devoid of fear.

A streak of light showed ghostlike through blackness as the commanding officer moved his luminous wrist watch and turned up the back of his hand.

"It's now quarter past four in the morning." His laugh boomed out startlingly. "You asked me that same question, Lieutenant, exactly six minutes ago."

"Why not?" said the Lieutenant. "There isn't anything else to do."

Voices began to fill the darkness with hollow raillery: —

"Whatchu kickin' about, Lieutenant? Submarine woik's the nuts. Nuttin' to do but set on our bottoms 'n' draw extra pay!"

"Join the Navy and see the world! Jeses!"

"Yeah. Me old lady got me in this because she said them airyplanes was fallin' all th' time. She's sure got me down about as far as I can go."

"Pipe down, you guys! You're using up the air!"

"That's a laugh. What air?"

"You tell 'em, Sandy. It smells like the pitcher show back home on bank night when all them dames comes in from the factories."

"Don't you never think o' nuthin' but dames? Jeses, Slim."

"Mebbe you ketch yerself a mermaid, eh, Slim?"

"That's a laugh. Get himself a piece of fishtail!"

"Pipe down, you guys! You're using up the air!"

Silence, and blackness, and breathing, and carbon monoxide creeping up on men about to die.

"Jeses. All you hear about in the Navy is how good them bastards in the Coast Guard is at rescues. They must be tryin' to gnaw their way through!"

The Lieutenant whispering: —

"—At the Gardners' party at New London, Skipper. You must remember her."

"There were twenty girls there."

"She wore that white swim suit with the red trim and took a double somersault from the high board. Susan Rowland."

"I remember that dive all right. She had a brother there, didn't she? Surly cuss that played contract so well."

"That's the one. Well—"

A plaintive voice saying: —

"What's the matter with Denny and that mouth organ? God knows it's the only time I've ever wanted to hear him play."

"He's playin' a harp, Cupie, in the other half of this can."

"Jeses. I've seen pitchers of guys like us using torpedo tubes."

"Pipe down, you! You're using up the air. We've been into all that crap about tubes before. The Coast Guard'll come through."

"And so will the Marines."

"You tell 'em, Sandy. We will find the streets all guarded by United States Marines."

"What streets?"

"Heaven's scenes, the song says."

"The song stinks. We ain't goin' to heaven no-how. We're goin' to hell in a hand basket."

"A sea casket!"

"Pipe down, you guys! You're using up the air!"

The Lieutenant whispering: —

"—And the last time I saw her was the night before we went away. She's sweet, Skipper. God! There's something about a girl like that that makes a man feel good all through."

"She's beautiful, all right, Mac, but I think she's older than you."

"It's the way she wears her hair. Funny thing, I had a letter from her just before we put out yesterday—"

"Yesterday, Mac?"

"Waiting for me at the base."

"I'll say it's funny. How did she know where to send it? Neither of us knew where we were going to be."

"She must have guessed, Skipper. Here, smell it. It reminds me of her hair."

Heavy note paper crackling in the darkness. Carbon monoxide creeping up on seventeen doomed men. The scent of violets faint in the fetid air.

3

Inspector Larry Davis of the New York Homicide Squad chewed reflectively on a toothpick. Supporting himself on his elbows, with his back against the side of Paul Gerente's grand piano, he kept moving his head in tiny jerks, watching the progress of Schnucke and her master about the living room.

Sunk down in a large easy chair, Sergeant Aloysius Archer was nervously trying to outstare Dreist. He had heard somewhere that dogs would turn away if you looked at them hard enough. It wasn't working out with Dreist. The Captain's police dog glared back at him unwaveringly from a point of vantage on the floor.

Under Schnucke's guidance, Maclain turned at right angles at the end of a divan and skirted it slowly. In passing, he brushed the cushions lightly with his hand. He turned again at the other end and stopped close beside the spot where Gerente's body had lain on the floor.

In the chair, Sergeant Archer started a yawn, felt that Dreist's glance was unfriendly, and choked off his yawn halfway.

"Look, Captain," he began pleadingly. "The guy's confessed, hasn't he? We've got his prints on a poker. We're rounding up a gal, who saw the whole thing. This egg Cameron's already on his way to headquarters. Let's go home. Be a pal and call this leg chewer off of me."

"What's your hurry, Sergeant?" A slight snip sounded as Inspector Davis broke the toothpick between his fingers. "We've watched him pace off every foot of this two-room-and-bath apartment for an hour and handle everything from bed to bottles, until the edges are worn off. I want to find out what the hell he's looking for!"

Maclain released Schnucke's brace and clasped his hands behind him. "So you've reached the stage of snapping toothpicks, eh, Inspector? It's been quite a while since I heard that noise. It's nice to meet you boys again."

Davis said: —

"Yeah, it's swell. Sometime we simply *must* have tea together—just Archer, and you and I. What the hell are you looking for?"

"Sit down, Inspector," Maclain urged. "You invariably get sarcastic when you're on your feet too long. I've already found you something, haven't I? What about that secret drawer?"

"With nothing in it," said Archer. "Yet how you found it still beats me."

"I found it, Sergeant, because unutilized space in the center of a desk is an inconsistency. Since I'm blind, I've had to train my other senses to be sensitive to inconsistencies. As a matter of fact, one brought me here tonight."

"That sounds just ducky, like everything you say, Captain—and it still leaves me up in a tree."

"Well, climb a few branches higher and keep your trap shut for a minute."

The Inspector left his place by the piano and settled himself on the divan. "Just what *did* bring you here tonight, Captain Maclain? You're beginning to interest me."

"I'm very glad." The Captain smiled. "That's a difficult thing to do. Countless thousands of innocent people are being murdered in Europe every day, Davis. When—"

"What's that got to do with us?" the Inspector broke in.

"Too much, unfortunately." The Captain's expressive voice was grim. "When murder becomes a commonplace—when the world begins to accept it with a shrug—then, God save us, the Homicide Squad needs help, Inspector, and I do too."

Dreist growled at the timbre of his master's words. The Sergeant shifted his honest bulk in the chair. "How long had you known this fellow Gerente, Captain?"

"I knew him only by hearsay, Sergeant. Paul Gerente was working for G-2."

"The Intelligence Department," Davis muttered. "Hell's broth, Maclain, what are we mixed up in now?"

"Something so deep that I can't even tell the whole of the truth to you. At ten-twenty tonight a man who was supposedly Paul Gerente delivered some Braille instructions to me in my office. He lengthened his stride as he crossed from the door to my desk—to make me think he was taller than he was."

"Then he'd heard of your methods before."

"Exactly, Inspector. He'd heard of my methods before. I had no reason then to believe that it wasn't Gerente, taking some extra precautions—or devising a means of testing me. I know now—"

"You're damn right it wasn't Gerente!" Archer exclaimed emphatically. "I know Gerente. I've seen him twenty times on the stage and I don't forget faces. At ten-twenty—"

"Quite," said Maclain. "We come now to the inconsistencies which put you up an imaginative tree." The Captain took a cigarette from his case, fitted it in a holder, and flashed his lighter. Guiding the flame adroitly to the tip by running his thumb along the cigarette, he inhaled deeply and put the lighter away.

"According to Mr. Cameron," he continued, "Paul Gerente was killed at seven forty-five. He and Cameron were good friends—so good that Gerente had given Cameron a key."

"We found it on him," said Davis. "That's true."

"Or partly true, Inspector. Anyhow, he had a key. To go on with the story—both Cameron and Gerente had been going with a girl—Hilda Lestrade. She came to call on Cameron; they had a few drinks in Cameron's apartment and came upstairs. Here, they had some more. Gerente got a bit drunk and high words followed. Gerente came at Cameron with a poker. Cameron wrested it away and struck him down. He fell right where I'm standing now."

The Inspector's heavy brows met in a frown. "What's the matter with that?"

"Inconsistencies, Davis. Incongruities. Impossibilities. It's full of them, and I can't even see. Where was Cameron standing when Gerente rushed him with the poker? If Gerente seized the poker from beside the fireplace, then Cameron must have been somewhere out in the room. Remember that, Inspector, when you question the girl.

"Did Cameron push Gerente back in front of the fire before he struck him down? If he did, it was a neat quiet job—for the struggle hadn't even rumpled Paul Gerente's dressing gown. And another point—before Cameron committed this foul deed he must have turned his victim around. It won't wash, Davis. Paul Gerente was struck down quietly from behind. Probably by someone who slipped out from the bedroom."

"But Cameron's confessed, Maclain," the Inspector reminded him stolidly.

"That makes everything easy, doesn't it? Will you hand me an ash tray, Sergeant? I don't want to get these on the floor." He flicked off his ashes, turned to the mantel, and set the ash tray down. "You can handle this any way you want, Inspector, but I'm going to tell you a little more."

"I can't stop you. Shoot. Mentally I'm putting it all down."

"Is it consistent that after committing a murder the murderer should wash three highball glasses and put them away again? That's number one. Number two is—somebody with wet feet stood for a long time outside of this apartment door in the hall, or left their rubbers there."

"Now, how—"

"Dreist sniffed the floor, Inspector, while I was waiting outside the door before Cameron let me in. I felt the floor. I think a pair of rubbers had been there, for I doubt if anyone could have stood so close to the wall."

"They belonged to the girl," said Archer with a sigh.

"She came upstairs from Cameron's apartment." The Captain put more ashes in the tray. "Did she keep her wet rubbers on until she came up here, and then suddenly decide to remove them and leave them in the hall?"

"There's something you're holding back, Captain." The Inspector's voice had an edge. "It isn't like you to take an open-and-shut killing and twist it into a nasty snarl."

"It's already a nasty snarl." The Captain snuffed his cigarette in the tray. "There was something inconsistent about that set of Braille instructions, Inspector Davis. It brought me here tonight, because I'd hardly expect to find it in G-2. There's something inconsistent here—in this room, and the bedroom; and traces of it in Paul Gerente's secret drawer."

"If there's anything in that drawer," said Archer, "it certainly doesn't meet the eye."

"Nor ever will, Sergeant," said Duncan Maclain. "I'm talking about an odor of violets!"

CHAPTER VII

1

THE THERMOMETER was dropping steadily throughout New England. A biting wind, rolling in from Maine, had sent the whole of Hartford to bed huddling under blankets, and turned the steep short hill up Asylum Street from the station into a dangerous incline of traffic-packed ice and snow.

Norma felt cramped and miserable when she picked up the brown-paper parcel containing Babs's galoshes and climbed stiffly down to the platform after three unhappy hours in the smoking car. The wind brought tears to her eyes. Getting what shelter she could from her furs, she lowered her head against the blast and fought her way downstairs. A porter, noting her clothes, started toward her, and seeing she had no baggage turned away disappointedly.

She had hesitated as long as possible before leaving the train, and so far luck had been with her. Neither in Grand Central nor in the Hartford station had she encountered a single person she knew. When she stepped out onto Spruce Street in search of a taxi, it came as a shock to find herself staring straight at a neighbor, Bunny Carter, who was leaning from the back window of his chauffeur-driven Lincoln car.

Bunny was president of the great International Aircraft works at East Hartford, where Gilbert Tredwill worked as a designing engineer. The sumptuous Carter home was built close to The Crags on an adjoining hill. Norma was extremely fond of both Bunny and his wife, Beatrice, but for the moment he was about the last person she wanted to see.

"Norma, my dear!" Bunny's jovial Billiken face twisted up into a welcome and he flung open the door. "Hop in! Hop in! I'm waiting for somebody else, who apparently hasn't arrived, but I'd rather have you."

Norma started to protest, and decided it would only make her late arrival in Hartford more conspicuous. She stepped into the car and sank back into the welcome seclusion of the corner, smiling a mechanical smile.

Bunny picked up a communicator beside him and spoke to Al Rutgers, his combination pilot and chauffeur. "Might as well go home, Al. Cranford isn't coming tonight. Stop at The Crags and drop Mrs. Tredwill."

The big Lincoln moved off with a swish of chains in slush, turned right up the Asylum hill, and started out Farmington Avenue for West Hartford.

"Well," said Bunny. "That's that. What have you been up to on such a day?"

"Shopping, of course." Norma lighted a cigarette, surprised to find how easy it was to lay the foundation for a complicated tissue of lies.

"Good Lord." Bunny chuckled. "You must love your home to take a milk train."

"Oh, I took in a show," said Norma, and regretted it instantly.

"Pretty soft to have a husband who gets tickets for everything," Bunny declared scornfully. "What did you see?"

Norma watched the great Colonial bulk of the Aetna Life building slip by. Her mind was a blank. Trying her best, she could only think of the name of a single show.

"*Hellz-A-Poppin.*"

"I thought you and Thad saw that before."

"We did." She opened the window a crack and dropped out her cigarette. Somehow she must end Bunny's questions. Everything she said gave her more explaining to do. She plunged on recklessly: —

"Thad wasn't with me. I went with some people you don't know. I could see it again, for that matter. It's a swell show."

Bunny leaned back beside her. The car was silent while he busied himself with a cigar. He pulled out an electric lighter on a cord. Norma felt that his habitually humorous round face looked grave in the reddish glow as he puffed on his cigar. He restored the lighter carefully to its place, and said: —

"Somebody told me Thad went to New York today."

"He did."

"Oh."

"*Oh* hell, Bunny. Don't you, of all people, get stuffed-shirty with me. Thad's twenty-five years older than I am—but I knew that when I married him. Just because I slip into New York on the sly to buy a few Christmas surprises, and happen to go to a show, is no reason for Hartford to be clucking its tongue at me."

"Norma, my *dear!*" His voice was hurt. The fine cloth of his camel-hair coat reflected his strong pull on the cigar. "You've got me wrong, entirely. I'd as soon cast aspersions on Bea."

"Forget it, darling." Norma felt she had blundered. She

reached across and patted his hand. "I'm always too sensitive about Thad and me when I'm tired—"

It was a temptation to go on; to share her secret with Bunny, who was clear-headed and competent. It would be heavenly to relieve the strain by talking things over with him and his wife. She could count on understanding from delicate, brilliant Bea. But that must wait. The first—and most essential—thing was to hear Babs's story. Until Babs returned, and talked, there was nothing that Norma dared to do.

They were passing through West Hartford center, deserted except for a few cars parked in front of the diner.

"Coffee?" asked Bunny.

Norma shook her head. "A steak wouldn't get me out into that snow."

"You're awfully quiet," he said with pleading seriousness. "Honestly, Norma, I'll feel terrible if you're annoyed over anything I've said, and so will Bea. I was really only—"

"I've told you, Bunny, it's *me*." Norma laughed, and hoped it didn't sound forced. "I've bought a television set for Thad, which he's been wanting for ages. All I ask is that if you and Bea come over to the house before Christmas, you won't give my trip to New York away."

"I'll do even better," Bunny assured her. "If anything comes up you can tell them that you spent the afternoon and evening at our house. I'll pass it on to Bea. Your nefarious schemes won't be given away."

"Thanks," said Norma. "You're a grand conspirator. How is Bea?"

"Not very well," he told her gravely. "I think I'll send her to Florida later on. The cold and the snow get her down. She's been in bed for a couple of days."

"Give her my love. I'll try to stop over tomorrow, or the following day."

"She'll be glad to see you."

The lights of West Hartford dropped behind. The Lincoln turned left at the Farmington cutoff. A couple of lights marking The Crags showed like crushed blurred dandelions hung above the road in the storm. At the edge of Tredwill Village, Al Rutgers, at the wheel, turned left again. With whirring chains the big car managed to fight its way up the snow-choked roadway to the top of Tredwill hill.

Norma gave Bunny and Al Rutgers a brief good-night and thanks, and stood in the doorway under the porte-cochere until the automobile drove away. The Crags seemed vast and vacant when she stepped inside. The servants occupied another wing, and Norma was grateful for the reassuring touch of Cheli's manuscript on a chair before the fireplace. At least, she wasn't facing the prospect of breakfasting alone.

About to start upstairs, Norma stopped with her foot on the bottom step. Bringing with it a disturbing premonition, the telephone began to ring in a closet, which served as a booth adjoining the downstairs hall.

2

"Babs!"

Young Stacy Tredwill stood just inside the door of the Ritters' apartment and listened to the sound of his own voice echo back down the length of the corridor.

A shaded table lamp was burning in the foyer. Farther along, to his left, more lights showed brightly from the living room. He put his hat on the table beside the lamp, slipped out of overcoat and muffler, and hung them up in the coat closet.

In the living room he turned out some of the wall lights, softening the glare. Babs must have come in and gone out again—probably for cigarettes. She always forgot everything—lights included, and he hadn't seen her mink coat in the coat closet. He shrugged his shoulders and walked to the window to stand for a while watching the automobiles speed along through the slush on Park Avenue ten stories below. It was fun to have the use of a six-room New York apartment while the owners were away. It gave one a feeling of importance. The Ritters were swell—realized that he and Babs were old enough to have a little sense. Not many people would have left permission for visitors to order what they wanted from the restaurant downstairs.

Stacy left his place at the window and turned on the radio. A midnight program of dance music was on, playing a hit from a current picture. He sat down at the Mason and Hamlin grand and swung into the melody. He had seen the picture that evening with a friend. It pleased him to be able to remember every passage of the song; to select the key the orchestra was using.

When the number was finished, he shut off the radio. Back at the piano, he played the piece over and over again, adding variations of his own, playing very softly. A clock chimed somewhere. He quit abruptly in the middle of a bar and walked out into the hall.

Packages, gaudy in Christmas wrappings, were piled along one wall—tokens of several hours spent shopping with Babs during the day. Stacy passed them by and stopped before a bedroom door. He listened for a second or two before he knocked lightly and called his sister's name. The hall light fell across an unrumpled bed when he opened the door.

His slim shoulders were set and a line of determination strengthened his youthful chin when he returned to the living room. He had a code of his own governing the relationship between brother and sister. It was simply that they let each other alone.

Babs knew what time he'd be back at the apartment from the picture show. She'd told him that she had a dinner date and would be home before eleven. It wasn't his province to check up on her if she stayed out until two, but for her not to telephone was unfair.

With a telephone directory spread out beside him on the piano bench, Stacy sat for a long time staring down at Paul Gerente's name. Babs had carefully avoided saying where she was going, but Stacy knew. He knew nearly everything that Babs thought, and did—except, possibly, why she persisted in treating him like a fool. He closed the book with a bang. Babs would never forgive him if he called Paul Gerente.

"She wouldn't be there, anyhow," he assured himself half aloud. "They've probably gone dancing in the Rainbow Room."

He took a current mystery from the bookrack and went to his own room feeling that Babs's unthinking lateness had brought a depressing end to a pleasant day. In bed, he read for more than an hour, lowering the book every time he heard the elevator stop at the tenth floor.

It was difficult to concentrate on the story. Accidents kept filling his mind. Such things were always happening in New York—taxicabs crashing—pedestrians getting run over—people slipping in the ice and snow. Finally he turned out the reading lamp and fell into a restless doze to awake some time between three and four.

His pajamas were damp with perspiration. He got up drowsily, realizing that he had neglected to open a window in the room. Barefooted, he crossed the hall and opened Babs's door.

The bed was still smooth and unrumpled. Stacy switched on the light and ran a hand nervously through his tousled blond hair. Babs was thoughtless in lots of things, but she had her own code, too. Nothing but tragedy, Stacy felt certain, would keep her out with a man until four.

His drowsiness fled as he looked about the room. With the light on, he noticed something which had not been apparent before. The room was disconcertingly bare. The dressing table was cleared. Babs's traveling bag was missing from the stand at the foot of the bed. Moved by a sense of panic, he ran across the floor and opened the closet. It was empty, and for dragging seconds he stood leaning weakly against the door.

His first thought of sudden illness in the family he put quickly away. If his father, brother, or Norma had summoned Babs she would have left a note. Even if she had forgotten it in her haste, someone would have phoned him. They all knew where he was.

Dazedly, he walked from room to room of the apartment searching for an answer. It came after a time—logical and most unpleasant, but the only possible reason he could think of for Babs to leave and take her clothes away.

Resolutely, he picked up the phone in the living room and put in a Hartford call. He was faced with something which only Norma could handle, something overwhelming which must be broken to his father with a woman's diplomacy.

He was shaking when the distant ringing of the phone bell finally stopped and he realized the call was through.

"Norma?" he said.

"Yes. Who is it?" Her familiar voice sounded strained, distant and faraway.

"It's Stacy. Something terrible's happened, Norma. I don't know what to do. Babs has eloped with a man. She's gone."

"Gone where?"

"I don't know. She took all her things and left no word. It's terrible, Norma. I don't know how to tell you—she's eloped with Paul Gerente!"

CHAPTER VIII

UTTER EXHAUSTION swept over Norma in an enervating wave as she ended her conversation with Stacy and hung up the phone. A night light burned dimly in the hall, lending an air of cavernous vacancy to The Crags. Norma went into the living room, swept Cheli's manuscript aside, and eased herself down into the comfort of the big armchair.

The embers of the fire had long since died. Half a log, blackened and grim, lay across the andirons. By the feeble light, shining in from the hall, she could see the gray film of ashes under the log. Not a vestige of pink remained which by careful tending might be nursed to a warming glow.

Her love for Paul Gerente had died that way, and now Paul was gone. He had burned brightly too, for a time, warming the hearts of the public. It seemed unbelievable that her love for him could have been so routine. Living, he would have said, "Ashes? Really, Norma, my dear! Why not the last fading sparks of a falling rocket—the last fizzing drops swallowed from a glass of dry champagne? Ashes are so hackneyed. My memory deserves something better than an aphorismic cliché!"

It was almost a pity that he could never know how much his

violent death had upset her. His capacity for enjoyment was great. What immeasurable pleasure he would have gained from the knowledge that his lifeless body had disrupted Norma's secure and peaceful existence; that, dead, he was stamped ineradicably on her mind at the end of a single day.

Stacy's excited call to tell her that Babs had eloped with Paul Gerente had come as a paralyzing shock. For a moment it brought back the uncertainty which had plagued her earlier, revived the thought that the dead man might not have been Paul. She tried to recall the details of Stacy's story. All she could remember was that Babs had left and taken all her things from the Ritters'—summarily run away.

Analyzing things more carefully, Norma realized that she was jumping at false hopes again. Stacy had known that Barbara was going out with Paul Gerente. He had no inkling that Gerente had been killed. He knew that Babs was meeting Paul surreptitiously. With Babs gone, Stacy's boyish mind had seized on an elopement as the only logical explanation of his sister's secret departure. That much was easy to see.

Norma set out on another mental labyrinth which conceded the fact that she had seen Paul Gerente's body. Then Babs had seen it, too, for Babs was there. Beyond that point lay nothing but conjecture—frightful conjecture. Why had Babs run away? Babs was poised, self-assured, and proud of her family's influence. She was the type who calmly smiled defiance at the police when they arrested her for speeding, conscious that Thaddeus Tredwill's fortune stood back of her.

Norma shook her head in defeated bewilderment. She had told Stacy nothing over the phone, except to hurry home. She was glad of it now. In the morning she could talk to him, tell him to say nothing about Babs's visit to Paul, try to explain it to him in some plausible way. She was certain of one thing—Babs Tredwill had not turned herself into a fugitive from the law just because she had blundered in onto Paul Gerente's body on the floor.

Chill had crept into The Crags. It clung about Norma's slim ankles like an invisible fluid rising slowly about the chair. When she stood up the weight of her fur coat dragged at her soggily, reminding her that she still had it on. Fighting an inclination to relax in the chair again and sleep until morning, she stood for a few seconds brushing at a damp spot on the coat with the tips of her fingers. The thought of her own bed finally proved incentive enough to take her back into the hall.

Her handbag and the paper-wrapped galoshes were on a small table where she had placed them when she answered the phone. She picked them up and put them down again. The night light and her tautened nerves were jesting with her. Both her gloves had been on top of the galoshes when she went into the living room. Now only one of them was there. The other one lay at the end of a big Oriental rug, halfway across the hall.

Norma picked it up, retrieved her handbag and parcel, and stood uncomprehendingly looking from the front door to the stairway. "I'd better get to bed," she told herself firmly. "I'm walking in my sleep. I dropped that glove way over toward the dining-room door, and I don't remember being there."

Not until she was in her room did she begin to wonder if one of the servants hadn't heard the phone and come downstairs. Christmas was near. Bella, the housemaid, was nosy. She might have tried to peek in a parcel if she saw one in the hall. The conclusion of Norma's talk with Stacy had probably frightened her away.

"There's no use questioning her," Norma thought. "She won't admit it even if it's true."

Once in bed, Norma found that all of her bones were aching. Wide-eyed, she lay listening to the whine of the storm, wondering if she were coming down with an attack of the flu. She finally surrendered entirely to her wakefulness, and laid it unreasonably to Babs's galoshes. She had slipped them under her bed, still in their paper wrapping. Sleep might come if she got up again and put them away.

By the pink-shaded glow of a table lamp, she put on slippers and a warm woolen bathrobe. The package was loosely tied and opened easily. Norma put the brown paper and string in a wastebasket beside her small desk and, acting with a furtiveness which wasn't quite clear to her, filled the top of the wastebasket with white tissue paper taken from a drawer.

The guest room, occupied by Cheli Scott, was near by, but Norma had no fear of disturbing her guest. Cheli slept soundly, and Norma's soft padded slippers fell noiselessly against the thickness of the carpet in the hall.

Holding the galoshes pressed against her breast with both hands, she stopped outside of Babs's closed door. Sheepishly, she admitted her oversight. Certain from Stacy's call that Babs had fled, she had neglected to look in the most obvious place where Babs might be—the girl's own room. Under the drive of panic, Babs might easily have taken her things from the Ritters' and caught an earlier train home.

Norma guardedly opened the door and went in. The lulling hum of an electric clock was the only sound. Uninterrupted by any breath or movement of a sleeping occupant, the steady whir of the timepiece attested to the vacancy of the room.

She switched on the lights and looked about her. The room

was in perfect order, undisturbed from its cleaning during the day. Its perfection and beauty reflected Babs. The girl had something of the same sleek comfort about her, the same exquisite warmth. Norma felt doubly depressed. Babs, like her boudoir, was a product of much money, and the products of much money were often fragile and in need of loving care. Like the shimmering satin coverlet on the bed, Babs belonged at home. It was doubtful that she could ever survive the racking ordeal of a fear-impelled flight through a winter storm.

Norma closed her mind against a thousand questions. Had the child any money? Would she seek the doubtful safety of friends in another city? If she hadn't struck down Paul Gerente, why had she gone? If she had killed him in a struggle, where in the name of heaven could she go?

An automatic light clicked on in the closet as Norma opened the door. A colorful line of dresses on hangers crowded the interior. On the shelf, a row of hats on separate holders vied with each other in an exotic display. Metal shoe racks fastened to the inside of the closet door held twenty pairs or more.

Norma decided against the shoe racks. The fur tops of the overshoes stood out too conspicuously among the dainty slippers. She pushed some of the dresses aside and placed the galoshes on the closet floor. The dresses swung back over them again, hiding them from view. With a feeling of lightness, as though she had rid herself of some dragging encumbrance, she shut the closet, put out the lights, and started back to her room.

Halfway down the hall she paused and wrapped her bathrobe closer about her. The wind whipped up outside in a sudden strong noisy flurry. Far downstairs, probably from the basement, came the slam of a door.

Her only reaction was to suppress a "Damn!" of annoyance,

for she had heard that particular door before. It led from the laundry into the storeroom, and the latch never held. Unless it was locked with the key, its irritating slamming began sooner or later when the wind started to blow. Once begun, the slamming kept up indefinitely.

She decided to go and lock it herself, rather than call Pierce on the house phone. But at the top of the steps she paused again, recalling with slight uneasiness the incident of her glove in the downstairs hall.

Stubborn dislike of weakness in herself urged her on. She had made that trip to the basement at night more than once. Certainly she didn't intend to have her life at The Crags disrupted by the hectic events of a single day. If Bella, the housemaid, had dropped the glove, then Bella might have unlocked the storeroom door as well. Bella was not only nosy, she had a deep-rooted love for jams and jellies. The storeroom contained quite a selection.

Norma pushed a switch at the stairhead and descended with more assurance when light streamed up from the lower hall. Habit, more than anything else, caused her to fasten the heavy brass safety chain on the double front door—a Tredwill habit which left a final lockup for the last one in. Interrupted by Stacy's phone call, she had overlooked it before.

She went through living room and dining room into another hall. There, the lights set high in a dome seemed dim. Great draperies of crimson swept down from the ceiling, held by medieval weapons against the walls. Burnished suits of armor stood on pedestals. Shells of ancient men, they watched her with vacant faces as she passed, saluting her with motionless halberds in their hands.

At the end of the hall she avoided the entrance to Thad's

miniature theater and took a door to the right which led to the basement stairs. A switch at the top landing lighted a bulb in the laundry below. Norma went on down. The cold of the concrete crept through the soles of her slippers as she crossed the laundry to the storeroom door.

The door was locked. Hanging on a nail beside it was the old-fashioned key. Yet Bella must have been there, for lingering above the clean soapy smell of the laundry was a trace of violet perfume.

In the boiler room to the right the oil burner flashed into action with a muffled pop, warning Norma that morning was very near. Out of a darkened passage to the left an icy draft swept through the laundry as though the starting of the heater had drawn it irresistibly toward the flame.

"Bella." Norma called the maid's name softly. Gil's workshop lay at the end of the darkened passage. Gil had used it since he was a boy of ten. It was forbidden territory to servants and family, but that rush of cold air must have come from the opened workshop door.

Norma groped her way down the passage, feeling above her for a light cord which she knew was there, but couldn't see. She found it at last, much farther along than she had expected. The bulb was gone. Ahead of her something creaked raucously. She was certain then that the big whitewashed door which Gil kept padlocked so carefully was swinging free.

A wall switch was at the left inside the door. Norma reached around the jamb, found the button, and pushed it. Two green-shaded droplights lighted, throwing white radiance down on a drafting table spread with drawings and blueprints, filling the balance of the workshop with an emerald glow.

Machines and a forge stood at the back of the workshop,

crowding the room in a double row. A wooden workbench, littered with tools, ran the full length of another wall. Two model airplanes hung from the ceiling, swaying gently from the opening of the door.

A huge old walnut wardrobe stood in a far corner behind the forge. It was piled high on top with remnants of a hand printing press, and filled to bursting with a haphazard collection of nails, screws, and type—relics of a print shop Gil had started as a boy. The only place where anyone could be hidden in the workshop was behind that wardrobe in the angle of the wall.

Norma picked her way carefully between the machines, watching the floor for nails and upended tacks. When she circled the forge and looked up, the greenish light from the emerald shades was flickering on the dull grimed finish of the wardrobe, drawing it closer to her. For the space of one dreadful second she felt that the wardrobe was tottering and about to fall.

It took another second for her to realize that her terrible thought was true. Then it was far too late. She stood motionless with feebly upraised hands, unable to scream from a throat that was tight and dry. The heavy press toppled and grazed her head. An instant later the lead-filled bulk of the wardrobe had crushed her to the floor.

CHAPTER IX

GOOD! COLONEL *Gray, the head of our defense plans, believes your ability to get around with your dog invaluable. Even under war conditions, a blind man could pass unquestioned where others might be suspected and stopped immediately. The vulnerable spots mentioned in there are in code. Before I leave would you care to name their locations for me as given you personally by Colonel Gray? I'd like to be sure you know."*

Captain Duncan Maclain made a noise with his lips and switched off the Ediphone record which was repeating his earlier conversation. With an easy motion, denoting long habit, he took a cigar box from the right-hand desk drawer. He dumped the contents—a hundred-piece jigsaw puzzle—on the desk top and irritably began sorting out the jumbled pile.

Stretched out luxuriously on the divan, Spud Savage watched his partner's quick fingers select a piece, trace the design of the cut, and begin their search for its mate.

"Well, go on with it, Dunc," he urged. "Did you tell this bird all the vulnerable spots?" A glint of humor lighted his curious yellow eyes.

"Since you came all the way into New York to protect me,"

said Maclain, "I'd appreciate a little help from you. Did you ever hear that fellow's voice before?"

Spud yawned. "On that record, he sounds like all the actors we heard in that movie house on the Cape last summer—but for that matter, so do you."

"I'll make a note of what you say." The Captain found a piece which fitted, and gave a tiny smile. His expressive face could reflect almost any shade of feeling when he so desired. The smile gave him a quizzical look, as though he might be listening to distant laughter. He fitted the two pieces of the puzzle together, and patted them down. "We live in a funny country, Spud," he began.

"If you're going to sit up all night, I suppose I'll have to listen." Spud shifted restlessly. He didn't like the look on the Captain's face. "What are you driving at? Politics, economics, or keeping us out of the war?"

"Sabotage and espionage," said Duncan Maclain. His fingers began to move more surely through the pile—selecting and rejecting; placing certain pieces to one side—pieces which were burned by touch into his memory.

"Don't tell me you've caught a spy." Spud lifted his slippered feet and tucked them under the heavy silk of his dressing gown.

"Sabotage and espionage," Maclain repeated. "That's what I'm driving at—that, and the levity of your tone."

"Of *my* tone, Dunc? Why pick on me?"

"Because, my very dear friend and companion, you unconsciously represent a norm."

"For God's sake don't get unctuous," Spud said pleadingly. "Did you say 'norm' or 'worm'?"

"There isn't much difference, is there?" The Captain wriggled his eyebrows thoughtfully. "You're intelligent—"

"Thanks."

"Strong and fearless—"

"Terrific!"

"Well-educated—"

"A certificate from Vassar."

"Widely traveled, and unusually familiar with the workings of organized crime."

"In fact," Spud admitted shrinkingly, "I'm known to my devoted wife, Rena, as Samuel Savage, the Magnificent Obsession. Why don't you hire me?"

The Captain clicked two pieces of the jigsaw puzzle together like castanets. "The Detecto-Dictograph is recording all this," he said. "The reason I don't hire you is—you're *dumb!*"

"After that recommendation you just gave me?"

"Certainly," said Maclain. "You're a norm. Like the rest of our nation, you begin to giggle and twist like a coy little girl at the mention of espionage. The United States is probably the best-hated country in the world today—because it's the *best*. It has more to lose—and consequently more to guard. Yet you don't believe in *spies!*"

"Now look, Dunc, that's hardly fair." Spud sat up hastily. "You worked with me in both London and Paris during the last war. What about that crowd with the house at Leeds? What about—"

The Captain raised a hand. "There are always spies in England, France, and Germany—and every other country in Europe, too. The American public accepts that as a fact. The magazines and the movies have told them that it's so. But here?" He shrugged his broad shoulders deprecatingly. "Hell, no! Your average American will swallow the most incredible feats of gangsters—because he's had them on his neck for years. He overlooks the fact that, compared to a spy, the biggest gangster who ever lived was playing for small dough."

"You're upset, Dunc." Spud's voice was quiet with an unusual note of concern. He came to the desk and placed a hand on the Captain's shoulder. "I had no idea this was so serious, Dunc. What do you want me to do?"

"If I knew the answer to that, I wouldn't be upset." The Captain broke up a dozen pieces of the puzzle he had fitted together, carefully returned the fragments to the cigar box, and replaced the box in the drawer. "There are no rules of criminology which hold entirely good for a spy."

"The F. B. I. nailed three of them in the Rumrich case," Spud reminded him. "A couple of Russians, Gorin and Salich, were convicted in Los Angeles, too."

"Yes," Maclain admitted, "that's true—but Rumrich turned against the others. Let's consider this business of catching and convicting the hidden spy. First, the motive's fairly obvious in an ordinary criminal case. Not so with the spy. Love of a mother country may be buried very deeply. The background of a suspect has to be thoroughly traced."

"You mean by that that everyone's a suspect until they're proved innocent?" Spud went around the desk and took a chair.

"Exactly," said Maclain. "If you're in contact with anything which may be valuable information to another country—then you're a potential spy. You may be selling out for money, patriotism, political disagreement with the government in power, or unwillingly for self-protection."

"Blackmail?"

"Crude, Spud, but terribly true. Government agents of a foreign power may have dug up some secret in your past—or in the life of someone very dear to you. They kindly give you a Hobson's choice of facing ruin and disgrace or accepting a nicely remunerative commission as a spy.

"Once you're in, you're devilishly hard to catch. Al Capone built up an organization which nearly stifled a city—but the government put him away. He was a piker compared to the humblest of spies. When you become a secret agent—you have a *government* back of *you*.

"All the resources of a powerful nation are at your command. False references, false passports, or any necessary records to give you a seemingly authentic background are easy to obtain. Money? You're drawing on a national treasury."

"And where's the weakness?" Spud asked.

"That's what I'm looking for." Maclain thoughtfully tucked in his under lip. "It seems to me there are two. An ordinary criminal often has a police record—but a record is fatal to a spy. Once a spy is caught, his usefulness ends immediately. Let him become known to the authorities—and they're forever more on guard against him."

"What's the second?"

"It's even more important." The Captain spread his restless hands flat on the desk and for a moment left them in repose. "General knowledge, available to the public, is of no value to the secret agent. His field is limited. The *saboteur* must confine his destruction to objects of military or naval importance—things which are carefully protected. In other words, Spud, the authorities always know where to look for threatened espionage, and sabotage. Locate the *raison d'être. Saboteurs* must have something to sabotage. Spies must have something worth-while on which to spy."

"I suppose you're telling me, in your own peculiar way," Spud declared, "that this fellow, Gerente, was killed by a spy."

"Don't put flat statements into my mouth," the Captain remonstrated patiently. "Form your own conclusions, as you usually do. Gerente had some Braille instructions to deliver to me from Colonel Gray, the head of our defense plans for New York City. Gerente was killed and those instructions stolen from his rooms—"

"And brought to you anyhow," said Spud. "Why?"

"Maybe they were photostated on the way. Braille can be deciphered, you know," Maclain reminded him drily, "even by people who can see."

"Just because I have eyes, you needn't get sarcastic with me."

The Captain laughed softly. "A few things are clear. The man who brought those instructions here knew exactly what arrangements had been made for Gerente to talk with me. He knew also what the instructions said—except for the part in code, and that's the part he most wanted to know. He took a chance—"

"A long one."

"But a good one, that he might trick me. And another thing, if I hadn't become suspicious of receiving delicately scented instructions from G-2—Gerente's murder might have gone undiscovered until the following day."

"It's the following day now," said Spud. "It's half-past four." He stood up and stretched.

The Captain followed suit. "We'll have four hours' sleep at any rate. Colonel Gray is coming here at nine."

"He wants to see you, not me."

The Captain smiled. "I promised you'd be there too."

Spud picked up the sheets of Braille and sniffed them as he took them to the safe to put them away. "Violets, eh? None of this makes sense, Dunc. It's unbelievable that a man would confess to a murder he didn't commit. Yet when you say this fellow

Cameron isn't guilty—well, if I personally saw him blow a guy's head off, I'd still be inclined to let him go." Spud stopped in the middle of the floor. "Say, Dunc. Do you remember the Axel Fish case four years ago? Fish confessed to a killing he didn't do—but he confessed to save a girl."

"Your back is about to run into something," said Maclain. "You're traveling the right road at high speed—but you're in reverse."

"Reverse?"

"Certainly." The Captain pressed his temples wearily. "When the police pick up this Lestrade girl as a witness she's going to swear by all that's holy that she never even heard of Paul Gerente."

"Did she?"

"What the hell's the difference?" asked Maclain. "Davis will probably have three highball glasses out of Gerente's apartment with her prints all over them—and a *moulage* of her teeth where she bit Gerente on the neck after he fell to the floor. If that isn't enough to hold her, they'll set a bail that Garbo couldn't raise—and spray the irate Miss Lestrade all over with violet perfume."

"I take it," said Spud. "They mean to hold her in jail."

"Check," said Duncan Maclain. "Cameron didn't confess to a murder to save a girl—he confessed to a murder to get a girl out of his way!"

CHAPTER X

COLONEL MALCOLM W. GRAY arrived at Maclain's penthouse apartment while Spud and the Captain were still busy with eggs and coffee. At Maclain's suggestion, they transferred their coffee to the office from the dining room.

The Colonel was far from being the erect military figure which anyone awaiting the head of New York's defense plans might have expected to see. Instead, he turned out to be a chubby little fellow clad in an expensive salt-and-pepper business suit more reminiscent of Bond Street than Fifth Avenue. His cheeks were red from the cold outside and recent shaving. His graying hair brought to Maclain's keen nostrils an inkling of the barber's chair. The roundness of his chin and face and the crinkled corners of his eyes gave Spud the impression that the Colonel was always stopping on the verge of a smile. Oddly at variance with his other characteristics, Colonel Gray's grip and voice were steel.

He sat in the chair in front of Maclain's desk and kept leaning over to make a point by gazing intently into the Captain's eyes. Each time he did so, it seemed to disconcert him to find that Maclain couldn't see. He'd turn away and make his point a second time by gazing toward Spud on the divan and speaking more forcefully.

"I need good men," he declared suddenly, breaking up the amenities. "I presume Mr. Savage is a good man, Captain Maclain, or he wouldn't be associated with you."

"Last night he told me I was beautiful but dumb." Spud blew a smoke ring up from the divan and watched it admiringly.

"Dumb?" Again Colonel Gray almost broke into a smile.

"Slightly exaggerated," said Maclain. "—Spud has a tendency. I was figuratively speaking, that's all—pointing out to him that the American public doesn't believe in spies."

"Well, I do!" The Colonel took a straight-stemmed pipe from the pocket of his coat, put tobacco in it, and tamped it down with a well-manicured thumb. For a time he sat sucking on it moodily.

Spud said, "There are matches on the desk, Colonel."

"I seldom smoke," the Colonel remarked, staring at Maclain, "but I like to feel a pipe in my mouth. It gives me something to chew. Somebody killed one of my men last night, Captain Maclain. That's the main thing that brought me here to you."

The Captain leaned back in his chair and clasped his hands on top of his head. It was always a sign of interest in Duncan Maclain when his fingers were still.

"I wonder," he remarked, "if you'd have any objection to my taking this conversation down?"

The Colonel looked hastily around the office and said, "Down where?"

"On a record," Maclain told him. "I have Detecto-Dictographs set behind some panels in the wall. I find it very helpful, since I can't make notes, to be able to go back later and hear what people had to say."

"Well, if you can get any help out of what I'm going to tell you, go ahead!" the Colonel said placidly. "Although I'm not particularly fond of having machines eavesdrop on me."

He swung around suddenly on Spud. "I wouldn't be saying anything if I thought it would get beyond you two!"

Spud grinned. "Go ahead—Dunc's blind, and I'm deaf and dumb."

"And sometimes," said Colonel Gray, "I think I'm all three."

He turned back to Maclain. "Do you happen to remember what this fellow who brought my Braille instructions said to you?"

"Certainly," said Maclain. "I can do even more; I can play the entire conversation back to you."

He reached down and took a record from a bottom drawer, slipped it onto the Ediphone, and a moment later the sound of the conversation was filling the room. "I have a hookup with the Capehart," Maclain explained.

The Colonel sat nursing his fireless pipe until the record was through. "Well, thank God for one thing!" he remarked as Maclain clicked off the machine. "He didn't get much out of you. Look, Captain, the police have told me about your visit to Gerente's last night. I'm going to be frank, dangerously so, with you and your partner too. I'm pretty good at defense strategy, but I don't hold myself out to be much of a criminologist. I'm forced to leave that unpleasant phase of my work up to the police, the F. B. I., and men who have made a study of it such as your partner and you."

The Captain leaned back still farther in his chair. "We'll do everything we can."

Spud said, "That goes for me, too."

"I'm in a peculiar position," said Colonel Gray. "Gerente was killed, and I want to know why, but I can't tell everything I know to the police. Nor can I tell everything I know to you."

He put his pipe away and tried to move his chair.

"I'm afraid you'll have to leave it where it is," said Spud with a grin. "It's screwed down to the floor."

"What the—" the Colonel began.

"When I walk around the room," said Captain Maclain, "I want to know where the furniture is."

"I was speaking about Gerente," said Colonel Gray. "First, let me say this. To find out the key points which could sabotage this city, there are a hundred people in the United States who would have killed Gerente in the handiest way."

"That sounds like a man-sized undertaking to me," said Spud.

"What?" said Colonel Gray.

"To sabotage New York City."

"That's just the trouble," the Colonel told him bitterly. "It's just about man-sized. That's what's keeping me on hot eggs every day. Half a dozen power stations and four main water tunnels that could be valved down in two hours control the life of this town. One single electrical station in the northern part of the state can be thrown in, and that's all we have in case of emergency. There's a method of cutting off the sewage disposal, too. You'd be surprised, Mr. Savage, to know how many men it would take to accomplish such a project. Perhaps I'd better say how few."

"While you're at it, Colonel," Maclain suggested quietly, "why not tell him just what such sabotage would do?"

"Do! Why—" The Colonel seemed to be feeling around for some strong enough expletive. He finished by saying, "It would raise hell. That's what it would do. Do you gentlemen play chess?"

"Dunc does," said Spud. "He calls out his moves and I push around the pieces so he can checkmate me."

"All right," Colonel Gray continued. "New York City's like a Queen. She's so strong and powerful, and so mobile, that she's constantly subject to attack. It's wise to remember that a single pawn can take her out of the game.

"Suppose some organized band struck effectively—simultaneously ruined the six power stations, cut off the sewage disposal, and valved down the four main water tunnels. In an incredibly short time the streets of New York would be tied up in an inextricable traffic snarl.

"Automobiles would begin to run out of gas—there are hundreds just at that point on the streets at every hour of the day. They couldn't get any more—because filling-station pumps are operated electrically. The ones which have gas couldn't get out of town. The pumping systems in the tunnels would cease—immediately fouling the air. Bridges and ferryboats would be hopelessly jammed. Anyone will know I'm not exaggerating, if he's ever crossed the Queensborough Bridge on a holiday. It can be tied up for hours by a single stalled car."

The Colonel paused. Maclain heard his quickened breathing, and Spud's uneasy moving on the leather divan. He said softly, "Tell him about fire, Colonel Gray."

"Havoc!" the officer exclaimed sharply. "Devastation! The engines couldn't get through the impeded streets. If they got through the water would be gone. Milling mobs would take possession—mad with fear. Police can't move. Troops can't move. Then, with the sewers out of commission—comes pestilence." He lowered his voice. "The terror by night. The Queen is dead. New York City is gone."

Spud asked: "What about the telephone? I suppose it would go too."

The Colonel shook his head. "That's one of the companies which have had enough foresight to prepare for emergency. They have a secret power plant of Diesel engines safely hidden away." He swung around on Maclain. "I hope you understand how invaluable you can be—a trained intelligence officer who can move around in darkness as well as in the light; a man who knows every street of this vast city."

Maclain nodded soberly. "Yes, Colonel Gray. I know."

"Good." The Colonel took out his pipe again, lighted a match, and let it burn down without applying it to the tobacco. When the match was out he threw it away. "Gerente was working on two things," he said. "He was helping me on defense plans for one. Secondly, he was playing around with a girl."

"Hilda Lestrade?" Maclain sat up straight in his chair.

On the divan, Spud grinned quietly.

"Maybe." The Colonel bit down on his pipe-stem. "The police have her in custody along with a chap named Cameron, who has confessed to Gerente's murder. Have you read the morning papers?"

"No," said Spud. "They weren't delivered. We're supposed to be out of town."

Maclain asked, "What did they say?"

Colonel Gray hesitated. "They gave Gerente a big play. He was well known on the stage a few years ago. Crime of passion—"

"I mean about the Lestrade girl."

"Not much, Captain Maclain. Mysterious woman—and all that sort of thing—"

"But he *was* playing around with her," Maclain persisted—"at least from what you say."

"You misinterpreted my statement, Captain. I said Gerente was playing around with a girl. It was you who mentioned Hilda Lestrade, and I said 'Maybe.' I still mean it. Maybe she was girl number two. Her appearance in this affair has rather complicated things for me—another reason I came to you."

"Perhaps there're more," Spud suggested. "This Gerente seems to have been quite versatile with the ladies."

"A valuable trait in some phases of my unpleasant duties," said Colonel Gray. "For the moment, I want to concentrate on a young lady from Hartford, Connecticut. Her name is Barbara Tredwill." He paused and added, "Did you ever hear of her before?"

The Captain thoughtfully shook his head.

"Was she the girl that a columnist hinted about in the paper yesterday?" asked Spud. "I noticed Gerente's name."

"That's the one. Her father's Thaddeus Tredwill, a prominent producer. Oddly enough, his present wife was married to Paul Gerente ten years ago."

"But what—" The Captain took up a flexible ivory paper cutter and began to bend it back and forth.

"Barbara Tredwill's brother, Gilbert, is a designing engineer with International Aircraft," Colonel Gray supplied. "There have been leaks from that plant. Gilbert Tredwill invented the bombing sight used on our planes. He has an even better one almost perfected today. Young Tredwill has a workshop in The Crags, his father's home."

"He lives there?" asked Maclain.

"With his wife, Helena. She's naturalized French—maiden name of Helena Corte."

"You sound suspicious of her," said Spud bluntly.

"I'm suspicious of everyone," said Colonel Gray. "I'm even suspicious of Gilbert Tredwill himself. He might be inadvertently giving information away. That's why Paul Gerente made it his business to become acquainted with Gilbert's sister, Barbara. He's been trying to learn all he could about the Tredwill family from the girl."

Maclain laid the paper cutter down with a snap. "You mean he might have learned too much to stay alive?"

"You're quick to get an idea. Gerente had an appointment with the Tredwill girl for dinner last night—and later, he had an appointment with you."

"Then the girl was in New York?"

"And most of her family, too," said Colonel Gray. "Her father was at the Waldorf-Astoria. Gilbert Tredwill and his wife stayed there too. Barbara Tredwill and a younger brother, Stacy, were guests of Frederick Ritter, who has an apartment on Park Avenue—but the Ritters are away. They turned over their apartment to the girl and her brother."

"I presume, since you have all this information," Maclain said slowly, "that you've questioned the girl."

The Colonel regarded a crease in his well-tended trousers and sharpened it between finger and thumb. "I talked with Gilbert Tredwill on the phone this morning, before I came here to see you. There are strong reasons why I don't want anyone in the Tredwill household to know why Paul Gerente scraped up a friendship with Gilbert's sister. I'm telling you this, Captain Maclain, because I need your help right now."

"I've promised it," said Maclain.

"Watch your step, Dunc," Spud warned. "I'm afraid you're dealing with a very clever man."

"Me, Mr. Savage?" The Colonel's friendly face grew even rounder than before. "My superiors have accused me of childish naïveté. I've—"

"Undoubtedly," Maclain broke in, "that's why they put you where you are. What were you about to say?"

"Paul Gerente's dead, but the country is very much alive. Someone must take up his work, Captain Maclain. I want you to go to Hartford today—right now. I've made arrangements for you to stay at The Crags—the Tredwill home. People who don't know you are more than apt to underrate you, if you don't mind my saying so. That's beyond price in what I want you to do."

"Yes," said Maclain.

"I want to find out who's getting information about the International Aircraft, and Tredwill's plans—and how. That means painstakingly accumulating everything possible about the Tredwill family, and everyone in the vicinity. Mr. Carter, president of International, lives close by. He'll co-operate with you." The Colonel was still long enough to put his pipe away. "I want to know if, before he was killed, Paul Gerente saw the Tredwill girl. I—"

"Just a minute, Colonel Gray. Tell me this: What am I supposed to be doing in Thaddeus Tredwill's home?"

"You've been retained by Thaddeus Tredwill to solve the disappearance of his only daughter," the Colonel stated briefly. "Barbara vanished from the Ritter's apartment last night and took all her clothes with her."

"I'll go," said Duncan Maclain, "but my dogs must go with me."

"Arrangements have been made for them, too." The Colonel stood up.

Spud helped the Colonel into his overcoat, and asked, "How much does Thaddeus Tredwill know?"

"He's expecting Captain Maclain," said Colonel Gray. "I talked to him this morning as well as his son. I wanted to question his daughter privately. He got in touch with his younger son, Stacy, and learned that Barbara was gone. He called me back. It was then I arranged for Captain Maclain."

"You still haven't said what he knows about Gerente," the Captain reminded him.

"Not much, I hope," said Colonel Gray. "He knows that Gerente was friendly with Barbara—but he doesn't know the real reason why. He knows from his son that Barbara had a date last night with—" The Colonel broke off abruptly and stood holding his hat in his hand.

"Yes," said Maclain, "that's quite a possibility. Other fathers have done it before."

"What's a possibility?" the Colonel demanded a shade impatiently.

"What you were thinking," Maclain told him unruffled. "That Thaddeus Tredwill killed Gerente for fooling around with his daughter."

"Damn it, sir," said Colonel Gray, "I'll thank you to quit reading my mind." He started toward the door and turned back to Maclain. "It's only fair to warn you, Captain. I'll give you all the protection I can—but that may not be enough. The last war blinded you. The one going on now may end your career. The disappearance of that Tredwill girl wasn't on the cards at all!"

CHAPTER XI

INSPECTOR LARRY DAVIS adjusted a window shade so that the slanting rays of the morning sun would keep out of his eyes. Under cover of the operation he winked at Sergeant Archer.

The Sergeant received the wink impassively and began to drum his heavy fingers on the wooden arm of his chair.

For a time the Inspector's office at Police Headquarters was silent.

Spud Savage broke the quiet with the scratch of a match. "They've now reached the stage of signaling each other with their eyelids, Dunc," he remarked to Captain Maclain beside him.

Maclain's lips crinkled at the corners. "I heard it click. Davis always makes a noise when he winks."

"It's an affliction," announced Davis. "A *tic*." He tried to look pleased with himself and succeeded in donning a Machiavellian expression. "It's brought on by worry at the thought of you going away."

"Not bad." The Captain looked like a school-teacher pleased with a boy. "Although the spelling is dissimilar—and the French pronunciation is tēk. Usually—"

"Quit spoiling his fun, Captain," Archer put in. "Who ever

heard of an Irishman speaking French? We're all upset because you have to rush off today."

"I have plenty of time," said Maclain. "At least enough to wait until I can talk with the Lestrade girl."

"Okay," said Davis. "It can't do anything more than waste time—and you're worse than a cockle-bur. She won't admit anything, but talk to her—talk to her all day. We have proof she was there."

"In Gerente's apartment?" asked Spud.

Davis nodded and said for the Captain's benefit, "Certainly. Where else do you think she was?"

"That's your little police wagon," Spud declared innocently. "I wouldn't know."

The Inspector pushed a button. "Bring up the Lestrade girl," he ordered the man who looked in the door.

The man saluted and disappeared quietly.

"It was time you gave him a promotion." Maclain shifted uncomfortably on the hardness of his chair. "Shaugnessy's always been a good man."

The Inspector picked up a sheaf of papers from his desk and irritably thrust them into a drawer. "There are thousands upon thousands of cops in this city," he declared, shaking his head. "Do you spend your spare moments having a list of promotions transcribed into Braille just to annoy *me*?"

"Yes," said Sergeant Archer ponderously. "I'll bite, too. I hate guessing games. How did you know Shaugnessy was promoted? How did you know that was him just now at the door? He's been out of the building for an hour or more."

"I'm sorry, Sergeant. I didn't realize that my unfortunate habit of thinking out loud might upset you."

"You and F. D. R.," said Davis. "Both of you think out loud when it's something you want the public to know."

The Captain saluted him gravely, military fashion. "At least you've compared me with a remarkably able man, Inspector. There's nothing mysterious about Shaugnessy, I assure you. You saw him and I heard him, that's all."

"I thought maybe you smelled him," Archer suggested. "You kept us long enough last night while you were chasing down a smell of perfume."

"Which I'll thank you not to mention," Maclain retorted in a tone both officers knew.

"You mean that, Captain Maclain?" Davis's heavy eyebrows were set in a straight line.

"Yes, I most certainly do." The Captain tempered his admonition with a smile. He turned his head in the direction of Sergeant Archer. "Speaking of smelling Shaugnessy—it's not impossible. There's a distinctly spicy odor to you. Shaving cream, unless I'm wrong."

The Sergeant grunted, and Davis laughed. "What about Shaugnessy at the door?"

"Spud can tell you that," said Maclain.

"Shaugnessy was wounded in a gun fight," said Spud. "That's why you have him working in your office. He limps. Dunc heard his step outside the door, that's all."

"Oh. And you tasted his promotion, I suppose—or felt the stripes on his arm."

"Hearing again, Inspector. As Spud and I came through the outer office, somebody asked where Sergeant Shaugnessy was. He was Patrolman Shaugnessy—not Sergeant—the many times we've been here before." The Captain's head moved slightly up and sideways. "I hear him coming now with the girl."

"I'd like you to listen to Archer's belly when you get a chance," said Davis. "I've been suspicious for some time that there was more in there than beer."

Archer's protest was cut off by the opening and closing of the office door.

"You can wait outside, Shaugnessy," Maclain heard Davis say. "Sit down, Miss Lestrade."

There was a rustle of silk, then the sound of Shaugnessy's departure, and the creak of an occupied chair.

A room was always audibly alive to Duncan Maclain. People about him breathed in different tempos; marked themselves by tiny coughs and unnoticed sniffles. Some of them clicked their teeth. Others had bones which cracked sharply when they moved.

Even when people thought themselves in utter repose, they were inclined to shift in unconscious embarrassment before Maclain's blindness. Inevitably, their presence was betrayed by a dozen or more lifetime habits of movement, which couldn't be controlled in a single day.

"This is Captain Duncan Maclain, and Mr. Savage," Inspector Davis told the Lestrade girl. "Captain Maclain's blind."

"So are the police," said Hilda Lestrade. "I'm being held for something I know nothing about. At least I can refuse to be questioned by everybody in New York every hour of the day."

"We all make mistakes," Spud remarked in his friendly disarming way. "If you're being detained in error—certainly you can't be harmed, Miss Lestrade, by anything you might say."

"Unless," Maclain added, "you insist on saying something which is untrue."

"And where do you fit into the picture?" Hilda demanded

frostily. "So far, the police, and that louse, Cameron, are the only ones who have said anything untrue."

"That's what I'm trying to prove, Miss Lestrade. I'm a private investigator, who happens to believe that somebody has taken out a private grudge on you."

"Now, hold on, Maclain," the Inspector interrupted. He stared from Maclain's bland face to the troubled features of the girl, who glared back at him defiantly. "There's a little matter of some fingerprints on highball glasses in Gerente's apartment which needs some explaining away."

"Were there any teeth marks on the dead man's neck?" Spud wanted to know.

"This is a hell of a time for cheap humor, Spud," Archer whispered loudly.

"Excuse me." Spud looked contrite. "It was just a passing idea of Captain Maclain's."

"Well, let it pass." Davis searched for a toothpick and failed to find one. "Cameron claims Miss Lestrade was in the apartment when this fellow was murdered."

"And I say he's a liar!" exclaimed the girl.

"That's your privilege," Davis continued with his cold eyes fixed on Hilda. "We work on proof. If either you or Captain Maclain can tell me how your fingerprints—"

"Obviously we can't," Maclain broke in, raising his hand. "Still, I'd like to hear what Miss Lestrade has to say."

"I've plenty to say, mister." Hilda's voice had a slightly hopeful ring. "I've known Arnold Cameron for two or three months— that's all. He's a phoney and a four-flusher, if you're asking me— an egg importer."

"A what?" asked Archer.

"Eggs," said Hilda, giving him a disdainful glance. "Eggs."

She held her thumb and forefinger up in the shape of one.

"Get it, Sergeant?" Spud asked eagerly. "The things that roosters don't lay."

"From Australia," the girl went on. "At least that's what he told me. We had dinner together last night and—"

"Where?" asked Maclain.

"In Cameron's apartment. I cooked it for him—"

"What?" The Captain stopped her again.

"*Blini*," she said. "That's pancakes served with caviar and sour cream. I've told them to check the garbage if they don't believe me. They'll find the empty glass caviar jar I threw away."

"We found it." Davis was impatient. "That part of your story is probably true."

"*Blini*." The Captain pursed his lips and meditatively scratched a place over his right eye. "That's a Russian dish, isn't it?"

"Yes," Hilda answered promptly. "And I think that Cameron's a Russian, too. He took me to a Russian café on Second Avenue several weeks ago. I got the recipe for the *blini* there. The place is full of long-haired reds. They knew him, too."

"And after dinner last night?" Maclain persisted.

"We had a few drinks when the dishes were cleared away. Then he got a phone call from some girl and told me I had to go."

"And you left without going to Gerente's apartment upstairs?" asked Maclain.

"I've told the police, and I'm telling you, I've never seen this man Paul Gerente, dead or alive, nor have I ever heard his name before."

"And suppose your fingerprints weren't only on the highball glasses?" the Inspector asked smugly. "Suppose we found some on the grand piano, too?"

"I don't give a damn if you found them all over the bathtub

and the john," the girl declared hysterically. "I didn't put them there."

The Captain took out a fountain pen and removed the cap. A leather-bound notebook followed from his side coat pocket. He flipped the notebook open in his left hand and braced it on his knee. Guiding his right hand with outstretched little finger, he scribbled hastily.

Conscious that the occupants of the room were watching him, he deliberately recapped the pen and put it away. "Inspector. Do you mind if I show Miss Lestrade what I've written here without revealing it to you?"

Davis indulged in an official frown. "She's a witness, not a criminal, Captain Maclain," he said after a moment. "We have no desire to read her personal mail."

"Thank you, Inspector." The Captain extended the notebook toward the girl.

She took it from his hand, glanced at it quickly, and passed it back again. Suddenly she twisted around to face Davis and sat up straight in her chair.

"If you'll get a stenographer," she said venomously, "I'll tell you the truth about what went on last night in Gerente's room. Cameron's a rat. He found out that I was seeing Paul—and—and—" Her voice broke and she steadied herself with an effort. "He struck Paul down without giving him a chance."

Davis's eyes narrowed. "Go on."

"It was premeditated murder, Inspector—murder in the first degree. I don't care about anything now, except to send Arnold Cameron to the electric chair!"

The Sergeant jumped to his feet with astounding agility. "Listen, lady! You better be sure of what you say!"

"Take her outside, Archer, and get a statement." Davis waved a commanding hand, and waited until Archer and the girl had gone. "Now what the hell did you write?" he demanded of Maclain.

A muscle moved in the Captain's chin as he handed over the notebook. The inspector stared at it gloweringly.

A murder suspect with a single witness is in a much worse fix than you.

Davis shook his head. "How the devil could that make her switch her story that way?"

"Search me," said Maclain. He stood up. "I'm afraid we'll have to go."

"You'll get out of here over forty dead policemen unless you tell me what that means," the Inspector warned him.

"It's a sympathy note." The Captain smiled. "A note to bring her cheer. She's a quick girl, Davis. Almost as fast on the uptake as you. Cameron decided to drag her into this mess—and I, speaking as a friend, implanted the idea in her head that she might make things tough for Mr. Cameron, too."

"Speaking as a friend," Davis mimicked. "What ever gave that wise baby the idea she had a friend in you?"

"I'm not quite sure, Inspector,"—the Captain took a step toward the door,—"although I'd give a lot to know. I think it was the ink which Spud put so carefully into my fountain pen this morning."

"The ink?" said Davis. "What ink, Captain? I think you'd better tell me before you go."

"The violet ink," said Duncan Maclain. He sniffed with deep appreciation. "Violet, Inspector—the color of that strange elusive smell!"

CHAPTER XII

HUMANS, THROUGHOUT the ages, have found it comforting to huddle about a fire. Warmth and propinquity minimize life's tragedies and multiply its joys. Barbara's disappearance had gathered the Tredwills together in the living room.

Thaddeus Tredwill stood in front of the fireplace gazing at the semicircle of faces which looked to him for leadership in a crisis. Outlined against the leaping flames, his tall aristocratic frame showed gaunt and spare.

Gil's wife spoke from out of the shadows beyond the group: —

"But it's too fantastic, Thaddeus. The man's blind. What does he expect to find with that dog—groping around in Barbara's room?" Her accent was a shade more noticeable than usual, although her English remained precise and clear.

Thaddeus looked toward his son with an expression which seemed to say, "You answer her, Gil. You brought her here."

"There's a State Trooper with him, Helena," Gilbert reminded her. The engineer, when he spoke seriously, looked much like his father. Both had a high forehead and jutting nose. Both used their hands to make their points clear. Gilbert, on the surface, appeared more stable. Thad had a touch of wildness at times, probably due to his frenzied thatch of whitish-gray hair.

"I'll bet he's good," said young Stacy from his place on the bearskin rug. "I wouldn't want his dogs after me."

"Good," Thad repeated slowly, weighing the word. "Fantastic. Words—words—words." He gazed down at his younger son. The boy moved uneasily and put one hand in the open mouth of the bear.

"Fantastic," Thaddeus repeated, and fixed the slightly square face of his daughter-in-law with an accusing stare. "What can be fantastic, Helena, after what's happened in this house since yesterday?" He swung his head around from person to person with the gesture of a minister daring some member of his congregation to reply.

"I find that my only daughter is consorting with a *man*." Thaddeus decided to sum things up for the fifth time, since no one had the temerity to answer him. He paused just long enough to let his audience grasp the full implication of the word *man*. Few orators could condense more vitriol into a single tone.

"A man," he reiterated. "My wife's ex-husband—a brute and a libertine—and everybody knows that he's seeing my daughter—everybody except me."

"Nobody knew it, Dad," said Gilbert placatingly.

"The world knew it—and the press knew it. I suffered the humiliation of having a blind man point that out to me. Now my wife's been badly injured in her own home, and my daughter's gone. Where? Who can say?" He broke off with genuine grief in his voice.

"Norma's awake, Thaddeus."

Gil moved on the settee to make a place for Cheli Scott, who had come in from the hall.

"I'll go up," said Thad.

"I wouldn't." Cheli sat down. "Better let her rest. She's still frightfully nervous. I had Pierce bring her some tea."

Thad questioned the girl with his eyes.

"She'll be all right in a day or two," Cheli told him. "Dr. Trotter said this morning that she'd suffered a shock and a shoulder sprain—"

"I feel guilty as hell," Gil interrupted morosely. "I've been intending for years to move that wardrobe out of the way. It was always tottery." He turned to Cheli. "You had plenty of nerve to go down there alone last night when you heard that thing fall."

"I thought that Pierce went with you, Cheli," Helena remarked, with a smile that missed her china-blue eyes.

"He certainly did." Cheli crossed her legs and smoothed her house coat over her knee. "Norma was the one with nerve, Helena. I wouldn't go into that basement alone in the daytime—not me." She looked at Gil. "I don't like to pry, but will someone tell me what that man with a dog is doing upstairs in the hall?"

"He's Captain Maclain, a detective," Stacy volunteered eagerly. "He got here about an hour ago in his car. He's trying to find out where Babs went. He was blinded in the last world war."

"A blind man—" Cheli began incredulously.

"He's world-famous," said Thad. He spoke with automatic preciseness, as though he had determined to drop the one subject which had torn at his heart all day. "Maclain's a challenge to any playwright, Cheli. Someday you should put him into a show. Humanity has become too dependent on the old phrase 'seeing is believing.' The Neanderthals knew what the four other senses could do. Without them man wouldn't have survived until now."

"Quite right, Mr. Tredwill."

The group before the fire turned to see Captain Maclain standing in the doorway.

"Come in, Captain," Thad said quickly. He started to ask a question, and added instead, "Cocktails will be along presently. Won't you take a chair?"

Schnucke moved forward, eyeing the Tredwill family with canine dignity. Helena stood up, and the dog unerringly directed the Captain past the barrier of a library table to Helena's proffered chair.

"I couldn't help overhearing part of your remarks as I was crossing the hall," Maclain apologized with a smile. He sat down and continued, "You mentioned the old phrase 'seeing is believing.' That's a true statement, Mr. Tredwill. I can't use my eyes. Will it surprise you to learn that I believe only what I can see?"

"You've already proved surprising in many ways, Captain Maclain." Again Thad stopped just short of speaking impatiently.

"I'll try to prove my contention."

Schnucke watched her master settle back in the chair. Maclain gestured with his hand and she lay down beside him. "The unabridged dictionary gives more than a dozen definitions for *see*," he announced. "Only the first two relate to the eyes. I depend on the others. Particularly on mental perception—definition number three. My vision is communicated to my brain through other mediums. I venture to say that, excluding color, it is just as clear as the vision accorded you."

Gilbert said, "That's a fascinating idea."

"It's true." The Captain sat silent. He had the rare ability to relax utterly at will, to become almost a component part of lounge or chair. "There are five people here with me now," he said after a time. "When I first arrived, an hour and twenty minutes ago,

I was introduced to four. The young lady on the settee to my left passed me in the upstairs hall."

"I'm Cheli Scott, a playwright, Captain Maclain. I'm visiting here."

The Captain acknowledged the information with a nod and a smile. "You're wearing a taffeta house coat, Miss Scott. You're in your early twenties. You have a bracelet with bangles on your right wrist, and woven Mexican slippers on your feet. You're holding a manuscript in your lap. You're slender and about five foot seven or eight—more than average tall."

Cheli laughed a trifle uncomfortably. "You must have questioned the trooper closely when I passed you in the upstairs hall."

"Not at all," said Captain Maclain. "Taffeta has a distinctive rustle, and house coats have zippers. You pulled yours up closer about your neck as you passed us upstairs. The house coat might have been a dress—except for its extra length swishing about your ankles, and the fact that you're wearing Mexican house slippers. The weave of them creaks unmistakably."

"What about her age?" Helena asked.

"Her voice," said Maclain. "It's young. Yours is too. The timbre changes with the years—just as the vocal cords alter with maturity. Stacy, on the bearskin rug at my feet, is still earmarked by his voice as a boy. Mr. Tredwill can never pass vocally for anything but a most mature man. In addition, the voice, more clearly than the face, expresses fear and hope, happiness and pain, excitement and calm."

Stacy asked, "How did you know about the bearskin?"

"My feet are on it. I can touch the head with my toe. See? And the first time I came in the room Schnucke shied slightly away."

"I suppose you heard the bracelet and the manuscript, too," Cheli remarked with a reflective glance at her wrist. "But my height and weight? I still don't understand."

"The bracelet jingles only when you turn a page. You've been leafing them over unconsciously. That placed it on your right wrist. Your height and slenderness were comparatively simple. I counted your footsteps—then compared them with my own as I walked the length of the upstairs hall. I live in blackness, Miss Scott, but it frees me from many distractions of those who use their eyes to see."

"And what, if anything," asked Thaddeus, "did you see in my daughter's room?"

"Nothing that can be of much value, I fear." Maclain stood up. "This is very pleasant, but I have a little more exploring to do. Before we have cocktails, I'd like to have Mr. Tredwill take me down to his workshop." He turned in Cheli's direction. "You found Mrs. Tredwill this morning, Miss Scott. I wonder if you'd come too. The trooper arrived later, I believe. He wasn't quite sure where Mrs. Tredwill fell."

"Would *she* refuse?" Helena murmured as Cheli followed the two men from the room. She answered her own question softly, "*Jamais de la vie!*"

The Connecticut State Trooper joined them in the hall. He gave a polite nod to Gilbert and Cheli, and asked, "What are we up to now?"

"More looking around, Stinson," said Maclain.

"I hope you find something," Trooper Stinson replied. "I've been over this house three times today."

"Why don't you go?" asked Gil. "Mrs. Tredwill met with an accident, that's all. There's nothing to keep you here now."

The trooper looked doubtful. "If you need me, Mr. Tredwill,

I've orders to stay." He hesitated and added, "But I'm inclined to agree with you."

"About the accident?"

"That's it, Captain," said Stinson emphatically. "Trooper Halick and I got here early this morning in answer to a call. One of us has been here off and on all day. When we got here the butler, who let us in, had to take a safety chain off the front door. Every window was locked inside, on the basement and ground floor. I'll stake nine years in the State Police that nobody got in and out of this house at all."

"Mrs. Tredwill got in late last night," Cheli reminded him. "She'd been with some friends, the Carters. Couldn't someone have come in the front door before she got home?"

"How'd he get out?" The officer shrugged. "We saw the tire tracks of Mr. Carter's car. It snowed here all day long and most of last night, too. There was that one set of tire tracks up the driveway from the village—no more."

"Which doesn't mean much, Stinson," the Captain said. "Any former tracks might have been effaced by passage of the Carter car and the snow. I suppose you and Halick checked for footprints, too."

"Captain Maclain," said Stinson earnestly, "I've been in this racket nine years, as I said before. We not only checked for footprints, we checked for fingerprints, and pick locks, and breaking and entering, and marks on the window sills—inside and outside on the ledges in the packed-up snow. I'm telling you now—if anybody got in here last night without leaving a trace, then he's still in here. Either that—or he flew."

"Maybe he had on winged galoshes," said Duncan Maclain. "I think he'd have needed them with all that snow."

CHAPTER XIII

CHELI AND Gilbert watched with interest as Maclain followed Schnucke's imperceptible signals down the length of the high domed hall. The Captain proceeded slowly. Twice he stopped and explored the mounted suits of armor with fluttering touches of his fingers. Each time, Schnucke's dark eyes turned up inquiringly to the glittering metal men.

"I don't think she likes them," Cheli said in a low tone to Gil.

Maclain's keen ears caught it. "I don't like them much, myself." He spoke for the first time since the State Trooper had gone. "Do you think it was the best thing to do, Mr. Tredwill—sending that officer away?"

"My father's been anxious to get rid of him ever since we got home this afternoon."

"Why?" Maclain stopped at the end of the hall with one hand resting on the ornate knob of the theater door.

"He thinks my sister's been kidnaped," said Gil.

"Kidnaped," Cheli whispered, and uttered a stifled "Oh!"

"Can I take it, Miss Scott," Maclain inquired with a quick turn of his head, "that you're inclined to disagree?"

"I don't know why, Captain Maclain, but somehow it seems preposterous. Babs didn't know she was going in town herself until yesterday. I thought that kidnapers—"

"Planned their coups in advance," Maclain supplied. "That's quite true. But Mr. Tredwill's father must have some justification for his idea."

"He hated Paul Gerente," Gil said simply. "Dad thinks that's why Gerente was seeing Barbara—that he planned this kidnaping and something slipped. Dad believes that the kidnapers killed Gerente. He was certain he'd hear something from them today."

"If he's right," said Cheli, "maybe he will, Gil, now that you've sent the police away."

"That's why I let Stinson go."

"Perhaps it was the best thing to do." The Captain opened the theater door. "What's in here?"

"Dad's theater." They had stepped inside and Gil's voice echoed in the resonant room.

"Your father's wife was an actress, wasn't she?" asked Maclain. He walked down toward the stage counting the rows of seats by touching them with his hand.

"Norma? She played the lead in *Dawn before Darkness*. Thad married her after the close of the play."

"I wish I could get her for the one I'm working on now," said Cheli.

"I doubt if she'll ever return to the stage," said Gil.

The Captain turned at the first row and came back to join them. "Can you get outside of the house from this theater?" He rested himself against the back of the aisle seat in the last row and addressed his question to Gil.

Cheli said, "There's a door at the back of the stage. The police examined it today and said it hadn't been opened for a long time."

"It was locked?"

"Barred," corrected Gil. "It's fireproof and fastens with a big iron bar inside. Nobody could have come in there—or gotten out without leaving it unbarred."

"I'll take your word for it. Let's go downstairs." The Captain stood erect. They left the theater with Gilbert leading the way.

The Captain was silent until they reached the basement. He spoke when Gilbert started across the laundry toward the passage Norma had taken the night before.

"If you don't mind, I'd like to get a little more information, Miss Scott. I understand that Mrs. Tredwill came down here last night because she heard the slamming of the workshop door."

"That's not quite right." Cheli glanced at Gil, who was watching the Captain with a wondering frown. "Norma thought the storeroom door was open. She had been down here to close it before."

"Last night?" Maclain asked quickly.

"No. I meant in the past."

"That's true," said Gil. "Unless it's locked it has a pesky habit of banging. I've fastened it more than once when I've been working late down here."

"Where is the storeroom?"

"Straight ahead of you," said Gil.

Maclain moved forward until Schnucke paused, signaling his nearness to the door. He found the knob after a single try. "It's locked now. Who keeps the key?"

"It was locked last night," Cheli told him. "The key hangs on a hook to the right of the door. Norma saw it there when she came down."

The Captain ran his hand upward along the wall.

"Farther right," said Gil. "Here, let me." He stepped up beside Maclain and handed him the key.

The Captain unlocked the door, stepped back, and slammed it to. The lock clicked but slipped out again, and the door swung free. For a moment Maclain stared at the door almost as though he had the power to see.

"Leave it open, please," he said. "Something about this interests me. Suppose we go into the workshop now."

He followed Gil and Cheli down the passageway. Keys tinkled on a ring. "The state policeman padlocked the door again," said Gil. "I have a key."

"Do you mind if I open it?" The Captain extended a hand.

"Not at all." Gil handed him the ring after locating the proper key.

The Captain took his left hand from Schnucke's brace, steadied the padlock, and inserted the key. He removed the heavy padlock and briefly hefted it in his hand. Freeing the hasp from the staple, he pushed on the workshop door. It opened with a creak. Maclain pushed harder.

"Engineers never do anything," said Gil. "For a year I've intended to oil that door."

"And line it up, or plane it," the Captain advised. "It scrapes along the floor."

Caught in a draft, the storeroom door in the laundry banged noisily.

"There!" said Cheli.

"There was somebody in this basement when Mrs. Tredwill

came down last night," the Captain declared. "Somebody who locked that storeroom door."

"It's almost impossible, Captain," said Gil.

"It's impossible for a scraping heavy door to slam. This one in particular." The Captain opened and shut the workshop door again. "It's also impossible for storeroom doors to lock themselves, Mr. Tredwill. That much I *know*.

"Mrs. Tredwill heard that storeroom door slam, as she thought. Not this one, here. It blew shut, as it did just now—from a draft caused by someone opening this workshop door. Yet that storeroom door was locked when Mrs. Tredwill got downstairs. If no one was down here, who removed this?" The Captain held up the padlock with a questioning air.

"I thought that I might have forgotten to lock it," Gil said without much conviction. "I don't know of any other key."

"Nor of anyone who might be interested in the work you're doing here?"

"I know of nations who might be interested, Captain, but I can't name any one person whom I know." He turned to Cheli with a touch of defiance and asked, "Can you?"

For a second her eyes showed sympathy. "No, Gil. I certainly can't." She flushed and turned away.

Maclain located the drafting table and set the padlock down. Moving one hand in a circle, he found the cord of a hanging electric light and traced it down to the shade.

"This is on," he remarked absently. "I suppose it's controlled by that switch you clicked as you came through the door."

"That's right," said Gil. "There's a second light near the other end of the drafting table."

Cheli said, "The wardrobe that fell on Norma is behind the forge at the far end of this room."

"I'm interested in lights right now," said Maclain. "Are these the only ones controlled by that switch?"

"Yes," Gil answered. "The lights over the machines turn on individually."

The Captain's sedulous fingers were surveying the table top, touching drafting boards, T squares, and triangles; delicately locating bottles of India ink, drawing pens and erasers, and, with equal delicacy, passing on again.

"Tell me, Miss Scott." The probing fingers were momentarily still, resting on the surface of a half-completed plan. "What lights were on in here when you found Mrs. Tredwill?"

"Just those two over the table."

"Do they illuminate the entire room?"

"Enough to get around," said Cheli. "Pierce turned on some others before we moved the wardrobe off of Norma."

"But these two give sufficient light, don't they," Maclain continued, "to see anyone who might be hiding in this room?"

"There's no place to hide," said Gil. "At least not with that wardrobe down on the floor."

"Ah!" The Captain reached down for Schnucke's brace. "That's what I wanted to know. Forward, Schnucke!" He followed her cautious course through the rows of machinery.

The wardrobe had been turned up on one side, but its spilled-out contents lay strewn about on the floor.

"Norma lay right here." Cheli hesitated, then finally took the Captain's hand. "Her head was here—her feet here. She was pinned down helplessly."

The Captain gave a few quick pats to the floor, then straightened up without comment and ran his fingers along the length of the fallen wardrobe. Schnucke watched him with a disapproving eye.

"Norma must have been trapped in the corner," Gil pondered aloud. "The forge was right behind her and when that wardrobe fell she couldn't get out of its way."

"If she wasn't hunting for somebody in here—why did she go near it?" asked Maclain.

"I don't see why she went near it anyhow." Gil stared down at the mess of type and metal on the ground. "Most women would be scared stiff if they thought someone was hiding back of that thing."

"Unless," Maclain suggested quietly, "it was someone she wasn't afraid of—someone she knew."

"That's it exactly, Captain," said Cheli. "Norma told me she thought Bella, the housemaid, was down here raiding the storeroom. I hadn't thought of it before."

"Good," Maclain exclaimed. "I'll talk with the girl." He turned quickly to Gil. "Mr. Tredwill, what valuable plans are you keeping down here now?"

"None." Gil hesitated, then went on, "That is, none outside. The ones I have completed are in the safe—"

"They were there night before last," said Gil. "But it won't take a moment to look and see."

He hurried off toward the drafting room. Cheli and the Captain followed more slowly. Maclain heard the turn of a combination and the clink of an opening safe door.

"They're all here." Gil spoke with relief. "If anything happened to these—"

"Quite," said Captain Maclain. He held out his hands. "Before you return them, do you object to having them examined by me?"

"But there's nothing you can—" Gil left his statement unfinished.

"No, Mr. Tredwill—nothing I can see." The Captain snapped the rubber bands from the rolled-up sheets of Bristol board and spread them out on the drafting table in a pile.

He found a heavy paperweight and placed it on one side of the sheets to flatten the springy curl. The other side he held down with his left hand.

"Have you a piece of waste and some gasoline?" He extended his right hand, palm up. "I'm afraid my fingers aren't very clean."

"They're not," said Cheli.

"Right beside you, Cheli." Gil pointed. "In the workbench drawer. Moisten it with some gasoline from that copper oilcan."

Cheli found the waste, moistened it, and wiped the Captain's fingers clean.

"You've wonderful hands," she told him.

"I'm fond of them myself," he said, with a smile which brought out the humor in his sensitive features. "They've been very good friends to me."

He sobered instantly. For twenty minutes his fingers roamed swiftly over the Bristol board, front and back. One by one he lifted the sheets from the pile, rerolled them, and fastened them with a rubber band.

Finally he lighted a cigarette, secured it more firmly in his holder, and drew a circle of smoke in the air. "What did you do with the tracings, Mr. Tredwill?"

"There haven't been any tracings," said Gil.

"Maybe not by you," said Duncan Maclain. "I think we'd better go up. Somebody's been eavesdropping on the basement stairs, but there's no use running out. They've gone." He picked up one of the rolls and held it to his nose. "I'm awfully sorry, Mr. Tredwill. I'm afraid your plans all smell of gasoline."

CHAPTER XIV

NORMA STIRRED against the softness of her pillows. A weight was pressing down on the covers, binding them unpleasantly about her. She laughed when she recognized that the pressing weight was her untouched dinner tray. The laugh had a ring of hysteria.

Each piece of familiar furniture in her bedroom stood out harsh and unnatural, with deep, clearetched lines. Usually they blended into a harmonious picture, comforting and secure. Now they clashed—had clashed all day. Dr. Trotter's so-called sedative had made her bed and bureau ugly; had given her a daytime nightmare of resting in the window of a secondhand furniture store.

She reached out beside her and rang for Pierce, then closed her eyes and lay motionless until the butler's knock aroused her. He came in and said, "Perhaps I'd better call Dr. Trotter again, madam," when he looked at the tray. "Or can I get you something else? You've had nothing but tea all day."

"I'll be all right, Pierce, if they'll let me alone. Is there any word from Babs?"

"Nothing, madam." He started out with the tray.

"Pierce."

"Yes, madam."

"This blind man, Captain Maclain? Thaddeus said he wanted to talk to me."

"It can wait, madam. It's nothing important, I'm sure."

"He's a detective, isn't he?"

"I believe so, Mrs. Tredwill. He has two dogs with him—one which guides him and another one called Dreist."

"You've fed them, haven't you?"

"They're being taken care of by Cappo, the Captain's colored chauffeur." The butler moved toward the door.

"Pierce."

"Yes, madam."

"I've decided to see him now. That interview's worrying me. Ask him to come up, please."

"Alone, madam?"

"Yes, alone."

"Yes, Mrs. Tredwill. Just as you say."

Norma stopped him again at the door. "Before I talk to Captain Maclain, Pierce, there's something I'd like to know."

The butler waited expectantly.

Norma pulled her negligee closer about her shoulders. The unconscious movement sent a twinge of sharp pain up her injured arm.

"Pierce, do you think anyone could have gotten into this house last night or after I left here yesterday?"

"I don't know about yesterday, madam. The servants and I were in Hartford all afternoon. Miss Scott said we might go. Dominick drove us in in the big car. Bella was the only one here—she stayed to fix supper for Miss Scott. I hope you don't mind, madam. We had some shopping to do." Pierce shifted the weight of the tray.

"Not at all, Pierce. Go ahead and ask Captain Maclain to see me."

"Yes, madam. As to anyone getting in here last night—frankly, madam, I don't know."

"Where is Bella now, Pierce?"

"She's lying down, madam. The police questioned her this morning and she's had a headache all day. I sent her to her room."

"She's a little too inquisitive, Pierce—and a little too fond of the Tredwill jam."

"I'll speak to her, madam." He went out and softly closed the door.

Norma settled herself more comfortably and stared at the patterned wallpaper close to the ceiling. There was no point to involving herself and Babs in Paul's murder. Some man had already confessed. Babs was bound to learn about it shortly and reappear with some plausible explanation as to why she went away.

It was better to talk with Captain Maclain immediately and avoid any suspicion of reticence. She had managed, so far, to keep her trip to New York a secret. It was true Thad had learned from Stacy about Babs's appointment for dinner. But Norma had no intention of saying more; of breaking down the last doubt which Thad could cling to—a comforting doubt that Barbara had kept her date with Paul. If it was possible to fool the police and her husband's family, Norma reflected, she certainly had nothing to fear from this blind man, Captain Maclain.

Her voice was determined and free of worry when she called "Come in!" to his knock. The dog came first, a beautiful German shepherd with lolling tongue. The Captain followed and paused just inside the door.

"Mrs. Tredwill?"

"Yes." Norma stopped, touched with self-consciousness, wondering if she should direct him to a chair. The dog saved her the embarrassment by guiding Maclain directly to one near the bedside.

"I'm Duncan Maclain." He touched the chair with a movement almost too swift to follow, found it free of encumbrances, and sat down. "And this is Schnucke." The German shepherd acknowledged mention with a friendly wag of her tail.

Norma was silent, lost in the fascination of watching the Captain smile. Somehow she had formed an idea that blind men moved clumsily, and were generally shoddy. Duncan Maclain, quick and at ease, fitted the picture not at all.

His evening clothes were faultless. The neatness of his crisp black hair, and the insouciant touch to his white tie, attested to his chauffeur's additional skill as a valet.

Nothing overshadowed his smile. It brought his face to life with a striking animation which called for response. Caught by its charm, Norma realized that most people wore masks through life. Maclain's features spoke, showing character and pleasure, thought and ability, warming her with their pleasant glow.

"You wanted to talk with me, I believe," Norma began. "I'll be glad to tell you all I can."

"That's awfully kind of you. I'm up here trying to help Mr. Tredwill locate his daughter. I'm wondering if her disappearance had any bearing on what happened to you."

"To me?" she parried. Her trip to New York was uppermost in her thoughts. How much did this man know?

One of Maclain's long fingers reached down to touch the dog

beside him. Norma watched it, wondering if he'd noticed perturbation in her tone.

"Last night," he said, "when that wardrobe was pushed on you."

"Pushed on me?" She raised a hand to her forehead. "I've been puzzled about that all day. At first I thought it just fell."

"It couldn't have," he assured her gravely. "Someone was hiding behind it and took the only chance of escaping discovery. Who did you think was there?"

She was silent for a while, finding the unfathomable blankness of his eyes disconcerting. The longer she kept him on her adventure in the workshop, the longer he'd postpone questions about what happened during the day.

"I thought it was one of the maids," she said at last. "Something happened when I came in from the Carters'."

"Tell me about it, please. There are many things I need to know."

He sat unmoving while she related the incident of her glove in the downstairs hall. It was only necessary to remember that she had been at Bunny's—*not* in New York. There was nothing implicating after she got home. Her story flowed easily.

"You say you were playing bridge with the Carters?" he inquired casually when she was finished.

"Yes." Norma began twisting at the edge of the spread. "I didn't get home until very late. They wanted me to spend the night on account of the storm, but Cheli was here alone."

Maclain got up abruptly and Schnucke stood up beside him. Under her guidance he crossed to the windows. The draperies were drawn, but the Captain found them and pushed them aside. With his back to Norma he had the appearance of a man with sight staring out into a dark world covered with snow.

"You mentioned a package. I suppose that was a Christmas present from the Carters to you."

"Yes," said Norma. "I think that's what Bella wanted to peek at down in the hall."

"This was after two?"

"It was very late. It must have been well after two."

"Were you asleep when Stacy telephoned?"

"No. I couldn't sleep."

"Why? You must have been upset about something to lie awake after such a long evening."

"Too much bridge, I guess." It was like answering some impersonal machine that couldn't even see her smile.

"Stacy phoned about half-past four?"

"Maybe later." Norma made an effort to sound thoughtful and sincere. "I can't be sure."

"Then Bella might have dropped your glove any time between two and half-past four."

"Yes," said Norma. "I suppose so."

"That would give her plenty of time to open the package and look in it," said Maclain. "Did she?"

Norma pressed her fingers hard above her eyes. Did the girl look in the package? What had that to do with it? He never followed a single line. What was he getting at now? She said: —

"Really, I don't know."

"You said you missed the glove when you picked up the package to bring it upstairs. I can tell in a moment, by feeling the wrappings, if it's been opened before." His friendly voice was lowered when he added, "If the package is here."

"I put it away." That sounded frightfully weak to her. She said more firmly, "It doesn't make any difference, does it, Captain Maclain?"

"No." The Captain turned and rested himself against the edge of the window sill. "Why, after leaving your gloves and package downstairs for two hours and a half, did you decide to bring them up when you answered Stacy's call?"

Norma put a hand to her throat, feeling it would help her to answer steadily. "I saw that the glove was gone."

"But you said you didn't see that until you picked up the package. Why were you bringing that package upstairs, Mrs. Tredwill, after you answered the phone?"

"Does it make any difference?" Norma began to cry.

"None," said Maclain. "Young Stacy is a most observant boy. The description he gave me of his vanished sister included a pair of galoshes that she wore into New York yesterday. Those galoshes are in her closet now. How did they get there, Mrs. Tredwill? The police will certainly want to know, and lying will weigh heavily on your conscience if that girl should die."

Where hardness would have only stiffened her resistance, she broke completely under his sympathetic tone. The truth came sobbingly, but the welcome relief of telling it left her apathetically calm.

"You say your husband saw that notice in the paper yesterday morning?" he asked her when she was through.

"I think so. The paper was open to the column when I picked it up downstairs."

"That's strange," said Maclain. "I thought he learned about that notice from me. I think I'll go upstairs, Mrs. Tredwill, and talk with that servant girl."

CHAPTER XV

Darkness and blackness.

The blackness of the deepest mine, the lack of light which drives weak men mad in dungeons, was the world of Duncan Maclain.

There was no light in Norma's room; no light in the hall; no light in the great house built on a Connecticut hill. Neither were there night and day—just time, and sound, and feeling, and sometimes taste and smell.

There were trust in a dog, footsteps to count, voices to remember, and the tingling feel of fabrics when sensitive fingers brushed against a wall.

Twenty paces.

Twenty yards.

Sixty feet.

"Left here, Schnucke!"

You remembered it the next time. If you forgot it, then Schnucke warned you—or, by yourself, you risked barked shins and a nasty tumble. You had to remember. It wasn't nice when a blind man took a fall.

Paces and faces and talks and walks and what was said in

Norma's room—you had to remember it all. The faces you built by the voice, of course, because you couldn't see. The talks were always clear: —

"I'd better send for Pierce, Captain Maclain. The servants' quarters are upstairs in the other wing. The door leading in there is the last to the left at the end of the hall."

"I can find it, Mrs. Tredwill, thank you. I prefer to go alone. I went upstairs with the state policeman this afternoon."

"Bella's room is the second to the right at the top of the service stairs."

"Don't worry, Mrs. Tredwill. My dog can see. If I need something I can call."

The talks were always clear, like that one with Colonel Gray: "The last war blinded you, Maclain—this one may end your career!"

God, how careful you had to be—"I'm sorry, Mr. Tredwill. I'm afraid your plans all smell of gasoline."

Twenty paces.

Twenty yards.

And three times twenty is sixty feet.

"Left here, Schnucke!

"Good girl, you're right again! This is the door to the servants' wing."

Through it and close it and listen.

"Nobody here, eh, Schnucke?"

Thirty-two paces and then the stairs.

Darkness. Blackness. Silence. The carpet is thick. The kitchen's below. See that rattle of dishes. See that smell of cooking lingering from the day.

Twenty-nine. Thirty. Thirty-one. Thirty-two.

Five steps up and a landing.

Turn right.

Seven steps up and a landing.

Turn right.

Ten steps up and you're there. Or was it nine?

Watch your step at the top, Maclain! Next time you'll remember—twenty-one, or twenty-two. It's careless to confuse them with those thirty-two steps in the hall.

"Thank you, Schnucke. It's twenty-one, not twenty-two!"

Darkness. Blackness. Silence. The carpet is thick. Bella sleeps in the second room to the right at the top of the stairs.

One. Two. Three.

That's the front door, and it's open. Feel that change in the air?

One. Two. Three. Four. Five.

"Right here, Schnucke. Bella's door is open. The light would shine in. If she's sleeping, it must be dark here in the hall. I'll call her softly.

"Bella!

"Steady, Schnucke, and forward! What are you trembling for?"

One step onward and listen.

"Schnucke, my ears are better than yours. Quit your whining and balking. I'll call her again.

"Bella!"

Darkness and blackness and silence and a smell of violet perfume. Maybe Bella uses it. "My nose is as good as yours, Schnucke. I smelled it out in the hall. Forward, Schnucke! Forward, I say! All right, if you want to be stubborn I'll leave you here at the door!"

Another step into the room and stop.

A table here. A bureau here, but nobody breathing.

"Bella!"

Those are clothes on the back of the chair.

Another step—Merciful Christ, Maclain, what's that you kicked on the floor? It's rolled away! No. It's only rolled. It's right there close to your toe.

Down on your knees.

No. You'd better stand and reach down with your hand. It can't be what you think it is—a football would roll that way!

They do such things in Germany—but never do them here.

Merciful Christ—a football with teeth and a nose and hair!

Out in the hall and down the stairs and through the serving door.

"God, Maclain, you're deathly pale! What are you running for?"

That's Thaddeus Tredwill. Calmly now. Tell him about the girl.

"It's Bella, Mr. Tredwill—"

"Bella," he's saying. "Pierce said she was upstairs in bed."

"Her body's in bed, Mr. Tredwill—but her cut-off head's on the floor!"

CHAPTER XVI

1

POLICE.

Sergeant King was grim. Under his faultlessly tailored uniform of trim khaki his broad shoulders tapered down to a waist athletically small.

This was murder beyond the Sergeant's ken—brutal and bloodier than the swift striking thrust of a maniac. Decapitation—a genus of crime the capable Sergeant hadn't met before, and most heartily hoped he'd never meet with again.

"And you, Mr. Tredwill—you were on your way upstairs when you ran into Captain Maclain?"

The Sergeant's voice had roughened from the grating of endless questions. He seemed reluctant to move from his commanding post in front of the mantel; equally reluctant to relinquish his comforting grasp on the butt of his gun.

"Good God, man—yes—yes—yes!" Thad's affirmatives grew progressively louder. "Get someplace, can't you? Someplace that we haven't been before."

King eyed him unemotionally. "I'm doing my best. Your son sent Trooper Stinson away. If the trooper had stayed he might have saved that girl."

"I sent no one away," said Gil in patient contradiction. "I merely told Stinson he might go if he thought it safe to do so. How would his presence—"

"Have saved the girl? Maybe it wouldn't." The Sergeant turned his back on the room and made passes at the fire with his toe. "He was downstairs, it's true," he went on, speaking more to the fire than to Gil, "but it wouldn't have been so easy to get that broadax out of the hall."

"There's a back stairway, as I've told you," Thad put in. "Whoever killed her probably went up that way."

"A broadax," Sergeant King repeated as though the words were indigestible. "Why?"

Captain Maclain answered him. "It's quick and silent, Sergeant, and a method that's certain sure. The best executioners abroad are reviving it for political purposes, I understand. In addition, I believe I'm safe in saying that it fills potential victims with a certain sense of fear."

The Sergeant pivoted at the waist to look at Maclain. The Captain had drawn a straight-back chair up to the long table in the center of the room. He was sitting with his hands folded on the table edge, quiescent as a good scholar in school.

"What do you mean by potential victims?" King asked. "Are you hinting there may be more?"

In an end place on the settee, Bunny Carter squirmed uncomfortably, waiting for Maclain to reply. Bunny had arrived at The Crags shortly after dinner to be plunged into an evening of horror that would leave him with a lifetime memory. Now the Sergeant was asking if Maclain expected more.

The Captain's cheeks flushed faintly. "This murder struck fast enough. This girl was beheaded—"

"Merciful heaven, Maclain," Thad burst out. "Can't you say killed—murdered—anything but that. It's wearing on me."

"She's just as dead, Mr. Tredwill, whatever word we are forced to employ." The Captain might have sounded callous except for the sympathy in his tone. "She was killed some time around six or seven, as far as we know—maybe later. I arrived here about four."

"What has that to do with it?" King asked sharply.

"Nothing perhaps." Maclain raised his head. Brief as the life of a shooting spark up the chimney, the leaping fire brought a glint of flame to his sightless eyes. "Perhaps a lot. Bella may have been killed to prevent her talking to me."

"About what?"

"About the disappearance of Mr. Tredwill's daughter, Sergeant," the Captain announced, choosing his words. "Barbara Tredwill vanished last night in New York City."

"So! Kidnaping!" The officer whirled around on Thad and Gil. "I'm investigating a murder here, believe it or not. Why was this kidnaping kept from me?"

"It wasn't," Thad told him with cold preciseness. "You know it now. This isn't a precinct stationhouse. I've a right to withhold information, if I think my daughter's safety demands it. I've got a right to wait until someone communicates with me."

"And who has?"

"No one, Sergeant King." Thad's big head sank down in his hands. For seconds the living room was still.

"It's nearly midnight." Bunny Carter looked at his watch and put it away. "My wife's not well. Is there any reason, Sergeant, for detaining me?"

"No," said King. "You can go."

Bunny rose and flexed his stiffened muscles. King looked at him reflectively. "You came over here this evening to talk with Mr. Gilbert Tredwill, didn't you?"

"Yes," said Bunny. "That's so."

"Did you see him right away?"

"He was downstairs in his workshop. I waited in here with Stacy, Mr. Tredwill's younger son—"

"Oh, yes." The Sergeant opened a notebook and looked at it. "I remember now, Mr. Carter. You can go."

"Thanks." Bunny's round face grimaced. "You can reach me at the plant if you need me tomorrow, Sergeant King. You too, Captain Maclain."

"Why should Maclain need you?" King snapped out.

"He's rather well known as an investigator," Bunny said meekly. "I thought he might be helping you."

"Oh," said King.

The Captain covered the faintest of smiles with his hand. "The Sergeant has enough problems, Mr. Carter, without adding me."

King left his post in front of the fire and walked to the door, where he signaled Trooper Stinson in the hall to pass Bunny by.

"Now where are we?" Thad demanded when King came back into the room.

"Damned if I know." King leaned against the table by Maclain and said earnestly: "What do *you* make of this, Captain Maclain? What did that girl want to tell you that would provoke any human to murder her that way?"

"If I could answer that last question, Bella would still be alive, Sergeant. This is all I can say: you've questioned everyone in this house—and no one has an airtight alibi. I'd advise you to call in more men, Sergeant—enough to post one in every hall."

"But no one in The Crags—" Thad began brokenly.

Maclain stood up, flowed to his feet, with a motion so commanding that it dominated the room. "Your wife was in The Crags when she was attacked last night, Mr. Tredwill. Bella was asleep in her room in The Crags when she was murdered today. The Crags has become the battleground of a war. I'm warning Sergeant King to watch everyone in this house, servants and all, as he's never watched before. When a clever killer has started to work the end is never in sight. The worst murders in the history of crime were committed by a twelve-year-old boy."

2

Gilbert Tredwill deposited the butt of his second cigarette in an ash tray beside him and turned to watch Helena conceal her smooth skin in the sleek satin of a nightgown.

She had undressed silently, carefully draping stockings and underwear over a chair, fussing wordlessly over her hair and make-up removal. Gilbert would have preferred her usual inconsequential chatter. When Helena undressed without speaking it was a fair premise that sleep would follow a family row.

He lighted a third cigarette which he didn't want, making an elaborate ceremony of striking the match and throwing it away. Helena ignored his obvious dallying. He snubbed the cigarette after a single inhale, and said: "What's the matter with you?"

She swung around from her dressing table as though the question had startled her beyond endurance. "I'm frightened, Gil." Her round blue eyes moved toward the bedroom door.

"Why?" he asked with masculine unreasonableness. Helena's

remark aroused in him a quick irritation which he found it hard
to account for.

"Well—why *not?*" Helena countered. "After what's happened
here, Gil, you don't expect me to feel secure just because there's a
policeman pacing up and down the hall." She turned back to her
dressing table and began to brush her hair with quick petulant
strokes. "Let's get away from here, Gil. This place isn't good for
either of us."

"My work's here, Helena—and my family."

"Voltaire said—"

"Don't quote things, darling, please."

Helena left the dressing table and sat down on the edge of her
bed. She slipped the mules from her slender, high-arched feet
and turned to face Gil halfway. "There's too damn much family,
Gil. The more you love me, the less they'll like me. I'm an in-
truder and a foreigner. Families are like that. It's—"

"Nonsense, Helena. Who's said anything about—"

"No one has said anything—but you're changing, Gil, becoming watchful and hard. I want some time alone with you.
Even in New York we're not alone."

"You're being difficult now," said Gil. "Thad shared the suite
with us—but he paid all the expenses, too."

Helena slid into her bed and pulled the eiderdown quilt up to
her chin. "I see."

"Is there some hidden meaning back of that remark?" Gil
reached for another cigarette, then decided against it. Instead,
he sat watching his wife stonily.

"Not intentionally," said Helena. "It just seems out of place
to find a Tredwill considering expenses. Usually one finds them
flinging money about most recklessly. Is it because your father

also pays the expenses of the household that you don't want to move from here?"

Gil began to undress, removing his clothes with short vicious tugs expressive of disapproval. In shirt and shorts he stood at the foot of his wife's bed and said finally: —

"I'm broke, Helena. Thad holds the purse strings, not me. He's generous—but generous in his own way. Our honeymoon trip—"

"Cost a lot," Helena supplied. "I know. And the things you've bought for me." She held out one hand. A diamond and platinum wrist watch caught multicolored rays from the bed lamp. She put her white arm back under the covers. "How much did you spend for Christmas presents, Gil?"

"My dear!" His dark face became more pleasant with a smile of protest. "I'm not that broke. Why, my salary from International is—"

"Twelve thousand a year. That won't buy three-thousand-dollar wrist watches for me." Helena shielded her face from the glare of the lamp, and added, "Nor Christmas necklaces. It was sweet of you—but I canceled the order before we left New York today."

Gil's face darkened again. "Who told you about that necklace?" He slid into pajamas and tightened the sash about his waist. "That was to be a surprise." He waited expectantly.

"It was an accident, Gil. The jeweler phoned the hotel about delayed delivery and I got the call. Look, darling," she said almost entreatingly, "you've lost money in the market, I know. Where did you get the cash to buy such a necklace? It was going to cost you plenty."

Gil switched off the lights and got into bed. "I borrowed it, Helena."

"From whom?"

"My boss—if you must know."

"Bunny Carter?"

"That's right," said Gil.

"When?"

"Last night in New York."

Helena was quiet as the footsteps of the patrolling state policeman passed softly in the hall. After a time, she asked: —

"Where did you see Bunny?"

"At the banquet I went to—at the Biltmore."

Helena raised herself on one elbow and relaxed again. "I must have misunderstood Norma. I thought she played bridge with Bunny and Bea last night until after two."

"Bunny was in New York," said Gil.

CHAPTER XVII

1

Duncan Maclain leaned back farther into the softness of an armchair, clasped the heavy silk folds of his dressing gown closer about him, and for a time gave himself up abstractedly to counting the footsteps of the trooper in the hall.

An air of somber expectancy had settled about The Crags, muting the life of the Tredwill home. The Captain felt himself caught in its toils, and the feeling was most unpleasant. It rasped on his super-keen senses, tearing at his nerves as some bad violinist might draw discords from strings with an over-resined bow.

Maclain's very existence was composed of ordered patterns. Before he could move with assurance, articles of furniture must be mentally pictured, allocated to their proper places. The conduct of humans affected him in similar fashion. Men and women were governed by certain immutable laws and customs. It was Duncan Maclain's habit to study those about him, and judge, as a trained psychologist might judge, what they would do under a given set of circumstances.

Bella's murder had struck with terrific impact, shattering those immutable laws which served as guideposts. The murder formed part of a pattern; that, he knew. But the picture was broken—obscured by tiny lines, as broken glass becomes opaque. Somehow he must strip away the cloudy inessentials and make the picture clear.

The stripping process might prove dangerous. Broken glass held nothing but peril for a careless hand.

Bella's murder was most annoying, and clever, too. Before it happened the picture had been clear. Bella fitted neatly into it, smiling cryptically out of its tragic frame.

Maclain had come to Hartford searching for someone nosy—discreetly nosy. Bella had filled the bill. Cleverness, even ruthless astuteness, was easily hidden under the role of an ignorant housemaid with a predilection for raiding the storeroom to loot it of sweets and jam.

The State Police were certain that no one had left The Crags after Norma Tredwill was attacked the night before. Again Bella fitted into the frame.

The odor of violets fitted, too.

Maclain restlessly left his chair, went to his Gladstone bag, and took out a box containing a jigsaw puzzle. It was easier to concentrate when his fingers had something to do. Seated at a writing table, he dumped the pieces of the puzzle out before him and began to sort them swiftly.

The puzzle was more than half together when he paused to touch the chime button on his Swiss repeater watch. The timepiece tinkled half-past two.

He placed the watch on the table before him, touched the desk lamp, and found it was on. Switching it off, he sat for a moment listening to Schnucke's light breathing, then went to work again in the darkness. Piece by piece the puzzle grew, built by the uncanny prescience of fingers which could see.

The odor of violets was a means of identification—labeling its wearer as a spy. It identified documents, too—showed they had been traced, or earmarked them as originating from agents of the same unfriendly power.

"Those Braille instructions were deciphered before they were brought to me," he said under his breath as he patted a fragment of the puzzle into position. "Probably by another blind man—a member of the ring. That checks all the way through—but I have no proof, and no one will believe what I say."

He turned his thoughts to the missing girl. For several long minutes he sat holding another piece of the puzzle in his hand.

Why had Barbara Tredwill run away?

It violated the rules of normal conduct in the opinion of Duncan Maclain. Norma had thought somebody was in the other room of Gerente's apartment. If that was true, the same person must have been there when Babs found Paul. The murderer? Perhaps, but there was no immediate means of proving it true.

The Captain laid the piece he was holding down on the table and stirred it about in small concentric circles.

Why hadn't Babs raised an alarm?

Why hadn't she phoned her father, or Stacy, or Norma, or anyone, before she ran away?

There were other questions—too many of them. The Captain relinquished the piece he was moving about and leaned back wearily.

If the murderer was discovered by Babs, why had Babs been allowed to leave unmolested?

The Captain straightened up suddenly, found the piece, and fitted it into the puzzle.

Murdered in Gerente's apartment, Babs would have bathed The Crags in a searchlight of publicity. Publicity was bad for a place which had become an outlet of information which might affect the outcome of a war. Gerente was killed because he became too interested in The Crags. Then if Barbara had seen Gerente's killer, Barbara was allowed to leave the Twelfth Street apartment for one reason only—because a neater plan had been conceived to get her out of somebody's way, a plan which would allow a few days' leeway for work to be completed.

To get her out of whose way?

The Captain stood up and ran supple fingers through his hair. He felt that his reasoning was sound, but it presupposed one thing he had failed to consider. If Barbara had encountered anyone in Paul's apartment, it must have been someone she knew. No stranger could have argued her into leaving quietly. There was a chance, of course, that she had left in terror, as Norma had done, without seeing anyone at all.

There was another chance, which Duncan Maclain disliked exceedingly—a chance that Babs had killed Paul; a chance that Arnold Cameron had known Thaddeus Tredwill's daughter, and was taking a murder charge to save the girl. Babs had keys to The Crags—knew every inch of the great house—

The Captain's knuckles rapped sharply on the table and he irritably shoved back his chair. He crossed the room and opened the door to the hall. The trooper's footsteps approached quickly, and the officer said in a low tone, "Captain Maclain. Is there anything I can do? Sergeant King said I was to co-operate with you."

"I'm going downstairs to use the phone," said Maclain. "You might make sure that no one listens in the hall."

"I'll go with you."

"You'd better post yourself on the stairs. You can watch both upstairs and down."

"Okay," said the trooper.

Schnucke came up beside her master, but Maclain ordered her back into the room and closed the door. He was already familiar with the layout of the Tredwill home. Under the anxious eyes of the trooper he strode off confidently, stopped at the top of the stairs, found the banister, and unhesitatingly went down.

A few minutes later he had New York Police Headquarters on the phone. He got the Missing Persons Bureau and asked for Sergeant Kyle.

"Duncan Maclain calling from Hartford," he said. "A confidential report of a girl named Barbara Tredwill was turned in to you this morning by G-2. Have you turned up anything yet? It's important that I know."

"Hold it," said Kyle. Maclain could hear the rustling of papers. The Sergeant spoke again. "A cab picked her up on Twelfth Street and dropped her at Sixty-third and Park Avenue. She went in an apartment house there, and came out twenty minutes later, according to the doorman. She was staying there with friends. She had a traveling bag with her when she left. No trace from there."

"Did she take another cab?" asked Maclain.

"No. She walked off uptown toward Sixty-fourth Street. Beyond that the doorman doesn't know. Have you got anything?"

"A hunch," said Maclain, "that she's been kidnaped, but I wouldn't want to put it on the air!"

He left the booth and went back upstairs accompanied by the trooper. In his room again, he fitted a record onto his portable Ediphone which Cappo had set up in a corner. Twice he played the record through, marking the voice of the unknown man who had impersonated Paul Gerente; searching for unusual accents or pronunciations; listening intently for cadences and tones as a handwriting expert might take note of loops and whorls.

The man's diction was faultless, but the Captain's face was set in lines of satisfaction when he took the record from the Ediphone. The speaker had an unconscious trick of pronunciation, a quirk of speech so slight that it had almost escaped the analytical ears of Duncan Maclain.

Once or twice he had injected an extra syllable on the vowel *i*—"cap-i-tan" instead of "cap-tain"; "con-dish-i-uns" instead of "con-dish-uns." To Maclain's impressionable hearing it marked the speaker with an ineradicable scar.

The Captain got into bed and lay sleepless for a long time listening to the crackle of frost against the windowpane. Russia and Finland were battling desperately. England, France, and Germany were choked in the constricting coils of war. The smaller nations of Europe stood armed, in constant danger of invasion. Those nations were thousands of miles away, yet, in the brooding quiet of The Crags, Duncan Maclain felt them disturbingly near.

From somewhere in the direction of Boston he heard the drone of a late-flying plane. Lying rigid, he followed the swell of the sound, traced it overhead, and relaxed with its passing.

For one terrible moment memory had carried him away, tricked him into thinking that the roar of the motor would be blotted out by the whine and crash of a life-destroying bomb.

"We *are* at war!" he whispered into the darkness. "Every combatant in the world is against us—fighting our peace with every weapon they know." He sat up suddenly and shook his fist into the darkness. "I'll beat you," he exclaimed so loudly that Schnucke stood up and came to the bedside. "You think you've wrecked me with blindness—but I still have a brain. Your weapons of death and terror are helpless against it." He lay back on the pillow, then reached down and petted the dog beside him. "Go lie down, Schnucke, you need your sleep—you and a blind man versus a world full of fools!"

2

It was shortly after seven when Sergeant King rapped at the Captain's door. Cappo, bearing a tray of breakfast, was with the officer.

"I'm going upstairs to look over that girl's room again," the Sergeant said laconically. "After you eat I'd like you to join me."

"I'll come," said Maclain.

"Good." The Sergeant went out and Maclain addressed his giant Negro servant: "Did they make you comfortable last night, Cappo?"

"Yessah, Captain." Cappo's big hands moved with extraordinary delicacy as he arranged the breakfast tray. "I slept over the garage. This breakfast ain't exactly like Sarah would fix it, Captain."

Maclain laughed as he sat down and located the dishes on the tray. "There are other cooks besides that wife of yours, Cappo."

"Yessah," Cappo agreed doubtfully, "but seems like Sarah knows exactly what to do. That's hot cereal in the bowl, Captain, cream in the silver pitcher, and milk in the china one. You say the word and I'll open the eggs for you."

The Captain ate silently while Cappo laid out a suit, drew water in the tub, and found clean underwear.

"Where's Dreist?" Maclain asked when breakfast was nearly finished.

"He's chained up in my room, Captain."

"I want you to stay close by him," said Maclain. "I don't want anyone to get near him—nor anyone to see him if you can help it. What's the number of the house telephone in your room?"

"Number nine, Captain."

"If I give four short rings I want you and Dreist," Maclain said impressively. "Understand?"

"Yessah." Cappo spoke from the bathroom. "How'll I know where you're ringing from?"

"There are twelve phones in the house," Maclain told him after a little consideration. "I want you to locate each one and its number. I've done so already. I'll give four short rings—and follow with the number of the phone I'm ringing from. For eleven, I'll follow with two long rings—and for twelve, one long and then two more. Is that clear?"

"Yessah, Captain. If you gives four short and two short I come running with Dreist to phone number two."

"Right."

Cappo busied himself about the room for a moment, then he asked, "Are you going to need the car?"

"Badly, perhaps." The Captain stirred the last of his coffee and drank it down. "But I'm not going to use it for that very reason. I want you to let it out around here that something's wrong with the car. Ask about the nearest garage. If necessary, put some small thing out of adjustment—but keep yourself ready. You may have to drive to New York in a hurry."

"I'll be ready, Captain. You can trust me."

"That fact, in the chaos of a schizophrenic civilization," said Maclain, "is one of the very few things I *know*."

"You sure know a lot of words, Captain." Cappo's massive head shook admiringly. "Yessah. You suttinly do."

3

Duncan Maclain bathed and dressed hurriedly. When he was ready to leave the room, he sent Schnucke off to be fed and walked by Cappo. He didn't need Schnucke's help to find his way to that room on the upper floor.

In the top hall he paused outside of the door.

Sergeant King turned from his occupation of staring moodily out of the single window and said, "Come in."

The Captain took three steps and stopped just across the threshold. He stood palms out, his little fingers lightly touching the seams of his trousers. The position threw his powerful shoulders slightly back, giving him a most military air.

"Tell me, Sergeant King, when you searched this room last night did you find any violet perfume?"

The Sergeant opened his mouth and closed it again. Seconds of silence ticked away, and with each one the Sergeant found it more difficult to reply. He was bogged down in the noisome muck of a crime too sanguinary to be real. It belonged in a hovel, somewhere in the backwoods or the slums, to be listed in the category of crimes of lust and passion. It was decidedly out of place in a wealthy producer's home.

His watchful eyes trickled down over Maclain. Everything was out of place. The murdered girl was beautiful—yet through hours of intensive search the police had failed to locate a lover; failed to locate any motive, any family, anyone who knew anything about her. Now, added to his sack of assorted incongruities was a blind man—not an ordinary blind man, but one armed with highest authority from the Commissioner himself; blanket authority to pry, interfere, and ask questions—questions which the farthest reaching of the Sergeant's quick mind could only type as irrelevant, questions about violet perfume.

King drew a deep breath and managed to keep it from ending in an audible sigh. "There's a bottle of violet perfume on her bureau," he said with a trace of compassion. "Why?"

"I thought it might be a clue." Maclain shook his head. "I smelled it last night in the hall. If the girl used it herself it probably means nothing at all."

"It probably doesn't," King agreed with a shade more cordiality. "You made a remark about this method of murder last night. I asked you up here to talk to you. The murderer picked about the bloodiest method I've ever heard of—so bloody that he stood behind a screen and swung the ax around one end. I thought you might tell me why."

The Captain left his place just inside the door and took two steps toward the bureau at the left of the room. His fingers moved about the surface until he located the bottle of perfume. He sniffed it without removing the stopper, then put it down again. Slowly he swung about and with his left hand touched the fabric of the plain cloth three-panel screen beside the bed.

"Did you ever hear the story of the horseshoe nail that lost Napoleon the Battle of Waterloo?"

"Yes," said Sergeant King.

"This reminds me of it, somewhat," Maclain continued, as though the Sergeant had failed to answer. "The screen was here and the murderer saw it. The sight of it reminded the murderer that it might be used effectively as a shield against spattering blood. That pleasant thought reminded the murderer of the weapon in the armory hall. The weapon reminded the murderer of what happens to traitors in Germany today. Bella met her Waterloo."

"You're talking in riddles," said Sergeant King.

"And you're dealing in them, Sergeant," replied Maclain. "You can investigate this murdered girl from now until Hitler goes into a synagogue to pray. You'll unearth nothing but a carefully prepared labyrinth of blind alleys. Two nations stand in your way."

"Two nations?"

"She was working for both of them and both paid her, but she loved only one. You'll get no help from either this country or the country that killed her—Nazi Germany. She died on active service, and no human will ever prove that she was a counterespionage agent working for G-2. My problem is who killed her, not why. Yet you have to know the why to find the who." The Captain turned his back on the Sergeant and felt his way to the end of the bureau, where he found a chair. He sat down, crossed his legs, and seemed to be looking at his toes.

"This is a private home," said Sergeant King. "Do you expect the State Police to swallow a story that a maid was murdered in a private home by a spy?"

"No," said Duncan Maclain, "and neither does the spy. That's what makes it difficult, Sergeant, both for me and for you."

He raised his head with a sudden gesture which brought his chin out firm and strong. "The New York Homicide Squad is faced with the same problem, Sergeant King. Night before last, a man named Paul Gerente was murdered in a Twelfth Street apartment in New York. That was spy murder number one. Last night this girl was killed here—spy murder number two. If Barbara Tredwill fails to get back home alive, you can put her murder in the same class, as number three."

"And what am I supposed to do—arrest the whole Tredwill family because they were in New York and here too?" King's emotion was evident in the tightness of his fingers about the holstered gun at his hip, but his voice was ominously calm.

"It might prove efficacious in bringing matters to a head, but I'd hardly recommend it," said Maclain. "You'd be faced with the necessity of breaking several airtight alibis which keep this family in the clear in Gerente's murder. Gilbert Tredwill attended a banquet. His wife and his father had dinner together and went to a show. Stacy attended a picture with another boy."

"And what about Barbara?" the Sergeant snapped out. "She was in New York, too."

"So was Mrs. Tredwill." Maclain uncrossed his legs and placed his hands on his knees. "Would you be inclined to arrest either of them as a spy?"

The Sergeant turned to look at the bed where Bella had been murdered and suddenly said, "Hell, no!"

"Well," Maclain went on, "that brings us back to scratch."

He stood up. "I suppose you've searched this entire house for bloodstained clothes?"

"And found none," said King abruptly.

"It's a feature of these two murders that you find nothing." The Captain closed thumb and forefinger about the lower part of his jaw. "If you were going to hack someone up, Sergeant King, and didn't want to get bloodstains on your clothes, would you prefer to stand behind the inadequate protection of a screen or to remove your clothes entirely?"

"I'd remove them entirely."

"Check!" said Duncan Maclain. "So would I."

"So you've narrowed it down to someone in The Crags?" said Sergeant King.

The Captain stood up. "When I narrow things down that far, Sergeant, I make arrests. The fact that a murderer wishes to avoid bloodstained clothing is hardly adequate proof that that murderer is living in the Tredwill home."

4

Norma Tredwill was opening her morning mail when Pierce announced Duncan Maclain. Overwrought from an almost sleepless night, Norma pulled herself up into a straighter position on the chaise longue as the Captain came in.

His appearance was heartening. The terror of murder striking at The Crags the night before seemed to have passed him by. Impeccable in a salt-and-pepper suit of heavy weave, he greeted her with a smile which helped her put aside a burning desire to cry.

"Mr. Carter is calling for me at ten," Maclain told her. "He's driving me over to East Hartford. I don't want you to worry about anything you've told me. I can clear everything up with Mr. Carter. I really dropped in to see how you were feeling today."

"My arm's better, thank you. But, Captain, that poor girl—"

"Please!" Maclain raised a hand. "I'm going to ask you to try and forget that anything happened here last night, Mrs. Tredwill. You can help yourself and Barbara most by keeping your mind as far from worry as possible."

"Barbara?" asked Norma in a tight small voice. "You've heard something?"

"No," said Maclain. "Actually I hoped that you might have—in the morning mail. The officer on duty downstairs said that a letter addressed to you was scented slightly with perfume."

"It's an ad," Norma informed him with marked disappointment. "There was nothing but that and Christmas cards. I've already thrown it away."

She had a fleeting impression that Maclain had stiffened as she spoke, that under his urbanity her casual words had revealed for an instant hidden flecks of diamond-cutting steel. When he said, "That's too bad," she felt she must have been mistaken.

"Don't hesitate to call on me, Mrs. Tredwill, if there's anything you feel I can do." The Captain started toward the door. Halfway there he turned. "I wonder if you'd gratify a whim—let me smell that circular you received. Due to my blindness I'm extremely interested in various types of perfume."

"Certainly." Norma found it difficult to keep wonderment out of her tone. Pushing aside several Christmas-card envelopes in the wastebasket beside her, she located the letter and envelope. "I've had a couple of these before."

Maclain came closer and took the letter from her hand. For an instant he held it close to his nose. "It's very delicate," he said. "Were the letters always the same?"

"Really," said Norma, "I don't believe I read them. I throw most advertisements away. This is a recent pest—called the House of Bonnée."

"Some day, if I live," said Maclain, slipping the letter into his pocket, "I may buy some of their violet perfume."

CHAPTER XVIII

1

THERE WAS an air of somnolence about Duncan Maclain as Bunny Carter's Lincoln crunched down the driveway to Tredwill Village and turned its glistening radiator toward town. Watching him intently, Bunny thought that he could detect lines and indentations on the Captain's face which had not been there the night before. He started a line of inconsequential chatter in a friendly effort to smooth away the Captain's apparent worry.

"The Crags looks like some sort of medieval castle shining under the morning sun. Sometimes I wonder why I built my own home on the next hill. It's big enough, I guess, but The Crags sort of dwarfs it. Whenever I see the two of them together I feel as though I'm coming home to a caretaker's shack."

"There *is* something medieval about The Crags," said Maclain. "You have very vivid powers of description; something most people lack entirely." He closed his eyes as though he had felt the bright flash of sunlight which struck suddenly into the Lincoln from the windshield of an approaching car.

Bunny said, "Thanks. There's nothing much to describe right

where we're passing now. Just bare trees, a few hills and snow."

The Captain's right hand moved exploringly along the side of the car. He located a cigarette case in the fittings, and took one out without opening his eyes. Bunny started to light it for him, but found himself fascinated at the Captain's adroitness and sank back into his corner again. Obviously, in spite of his commendation of Bunny's descriptive powers, Maclain was intent on something deeper than the scenic beauties of the Connecticut hills. He lighted his cigarette with the ease of long practice, restored the lighter to his pocket, and for the space of half a mile let his strong hands rest tranquilly on his knees.

After a while, Bunny said, "We're coming into West Hartford now."

"I knew we were passing houses." Maclain smiled fleetingly, and explained, "Houses beside the road change the exhaust sounds of a car."

"That's interesting," said Bunny, "but I'm afraid that's a fact that won't ever be of much use to me."

"A Spaniard might say, '*Quién sabe?*'" The Captain snubbed his cigarette in an ash tray beside him, opened his eyes, and leaned slightly forward as though his attention were riveted on some particular noise he wanted to hear.

Bunny chuckled. "Why should I ever become interested, Captain Maclain, in the noise of the exhaust while passing houses in my car?"

"It might prove a diversion when you're driving in and out of town. You could close your eyes and try to locate exactly where you are."

"I usually have plenty to occupy my mind."

"Most people do," Maclain agreed. "But one man I happen to know of was able to direct the F. B. I. to the hideout of his kidnapers because he had listened intently to the sound of overhead planes."

"I've heard that you're a rather brilliant man," said Bunny in a quickly serious tone.

"Thank you." Maclain reached down and touched Schnucke's head. "You're lying on my feet," he told her. She looked up at him out of one dark eye and moved farther away.

"Yes," Bunny continued, "I got the information from Colonel Gray. I'm wondering if there's a warning back of what you just said—a warning that I might be kidnaped some day."

Maclain slowly turned his head toward the president of International Aircraft. The blankness of his eyes gave Bunny a false impression that he was being stared at with an expression akin to naive incredulity.

"Thaddeus Tredwill's daughter was kidnaped, Mr. Carter. She's not nearly as important as you."

Bunny's stocky frame tensed for a moment into immobility. "Great heavens, man! Why would anyone want to kidnap me?"

"Because you're in the same boat I am." Maclain turned away. "You're carrying around a great deal of dangerous information in your head, Mr. Carter. Information that certain people would like very much to know."

"What people?"

"That's a question I greatly deplore." The Captain interlocked his fingers and flexed them gently by bending his hands palms outward. "I rather hoped that you might have the answer for me."

"Too many answers," said Bunny. "The right one's buried someplace at the bottom of a sea of suspicion. The sooner you can dig it up, the happier I'll be."

"All right," said Maclain. "It's my turn to ask a question. I doubt if you're suspicious of two or three thousand people in International, as a group. Let's concentrate on a few. Who knows the final details of young Tredwill's bombing sight?"

Bunny considered the matter long enough to roll down a window and let in a blast of cold air. When the window was closed again, he said, "That's easy. Two people. Gilbert Tredwill and me."

"The answer's easy, too," Maclain told him unhesitatingly. "Information's been leaking out. If only one other person besides yourself knows that information, that's the man you're suspicious of—young Tredwill himself."

"I didn't tell you," said Bunny—"you wormed it out of me!"

"What do you think he's doing, selling out?"

Again Bunny pondered on a reply. Finally he said, "Damned if I know! He might be tipping off things inadvertently."

He swung halfway around in the seat and studied Maclain. The Captain's face was uncommunicative. "Men talk too much to their wives," Bunny stated emphatically.

"They talk too much to everybody." Maclain shrugged. "Go on."

"Well," said Bunny, "night before last I went to New York to attend a banquet at the Biltmore. Gil was there. He borrowed two thousand dollars from me." He stopped.

The Captain said nothing. Instead he touched the cold windowpane beside him and hastily drew his fingers away.

"I hadn't intended to go into town," Bunny went on. "That's what I meant by the sea of suspicion. It's getting me. Gil and his wife were in New York. Gil said he was going there to do some Christmas shopping and to attend the banquet. I thought I'd go in too and see."

"See whether he was attending the banquet or not?" queried Maclain.

"Well, more or less," Bunny admitted hesitantly. "I had a talk with Colonel Gray. He assigned a man to watch Gil's wife at the Waldorf-Astoria Hotel."

"Oh, it's the wife you're suspicious of now!" The Captain pushed back his hat, singled out a lock of hair over his forehead, and tugged at it thoughtfully.

"She didn't go out all evening." Bunny spoke almost morosely. "I came back on a late train and Al met me at the station with the car. Norma Tredwill came out just as we were about to drive away."

"She came back on the same train," Maclain broke in, "and asked you to say nothing about her being away."

"How did you know—" Bunny began.

"She told me the whole story," Maclain continued. "Even what she asked you to say."

"About playing bridge with Bea and me?"

"All of it." The Captain straightened up in his seat. "I think we can dismiss Norma Tredwill—rescue her from your sea of suspicion, as it were. But this loan you made to Gilbert Tredwill still interests me. What was it for?"

"Christmas presents," said Bunny. "I'm not worried about the money—he'll give that back to me—but I am worried about finding a financial soft spot in my best designing engineer. As a matter of fact, it rather frightens me. He's spending too much money on that wife of his, or she's spending too much for him."

He impulsively placed a hand on Maclain's arm. "I'm beginning to wonder if she's doing it purposely."

"If she is," said Maclain, "she seems to have missed her mark. I take it that you think Gilbert may have accepted some handsome offer to sell his country down the river because his foreign-born wife has him out on the limb of a financial tree."

"Doesn't it seem possible to you?"

"Possible," said Maclain, "but highly improbable. Such transactions, Mr. Carter, are cash-and-carry to a high degree. The cash price of Gilbert Tredwill's bombing sight must be a million dollars or more. I doubt if he'd sell that information on somebody's promise to pay. Then we have to assume that if young Mr. Tredwill's a traitor he's a wealthy man today. Yet night before last he borrowed two thousand dollars from you. I'm afraid that clears him, Mr. Carter. I've talked with him a lot, and he doesn't seem quite that subtle to me."

2

Louis Madoc, assistant foreman of construction, was watching a workman lay tile in a difficult corner of the new addition when Bunny Carter's Lincoln swung through the gates of the iron fence guarding International Aircraft from the state highway. It was not in the nature of Louis Madoc to miss much that went on about him. Workmen under him stuck diligently to their tasks, conscious that Louis had an ingrained instinct for loafers, and that he handled them ruthlessly. It was risky to idle on the job even when Louis was apparently far away. Too many men, stopping for a friendly chat with a fellow worker, had heard Madoc's smooth voice behind them saying—"Draw your time, fellow, and rest at home. There's a thousand men waiting to help build this new plant. I'll find workers that don't gab if I have to hire a new crew every day."

The assistant foreman moved about the vast addition with birdlike quiet and quickness. He was much like a great bird, anyway. Neck and nose predominated, and his eyes were piercing and glittery, with wrinkled lids which had a trick of starting to close and checking themselves part way.

Engrossed in watching the workmen, Louis Madoc missed the arrival of Bunny's car. The big limousine pulled up behind him unexpectedly. Madoc's head swiveled, filling his lean neck with wrinkles as Bunny stepped from the car.

"How are things coming?" asked Bunny. "I'm glad to see you're back to work after the storm."

"Good, Mr. Carter." Louis Madoc's glance at the Lincoln was timed to the fineness of a hair. It was more a movement of the eyes than a look—an erratic jump of the flat black pupils to the left, a muscular reaction that brought them back into focus to rest on Bunny's cherubic face again. "The work's progressing fine. I hired thirty more men immediately after the storm."

"That's the stuff," said Bunny. "While this addition's under construction, we're losing money every minute."

Louis gave a cackling laugh. "We can't put in much more time than twenty-four hours a day."

His mind was working swiftly. His single photographic glance at the Lincoln had printed a picture in his brain. Al Rutgers at the wheel interested him not at all. The thing which had whipped his thoughts into action was the sight of Duncan Maclain's lean profile glimpsed through the window of the car.

"Keep at it!" Bunny climbed back into the Lincoln and slammed the door.

"Who were you talking to just now?" asked Maclain.

"Madoc." Bunny was watching the progress of the new buildings as the car rolled on toward the main office door. "He's in charge of construction on Building Number Four—we've had some hard luck there. It's delayed us a month or more."

"That's too bad," the Captain sympathized. "That fellow has a curious trick of speech."

"Speech?" asked Bunny idly.

"Pronunciation," the Captain declared. "He says 'im-med-*i*-ately.' I've only heard one person with that same habit before."

"He's a good man."

"Undoubtedly," said Maclain.

The Lincoln pulled up outside the main office door. Bunny said, "We get out here, Captain." He slid open the glass between the chauffeur's seat and the back of the limousine. "Al, this is Captain Duncan Maclain. I'll want you to drive him back to The Crags in an hour or so."

"Glad to," said Rutgers with a grin.

Bunny gave a jocular laugh and opened the door. "Be sure you get him there. He's a good-looking devil—and this Lincoln smells like you'd been driving a van load of women around in my car."

3

A policeman halted them at the door, staring at the Captain and his dog inquiringly. Maclain stood slightly to one side, smiling inwardly at the volubility of Bunny's whispered explanation, which the president of International Aircraft blissfully thought he was pouring into the officer's ear alone. Even Bunny Carter was stopped at the door of International to explain the presence of a friend.

A moment later they stepped inside, Maclain doubly guided by Schnucke on his left and the pressure of Bunny's hand on his arm. They crossed a large lobby which the Captain judged to be a reception room and were stopped at another door. Bunny's whispered explanation was repeated again. It admitted them into a smaller room where a girl's friendly voice said, "Good morning, Mr. Carter."

Bunny introduced his secretary, Miss Tavestock, to Duncan Maclain. They went through another door.

"This is my private office, at last." Bunny conducted the Captain to a chair.

Maclain's left hand lightly brushed the flat-top walnut desk in passing. Once seated, he let his fingers rest on the leather arms of the chair and said, "Lie down, Schnucke." The dog stretched herself out close beside him.

"They certainly make you comfortable," he remarked, settling back at ease. "I suppose the importance of your office is indicated by the size of this room. A man could almost get lost in here."

A creak of a spring sounded as Bunny sat down in his swivel chair. "I'd be a sorry president if I couldn't pick the best office in the place for myself."

The springs creaked again as he leaned back a trifle too far and straightened up suddenly, bringing both his feet to the floor. "Damn it all, Maclain, you worry me! Who told you this office was big? You touched my desk as you passed by, but how do you know I didn't walk you clear across the room and set you close to the opposite wall?"

The Captain's eyebrows wiggled delightedly. "None are so blind," he said, "as those who have ears and won't see."

"Don't be cryptic," Bunny pleaded. "I honestly mean it—you worry me."

"I can judge the size of a room by the sound of my voice," the Captain explained. "It's a trick I learned by reading Bragg's book, *The World of Sound*. The late blind Justice Fielding and Sir Arthur Pearson both developed it until they could give the dimensions of any room they entered with amazing accuracy. Try it yourself, Mr. Carter. If you practiced it consistently for about twenty years, you'd find that it comes very easily."

"I don't know why Colonel Gray doesn't hire you as a spy instead of sending you up here to worry me!" Bunny tapped his toes thoughtfully on the heavily carpeted floor. "Ribbentrop would probably take you on a personally conducted tour of the Krupp Works—heaven knows what you'd be able to see."

"You might be surprised." Maclain leaned forward earnestly. "I've already learned the approximate dimensions of the buildings you're putting up, and of the one we're in now, by driving past them in your car. Would you like me to tell you?"

"No!" said Bunny emphatically. "You'll give me a headache if you're anywhere near right. I'm having enough trouble with espionage now."

"I noticed that as we came in," Maclain remarked drily.

Bunny slapped the desk top with the flat of his hand. "It would do this country a lot of good if everybody in it had to spend some time around a business that was meat and drink for a spy. One of the directors was howling his head off just the other day about 'foolish precaution.' I wish he could have been here this morning to get a demonstration of what even you can see. Not that I mean to be discourteous," he added quickly.

"Skip it," said Maclain.

Bunny left his chair back of the desk and began to pace the floor. "Things are so stringent here now that visitors to the plant on business aren't allowed to go to the rest rooms alone for fear of what they may see. The public doesn't realize that a single glimpse of wings hung up in a drying room can be built up to give an accurate estimate of how many planes we're turning out a day."

"That's interesting," said Maclain.

"It's maddening," Bunny assured him, "when you're trying to keep information quiet that the whole world wants to know. Supposing a trained agent sees finished planes through an open door. He can figure out how much space they're occupying on the floor. Photographs are taken of the plant as a whole from the outside and measured to scale. Watch is kept on how many hours the plant runs in a week. That information is compared with plants in the agent's own country and they know almost to a hair what will come out of this plant during the next few months."

"And what about your own employees?"

"They have to keep pretty much to their own departments," Bunny explained, "but of course information can leak out even there. Naturally we take every precaution we can—it's vital information like Tredwill's bombing sight that worries me. That's why I had him do a lot of his work at home. And now—"

"Yes, now," Maclain put in, "information has leaked out even there. Tracings have been made of Tredwill's plans. When we find out who did that, Mr. Carter, we'll find out who kidnaped that girl."

The Captain paused, crossed his legs, and smoothed his overcoat down. Bunny quit pacing the office and hoisted himself up on his desk.

For a time, he kicked his heels against the side. Then he asked, "Where do we go from there?"

"All over the United States." The Captain's voice lowered to a note which was grippingly serious and grim. "Catch a spy, Mr.

Carter, and you have nothing at all. To break up espionage, you have to catch a skillfully organized band. We're up against one now. They have one weak link. If they make tracings, those tracings have to be delivered somewhere, somehow. Tracings aren't easy things to get out of a house like The Crags by mail. Equally weak is the fact that somehow instructions must be sent to an individual spy."

Bunny sucked his upper lip in thoughtfully. "I see."

"That's gratifying." Maclain put one hand into his inside coat pocket. "Mr. Carter, I want a girl."

"A girl?" Bunny repeated incredulously.

"One who can type," said Maclain. "She has to have certain qualifications. Foremost among them is that she can keep her mouth shut. She has to have an unbroken record as an American citizen—a record that's known to you. She must lack curiosity entirely, and not be subject to temptation at the sight of a lot of money."

"Miss Tavestock will fill the bill," Bunny remarked without hesitation. "What do you want her to do?"

"I want her to copy a letter," said Maclain. "I want it copied exactly. Each line must be measured with a ruler and spaced to the fraction of an inch, and I want a stencil cut so that I can feel it all the way through the paper."

"That's easy enough. What sort of a letter is it?"

"It's a letter from a perfume house," said Duncan Maclain, "and that's the hard part about it. If Miss Tavestock gets curious and happens to mention it to her boy friend some night, or to anyone else, she's apt to wake up some bright morning and find that her head's been chopped off on the floor!"

CHAPTER XIX

1

WHEN DUNCAN Maclain left the International Aircraft plant he was carrying a brief case loaned to him by Bunny Carter. Inside the pigskin bag was the stencil cut by Miss Tavestock, and an Ediphone record from Bunny's machine. On that record was a verbal copy of the advertising letter as read to Maclain in Bunny's most formal dictating tone. The contents of the letter not only were engraved on the cylinder, but were equally impressed on the sensitive receptiveness of Duncan Maclain's brain.

For thirty minutes after Bunny had recorded the letter, the Captain had sat in the seclusion of the president's office with headphones clamped to his ears, playing the record repetitiously through and through. Once or twice Bunny had looked in from his secretary's office, where he was watching Miss Tavestock cut the stencil with conscientious accuracy. Each time, the Captain's head had raised alertly and one of his expressive hands had motioned Bunny impatiently away.

"What do you make of it?" Bunny had asked when he returned carrying the stencil and the original letter. "It looks like an ordinary enough circular to me."

"That's the beauty of it," said Maclain. "That's the beauty of everything we're dealing with. It looks so ordinary that even the most alert investigator is likely to glance at it but once, and then turn away."

Bunny asked him, "What are you going to do?"

"I'm going to take this record, the letter, and the stencil to Middletown, if you'll lend me a brief case to carry them in. That is, if you don't mind my using your car."

"Not at all," said Bunny immediately, "but why Middletown? What do you expect to find there?"

"A State Police laboratory." The Captain carefully put the letters and the record into the brief case and snapped it shut. "Sometimes there's more writing on a piece of paper than appears on the surface. Police laboratories have curious means of bringing it to light with chemicals and ultraviolet rays."

Word by word the Captain mentally sifted the contents of the letter as Bunny's Lincoln drove him on his way. There weren't more than a hundred and twenty words on the single sheet of fine bond typewriter paper embossed with the heading: —

THE HOUSE OF BONNÉE
TANNER BUILDING
EAST 57TH STREET
NEW YORK CITY

The words were simple, carrying no hint of espionage or intrigue, carrying nothing except some advertising man's conception of an angle which might induce a recipient of the letter to buy the products of the House of Bonnée.

The Captain gave it up after a while and relaxed in a corner of the car. He remained motionless, head back, with his finger tips pressed gently against his eyes, until he sensed by the sound of the car that they were crossing the long bridge leading into Middletown. Then he sat up and grasped the handle of the brief case beside him. There were still many things he couldn't understand. One of them was why that lingering scent of violets should be in Bunny Carter's car.

2

Dr. Jellicoe, a neat, precise man in his early fifties, tapped the edge of his pince-nez against his teeth and stared across his desk at Schnucke and Duncan Maclain.

"You think there's a message of some kind written on this piece of paper in invisible ink, Captain?" The Doctor replaced his pince-nez and stared down once more at the letter in his hand.

"I haven't any idea," said Maclain, "but it's something I'd like very much to know."

"It's a type of work that's a little outside of my field." Dr. Jellicoe's unlined forehead was momentarily marred with a tiny frown. "I've used iodine fumes for bringing out latent fingerprints, and I believe there's a process with a combination of sodium nitrate and silver nitrate solution that's very effective."

"Two solutions in the latter method, to be exact," said Maclain. "It's what they call a sulphate picture. After the sodium nitrate and the silver nitrate you'd have to use Formalin and sodium hydroxide, but I'm afraid it won't do. It's apt to destroy the visible writing which I want to keep particularly."

Dr. Jellicoe checked a question and said, "You might make a copy."

The Captain smiled. "I'm afraid that wouldn't do much good either. You see, I want to throw this letter away."

"Yes, certainly," Dr. Jellicoe agreed a shade too quickly. He began to wonder if Duncan Maclain knew that he was an accredited member of the staff of the Connecticut State Hospital for the Insane.

The Captain continued. "That may sound funny to you, Doctor, but I want to see who finds it."

"Oh, yes," said Dr. Jellicoe, studying a button on the desk by his side and wondering if an attendant was near. "Yes, I have that same urge at times, myself. I think it exists in everyone in a greater or lesser degree."

"Pardon me?" said Maclain.

"Oh, think nothing of it," said Dr. Jellicoe. "There was some writing you wanted to see?"

"That's it." The Captain felt himself slipping. "Suppose we try the ultraviolet ray."

The Doctor took his pince-nez off again and looked with twinkling eyes at Maclain. There were flashes when he almost thought that this blind man was really sane. He had letters from the Commissioner of State Police and Colonel Gray of G-2. At least, those documents seemed to be in order.

Dr. Jellicoe shrugged his shoulders and said, "Well, it might be a good idea at that. Come along with me."

He started to place a hand on the Captain's arm, but abandoned the idea precipitantly as Schnucke with gentle firmness nosed him out of the way. Instead, he took a position safely in front and led the way to a darkroom farther down the hall.

Once inside, he hesitated a moment before closing the door.

Then his years of practice came to his rescue. Duncan Maclain was powerful, but he was blind, and the agile little Doctor had gotten himself out of plenty of tight spots before.

He switched on a quartz lamp filled with mercury gas, seated the Captain in a chair, and searched around until he found a light filter.

"I'm going to test it with nickel oxide glass," the Doctor explained, keeping a wary eye on Maclain. "It lets through rays of about thirty-six hundred and fifty angstrom units."

"Yes," said Maclain placidly. "At least both of us are on an equal basis. Thirty-six hundred and fifty angstrom units are something that neither of us can see. I believe that four thousand angstroms are the least that are visible to the human eye."

"That's right," said Dr. Jellicoe. He felt a little easier. The blind man seemed to know what he was talking about after all.

He held the paper up in front of the filter for quite a while, then turned it so that the rays would strike the other side. "It's almost certain," he said, "that any invisible ink would show up luminescence in the ultraviolet ray."

He clucked disparagingly. "I'm afraid there's nothing here at all."

"I didn't think there would be," said Duncan Maclain. "I guess I'll just have to throw it away."

"By all means." Dr. Jellicoe switched on overhead lights and turned out the quartz lamp. He had reached the stage where he acted automatically when he restored the letter to Maclain's outstretched hand.

The Captain turned and unhesitatingly found the doorknob. "Thank you so much, Doctor," he said cordially as he stepped out into the hall.

The Doctor stood in the doorway and watched the Captain and his canine guide stride confidently away. Suddenly he reached a momentous decision. He put out the lights in the darkroom, closed the door, and almost scurried down the hall. In his office he sat down beside his desk and said, "Hell, I need a drink. This working around in an insane asylum is beginning to get *me*."

3

"Home now, Captain?" asked Al Rutgers when Maclain was back in the car.

"Except for one stop," the Captain told him. "I want to go to a drugstore at the corner of Albany Avenue and Burton Street. It's called the Ideal Drug Company."

He settled back in the car. The seventeen-mile run into Hartford seemed distractingly long. Maclain doubted that the scented letter in the bag beside him could be a coincidence in the chain of events which had already cost two lives and which might cost many more. He was a firm believer in cause and effect and for a brief moment the fact that the ultraviolet ray had disclosed nothing weighed on him heavily.

He was finally convinced that Paul Gerente's murder, Babs's kidnaping, and the guillotining of Bella, the maid, were steps in a definite plan of some highly organized band. Such a band must have a source, some recognized headquarters. If perfume was their signal, then what better source, what better headquarters, might be found than an outfit so innocent-appearing as the House of Bonnée? Yet his test of the letter had drawn a blank.

His strong teeth clamped down tightly, setting his jaw into fighting lines. He was using weak tactics by hoping for carelessness in adversaries who had shown none so far. Code letters were careless when a message could be detected by the pet of every police department in the country—the ultraviolet ray.

A small touch of ice started at his neck and traveled slowly down his spine. Once again he was face to face with the name of that tiny flower. He began to trace its course: the odor on the Braille instructions; the odor in Paul Gerente's secret drawer; the odor in the darkness of the Tredwill hall; the scent on the letter in Norma's morning mail; the perfume in Bella's room; and traces of it with him right now in Bunny Carter's car. Then once again he had run against it unwittingly—the ultraviolet ray.

His clenched hand pounded impatiently on his knee. There must be some tie-up, something about those violets, that would break the whole thing; some clue that would bring out a message cleverly buried in the letter from the House of Bonnée. He knew one man, or thought he did—Madoc, who had spoken to Bunny Carter at the plant; but that hung on a slender, easily broken strand—the inadvertent drawling of a vowel and nothing more. Far too little to set in motion the complicated machinery of G-2. He must wait. Piece by piece, as he built his puzzles, he must tie them up together.

"When I strike," he muttered viciously under his breath, "I can't be wrong, and I think I know the way to strike at them all."

The window slid back in front of him and Al Rutgers said, "Captain Maclain, here's your store."

CHAPTER XX

1

AL RUTGERS' swimmingly deep black eyes watched the Captain questioningly as Schnucke preceded him from the car.

"The drugstore's to your right straight ahead," Al volunteered. "Can I be of any help to you?"

"Thank you, no. My dog will find the door."

Maclain gave a curt direction to Schnucke, who followed the cleared-off sidewalk up toward the Ideal Drugstore, cautiously edging her master around a patch of snow-covered ground.

Rutgers' close-cropped military mustache made a straight dark line over lips set in a musing smile as Schnucke skillfully checked the Captain at the pharmacy door.

Inside the store, several girls were lunching in booths ranged along the wall. At the entrance of the tall, handsome figure moving so surely under Schnucke's direction, their chatter was suddenly stilled.

A white-coated boy came forward immediately and said, "Can I help you?"

Maclain smiled his slow likable smile and said, "I'd like to talk to the proprietor."

"Mr. Kaufman's in back," said the boy. "I'll get him for you."

As the boy moved away, Schnucke followed and led Maclain to a prescription counter at the rear of the store. The Captain, in passing, touched comfortable leather seats at an elaborate soda fountain.

A moment later, an amiable voice said, "I'm Mr. Kaufman. What can I do for you, sir?"

"You can help me very much perhaps." The Captain shook hands and introduced himself. "I'm a private investigator from New York." He spoke in a very low tone. "My name is Duncan Maclain."

The proprietor waited expectantly.

Maclain continued, "I judge from the voices that I heard when I came in that there are a number of people in this store. Perhaps it would be better if I went in back with you."

"Certainly," said Mr. Kaufman with an air of surprise. "You'll have to come around the counter, I'm afraid. The opening is right in back of you." He called, "Bill, will you show the Captain through?"

Maclain followed a directing touch on his arm, passed back of a counter with Schnucke pressed disapprovingly close to his leg, and entered a prescription room where the proprietor assisted him onto a long-legged stool. Outside, the chatter of the lunchers was resumed.

"I have a prescription here, Mr. Kaufman," said Maclain. He took a bottle from his overcoat pocket. "I believe it was filled by you."

The proprietor took the bottle from his hand and said rather nervously, "There was nothing wrong with it, I hope."

"Nothing, I'm certain," Maclain told him reassuringly. "This prescription was given by Dr. Trotter to a maid in the Tredwill home just west of Hartford. It occurred to me that she came quite a long way to have it filled. Her name was Bella Slater and I wondered if you happened to know the girl."

"I know her by sight, if she's the one who had that prescription filled. Is that any help to you?"

"Not much, I'm afraid," said Maclain. "I hoped her family might live around here. She's been killed, Mr. Kaufman, but apparently no one knows any more about her than you."

"Killed?" the druggist asked, shocked. "An accident?"

"Far from it, Mr. Kaufman. She was murdered in a particularly brutal manner. That's why I'd appreciate knowing any little thing you can tell me about her."

The druggist was silent for some time. Maclain could hear him fiddling with bottles on a shelf by his side. At last he said ruminatively, "I don't believe she lived anywhere around here. I've been in this spot for a good many years. It's only within the last few months she started coming into the store. . . . Bill!" he called.

Maclain heard footsteps approach the prescription-room door.

"Bill," said Mr. Kaufman, "do you know anything about a Bella Slater who's been coming here for the last few months once a week or more?"

"It was usually on Thursdays," said Bill, "and most of the time to register a letter, that was all."

Maclain slid down from the stool. "You have a post office here?"

"A substation," said the proprietor.

Maclain swung around in the direction of Bill's voice. "You

don't by any chance remember the address on any of those letters?"

"We don't give out such information," said Bill.

The Captain took a wallet from his inside pocket and flipped it open in his hand. "I'm here on government business."

For a few seconds there was only the sound of the proprietor clinking his bottles.

"Okay," said Bill. "It's all right by me. I know the address of all the letters she registered here. They all went to the same place—Box Q, Division Eight, New York City. Do you want me to write it down?"

"I couldn't see it if you did," said Maclain, "and I know what it is anyhow. Thank you, gentlemen. You have a fine store here and an efficient one, too."

"There was a man with her once, if that'll do you any good," announced Bill.

"It might, if you can describe him."

"He wore a camel-hair coat that was a honey." Bill thought for a minute. "Pleasant sort of a guy with hard gray eyes that sort of looked through you."

"You have a remarkable memory," Maclain commended.

"It's not so hot," said Bill. "This was only two or three weeks ago. I can tell you more than that. The girl called him Arnold. I happen to know because customers stick in your mind when they do curious things. He bought her a bottle of violet perfume, and that's not a popular perfume these days."

"Some people like it," said Maclain.

Back in the car, he told Al Rutgers, "You can take me to The Crags now, if you will."

He relaxed moodily, thinking that he had uncovered another piece of information which amounted to exactly nothing. Box

Q, Division Eight, New York City, had run him around in still another circle. It was the private mailing address of Colonel Gray, officer in charge of G-2.

2

Not until he returned to The Crags did Maclain remember that Christmas was only two days away. It was brought home to him forcibly when, coming into the house by way of a side porch after talking with Cappo in the garage, Schnucke signaled him to the right. He turned abruptly and reached out one hand to encounter the branches of a Christmas tree.

Ahead of him at the door, Pierce's smooth voice said, "We always have one, Captain Maclain. I ordered that from Hartford hoping that Miss Barbara might return home."

"I'm hoping so too." Maclain went on in and exchanged greetings with the policeman in the hall.

In the drawing room, Stacy was playing Debussy. The Captain stood still until the piece was finished, lending an appreciative ear. The music added a homey touch strangely at variance with the efficient state officer vigilantly alert to prevent the swift strike of some unknown catastrophe.

The Captain went on upstairs. A low hum of voices sounded from behind the closed door of Norma's room. Maclain paused long enough to identify Norma's visitor as Thad. Farther down the hall, an intermittent click of typewriter keys told him that Cheli Scott was working in her room. He went on into his own and closed and bolted the door against intrusion.

He took the record and stencil from the brief case and slipped the record on the portable Ediphone. Stretched out on the bed with headphones on his ears, he began to follow the cut words with his perceptive fingers, at the same time listening to Bunny's incisive voice reading the text on the Ediphone.

Five times he played it over, checking it letter by letter, syllable by syllable, word by word, sentence by sentence, and line by line; hunting for hidden meanings, trying vainly to evolve some complex mathematical key. Thoroughly dissatisfied, he got up, found several packages of paper matches, and lay down on the bed again.

He began to count the vowels, taking the letter word by word and tearing off a match each time a vowel appeared. The *e*'s predominated, as they should have, with sixty-three. Then came forty-seven *i*'s, forty-seven *o*'s, thirty-nine *a*'s, and sixteen *u*'s. He included the salutation "Dear Madam" in his count because he considered it an integral part of the letter, for the salutation might be easily changed if it had anything to do with a code. The sender could use "Dear Mrs. Tredwill," or "Dear Mrs. Thaddeus Tredwill," or any particular combination that might fit his purpose. For the same reason, Maclain eliminated counting the vowels in the signature, "By The House of Bonnée." He considered that the signature was unlikely to be changed even for the purpose of a code.

He played around with the idea of the vowels for two hours or more before he rejected it as not making sense. Disgustedly he left the bed, found his jigsaw puzzle, and dumped the pieces on the floor. He sat down beside them and carefully began to put them together while Schnucke watched uncomprehendingly. The afternoon light was fading fast when he rumpled the almost completed puzzle into fragments again and returned it to the drawer.

He took his small noiseless typewriter from its case, set it on

THE HOUSE OF BONNÉE
TANNER BUILDING
EAST 57TH STREET
NEW YORK CITY

Dear Madam,

      The problem of the well-groomed woman is to obtain, in the city's turmoil and grime, a complexion superior to, and more vital than, that of her country cousin.

      Unfortunately most modern cosmetics have failed on many points. Nothing is more detrimental than force when cleansing and purifying the delicate skin. Once use caustics and the entire defensive membrane is injured. The sight of rough pitted skin more often than not indicates some balm of injurious content. It's important to demand far more than economy when purchasing. Don't forget this pertinent fact—the integrity of the makers is an essential ingredient. In purchasing face cream look for these assuring words—

                               By THE HOUSE OF BONNÉE

the writing table, and inserted the stencil into the roller, carefully counting the lines as he began to wind it into the machine.

The salutation "Dear Madam" came up into writing position at thirty-nine.

Maclain's lithe body was seized with a strange rigidity. There were thirty-nine *a*'s in the letter, a coincidence perhaps, but he doubted if that were so. It must have something to do with the setup—must be some indication of where the letter began.

The room was dark when he went to the brief case and took out the envelope with the original letter enclosed. As he did so, his highly trained sense of smell was caught once again by the lingering violet perfume.

He propped himself up on the bed with two pillows, closed his sightless eyes, and held the letter out before him as though his wonderful brain, shrouded in darkness, might give him what his eyes forever lacked—the power to see.

Violets.

How in the name of the ancient gods could a code be buried in violets—a code which was hidden even from the searing penetration of the ultraviolet ray. Someone intended to get that letter, to decipher its contents. The only way they could know that its contents was important was by its smell. Yet how could a smell be applied to a code? How could an odor become something that a reader with eyes could see?

In the back of his mind, a picture began to form; a picture, not of flowers, but of letters wavering and burning with vivid intensity. One by one he shut them off and turned them on. They flickered and danced, then suddenly the first two of them stood out flashingly, like the only two letters left burning in a faulty neon sign. You could apply those letters to a piece of paper.

He jumped from the bed, startling Schnucke into a muffled

bark, and snatched the stencil from his typewriter. Coldly and without a quiver to betray his agitation, he ran a finger down over the perforated words and up again. Only once he paused to give a chuckle which was cold as a falling icicle snapping against a pane.

He selected a fresh record from the stock in his Gladstone bag, slid it onto the Ediphone, and began to dictate. The usual, pleasant cadence of his voice was gone, replaced by words sharp and metallic as the clip of a gardener's shears: —

"Spud: The game has changed. Go immediately to the Tanner Building, East Fifty-seventh Street. Be cautious, because it's dangerous as hell. Get everything you can on a perfume place called the House of Bonnée. Remember, they mustn't suspect you, because the fate of New York City and this nation may be in their files. The Tredwill bombing sight has become passé, and I've become the quarry now. If you find anything suspicious, get in touch with Colonel Gray. Tell him that I'm more important than anything for the moment, and to keep an eye on me. I've stumbled on a foreman named Madoc at International. I think he's the man who impersonated Paul Gerente and brought the Braille instructions to me."

He reached out in the darkness, found the button to Cappo's phone, and gave it a single ring.

When Cappo answered he said, "Come here, but leave the dog."

Twice more he ran his finger over the stencil. When Cappo knocked at the door Maclain admitted him instantly.

"Listen carefully," he told his chauffeur. "Do you know where they dispose of the trash here at The Crags?"

"Yessah," said Cappo. "It's down in the basement in a bin."

"Have they emptied the wastebaskets today?"

"I don't know, Captain. I can look."

"That won't do any good," said Maclain hurriedly. "I'll have to take a chance."

He handed Cappo the advertising envelope and letter. "I want you to take these downstairs without anyone seeing you and throw them away in that bin. As soon as you've done that, I want you to take this Ediphone record to New York in the car and deliver it to Mr. Savage. You can drive it in three hours, can't you?"

"Yessah," said Cappo. "In nearer two."

"Don't get arrested," Maclain cautioned him. "Keep this record beside you on the floor. If anyone stops you for any reason at all, smash it instantly."

"Yessah," said Cappo. He paused a moment and added, "Did you want someone to watch, Captain, to see who gets that letter out of the bin?"

"No," said Maclain. "I'll find out soon enough. Whoever gets that letter out of the bin is going to kidnap me."

3

Dinner at The Crags was marred by an overwhelming mantle of nervous expectancy. At the head of the long table alight with the flicker of candles against cut glass and silver, Thaddeus Tredwill carved the roast. Each slice was cut with fine precision, laid upon a plate with studied care, and handed to Pierce to be served. Gil, Helena, Cheli Scott, and Stacy mutely watched. Sitting quietly at the right of his host, Duncan Maclain listened to the butler's self-effacing steps passing behind his chair. It seemed as though the entire drama of murder and disappearance had distilled itself into one torturing hour, filling those at the table to satiety.

Maclain felt the urgent need of introducing conversation to break the terrible spell. "I'd like to drive into Hartford after dinner to register a letter, Mr. Tredwill. Would it inconvenience you if Dominick drove me in your car?"

"Certainly not."

The Captain sensed the instant relief engendered in those present by his simple question. Down the table, Helena giggled at nothing. It sounded slightly out of place, like the laugh of an overwrought woman at a deathbed scene in a picture show.

Cheli Scott said quickly, "I'll take you, Captain, if you don't mind women drivers. I'm going in anyway."

"Dominick can take you both." Thaddeus put down the carving set and hitched his chair closer to the table.

"I wouldn't be so impolite." The Captain smiled. "To assure you of my faith in women in all professions, Miss Scott, I'll be glad to have you take me in your car."

"You have more nerve than I have," Thaddeus told him. "Automobiles scare me to death, even when they're driven by a chauffeur."

"Cappo's one of the best drivers I know," Maclain remarked, "but that hasn't saved me from having trouble with my car. He had to take it to town to have some work done late today."

Pierce put a plate down in front of him and said, "I took the liberty, Captain, of cutting your meat for you."

"You're very kind." The Captain picked up his fork and added, "I wish you'd take any message for me if Cappo happens to call."

"Certainly, sir." Pierce moved away.

Stacy asked without warning, "Which dog are you going to take in town?"

For the space of a breath the dining room was still. Then Helena spoke up with, "What do you mean? I didn't know the Captain had two."

"Dominick says there's another one out in the garage," the boy told her importantly. "Isn't that so, Captain Maclain?"

The Captain moistened his lips with a sip of water, wiped them carefully with his napkin, and said, "Yes, that's true, but Schnucke always goes with me. The other dog, Dreist, is somewhat in the nature of a spare. He's not much good to guide me around, but he's dangerous as a loaded gun."

"Dangerous!" exclaimed the boy. "He looks just like Schnucke to me, and she'd never bite anyone."

"Dreist's trained for police work," the Captain told him. "He can jump, run, and trail; and without any command on my part he'll tear anyone to pieces the instant he sees me threatened with a gun. For that matter, I don't need to be threatened. He attacks at the sight of a gun in anyone's hand."

"How about other weapons?" Stacy asked.

The Captain smiled. "He'll attack anybody who *hasn't* a weapon if I give him the command. He jumps up sideways behind their legs and knocks them over if they try to run. Football players call it clipping."

"Gosh!" said Stacy admiringly. "I'd like to have a dog like that for my own."

"I'm afraid you wouldn't have many friends left," said Duncan Maclain.

Immediately after dinner, he went upstairs to his room. There he took an almost flat automatic in a shoulder-holster rig from his Gladstone bag and started to put it on. With his arm through a loop he changed his mind, took the gun off, and put it in a bureau drawer.

As he left the bedroom, Thaddeus stopped him in the hall. "If I don't hear something about my daughter by tomorrow, Captain, I'm going to report her kidnaping officially to the police and the F. B. I."

"If I don't know where she is by tomorrow, I advise you to do so," the Captain told him, speaking very softly, "but whether you know it or not, you're already in touch with the F. B. I."

CHAPTER XXI

1

CAPPO PUSHED the swift Packard to the limit of safety on the trip to New York, utilizing every trick of a splendid driver's skill. Once he thought that a sedan with New Hampshire plates was clinging too close to him on the Merritt Parkway. Losing inquisitive sedans was a joyous game to Cappo. The Packard flashed right on an exit to New Canaan, twisted around two more turns at nauseating speed, and stopped on a bridge above the highway.

Cappo's dark face was wrinkled with lines of amusement as he watched the New Hampshire car pass below him, hesitate, and finally take the New Canaan turn. The Packard streaked off the bridge, made two more turns, and was doing better than eighty when it rolled back onto the Parkway. Cappo ran five miles passing everything until a glimpse of a State Police car slowed him down to a legal fifty. At seven-thirty, two hours and forty-five minutes from Hartford, he placed Maclain's recorded message safely in Spud's hands.

It was characteristic of Duncan Maclain's partner, Spud Savage, to think that an hour's delay in carrying out the Captain's suggestions was an hour's wasted time. He took the wax cylinder into the Captain's office, put it on the transmitter, and flicked the switch connecting the Capehart with the Ediphone.

Maclain's short, clear-cut message filled the room.

There was a battling light, almost feline, in Spud's unusual yellow eyes when he called Cappo in from the hall.

"When the Captain gave you this, Cappo, did he say why he didn't phone?"

"Nossah, Mr. Savage. He's acting mighty careful like." Cappo related what had happened at The Crags. His eyes widened to show the whites in a frightening expanse as he told of the murdered girl.

"Hell's fire!" Spud snapped out when the Negro concluded. "He probably suspects that someone's tapped the phone. I'm going to take a look at the Tanner Building right now. Come on, Cappo."

He slid his arms into a heavy overcoat and said a trifle morosely, "I wish now that Rena was here. She might handle a cosmetic job better than I can. Is there a gun in the car?"

"A twenty-five automatic, but 'tain't much bigger than so." Cappo measured the size by extending thumb and forefinger.

"That's big enough. I probably won't need it."

"Ain't no telling, Mr. Savage," said Cappo.

Spud located the venomous little Colt once he was in the car. He slid out the clip, tested the loading, and replaced the clip again. Duncan Maclain was a man given to expressive understatement. Spud didn't even want to look at a building unarmed if the Captain termed that building "dangerous as hell!"

Yet the atmosphere of New York City was deceptively lulling. As the Packard crossed the junction of Broadway and Amsterdam Avenue at Seventy-second Street, Spud looked out of the window at the orderly crowd of people and indulged in a sheepish grin. The traffic officer, an old-timer on Seventy-second Street, recognized Maclain's car and waved them through the converging traffic stream. Reflecting on his mission, Spud was hard put to waive a feeling of participating in an *opéra bouffe* where he had the part of a clown to play.

New York City was part of the United States; the United States, its institutions, traditions, and all they stood for formed a deity to Spud. The deity was mounted on a concrete base of integrity, set apart from other countries of the world and their futile bickerings. To him, as to most Americans, its ramparts were unassailable, its defenses ineluctable, tried and true. He could understand the internal seething and boiling of politics and crime, but the belief that outsiders might strike against his country was a shade beyond his comprehension. That he willingly, without thought or question, would start on a quest which he considered a trifle childish was a high tribute to his confidence in Duncan Maclain.

East Fifty-seventh Street was comparatively deserted when Spud rapped on the window and Cappo pulled into the curb. The Tanner Building was across the street, less than half a block away. The neighborhood was devoted largely to art and antique dealers. Most of the shops showed darkened windows on the street-level floor. Farther east, beyond the elevated, the lighted canopy of the Sutton Theater cut a yellow box of white, making the block where the Packard was parked seemingly dark.

"You wait here, and keep your motor running," Spud told Cappo. "The building's probably closed, but I may be able to get in the lobby and see what names are on the directory. You say the Captain mentioned something about being kidnaped, Cappo, when he asked you to throw that letter away?"

"It sounded that way to me, Mr. Savage, but he jokes an almighty lot."

"I don't think he was joking then," Spud remarked a bit irritably. "The darn fool's up to something which he knows I wouldn't approve of. Otherwise he'd have sent me more information. As it is, he's keeping things to himself and telling me nothing except what he wants me to know."

"Yessah, that's certainly a way with the Captain," agreed Cappo.

Spud took a cigarette from his pocket and put it back again. A man in the uniform of a Protective Agency was coming down the street trying the shops from door to door. Spud sat back in the limousine until the watchman went by with no more than a cursory glance at the car. He got out when the man was several doors beyond, turned up his coat collar, and lowered his head against the sharp wind sweeping down Fifty-seventh Street from the East River. The traffic light turned red, and Spud cut diagonally across the street.

Closer to the Tanner Building, he saw that a light was burning behind wide curtained windows on the second floor. Outlined against the curtains, gold letters indicated the House of Bonnée. Spud went into the small office-building lobby through an entrance next to a decorator's shop. There was an elevator a few steps to the rear, but the bronze door was closed and no attendant was in sight. At the right was a staircase. A sign on the wall said

HOUSE OF BONNÉE

Second Floor

Spud walked up, going over in his mind a hastily concocted story about selling cosmetics which he hoped might get him an interview with the head of the House of Bonnée.

He stopped before stained-glass panels in a double door. It opened readily. He went into a reception room done in colored mirrors in the most modernistic style. To the left, arranged on steps of crystal shelves, were bottles and jars. Close by the shelves was a cashier's booth with a window of chromium bars. Straight ahead he glimpsed a line of curtained booths through an open door. The curtain of the third booth was drawn back far enough to disclose the back view of a woman with a waving machine spread out octopus-like above her head.

On the other side of the waiting room, a girl with slender legs revealingly crossed looked up from a magazine. She was dressed entirely in white except for a small apron of violet hue embroidered in one corner with "The House of Bonnée." The girl's blonde hair was clustered thickly to her head in a mass of becoming curls. She stared at Spud questioningly for a few seconds out of ingenuous blue eyes before she wrinkled her saucy nose with a smile and asked: —

"Was there someone you wanted to see?"

Spud switched his story, deciding it was too late for a credible salesman's tale. He took a chance and said, "I suppose I want to talk to Monsieur Bonnée."

The girl laughed and lowered her lids inquisitively. "Monsieur happens to be Madame," she said, "and Madame happens to be away. It's after hours except for customers with late appointments. Suppose you stop in tomorrow."

Spud gave an embarrassed smile and took another glance at the woman visible through the door.

"My name's Rogers," he said. "Perhaps you can help me. I just wanted to know if my wife's still here. I was to meet her sometime after eight, but I was delayed."

"What Rogers?" asked the girl.

"Stephen." Spud clutched at the first name which came to his mind. "I believe Mrs. Rogers comes here regularly."

"There are three customers inside." The girl stood up. "Wait just a minute while I see."

She went toward the booths and closed the door behind her, shutting them off from view.

Spud walked swiftly over to the cashier's cage and peered through the bars, taking in a telephone switchboard, a safe, a glass-topped desk, and a couple of files. He left the window and sat down in a chair, feeling that for once the Captain must be wrong. There was decidedly nothing suspicious, nothing out of the way, about the House of Bonnée. New York was filled with such outfits, catering to the city's women from the Bronx to the Battery. He stood up again as the girl came back through the door.

"Your wife's almost ready," she said. "Won't you sit down and make yourself at home? We carry a unique line in the House of Bonnée. I've been trying to interest Mrs. Rogers in this particular brand of perfume."

She took a bottle from the steplike shelves and adroitly broke the seal. Leaning over Spud, she smiled, removed the stopper, and held it to his nose. It was pungent, and strong with a sweet acidity.

"It's twenty dollars an ounce," said the girl, "and the newest thing in our line. It's called Black Violets."

"I'm sorry." Spud reached up and pushed the bottle away. "I wouldn't care if it cost seventy-five dollars a dram—it doesn't appeal to me."

"You get used to it in time." The girl stoppered the bottle and returned it to the shelf.

Spud reached into his pocket for a cigarette, took it out, and searched for a match. It was very peculiar how heavy the match seemed to be. He closed both hands tightly about it, trying to keep it from falling to the floor. With one last effort, before his hands dropped inertly beside him, he grasped the cigarette and broke it in two.

2

Cappo shut off the engine of the Packard at twenty minutes past nine. He had a streak of frugality when it came to spending the Captain's money on the car. The past thirty minutes had become ones of agony at the thought of high-test gasoline being uselessly burned. Twenty minutes more dragged by lingeringly before he once more started the motor. A short distance down the block a machine moved away, leaving a vacant parking space. Cappo moved the Packard on down until it was nearly opposite the Tanner Building and backed it in. Not until then was he able to distinguish the lettering on the windows of the House of Bonnée. Again he put out the headlights and shut off the motor.

Spud had been gone an unconscionably long time, but he had given Cappo no orders to investigate or interfere.

The man in the Protective Agency uniform came back again. Cappo shivered under the warmth of his chauffeur's driving coat and turned away.

Upstairs in the Tanner Building, the lights went out in the windows of the House of Bonnée.

Cold air struck in sharply at the Negro. He twisted around with relief, thinking that Spud had returned, and found the blue-uniformed watchman holding open the door of the car.

"Waiting for someone?" the watchman asked.

"Yessah," said Cappo.

The man got in beside him and closed the door. "You've been here an awful long time. Who are you waiting for?"

"The gentleman I drive for."

"Oh," said the watchman. "Who's he?"

"He's my employer," Cappo told him steadily. "The man I work for."

"You said that before. What's his name?"

"That's his business. I don't see that it means anything to you."

"Where did he go?" the watchman asked sharply. "You sound suspicious to me."

"I don't care how I sound. It's his business where he went. I don't even know."

"Oh, you don't?" The watchman's voice rang with quick unfriendliness. "I don't suppose you know anything about a lot of robberies that've been going on around here either."

"Nothing," said Cappo.

"I think we'll see about that. Start your car, you're coming along with me."

"What's your authority?"

"This," said the watchman. He clicked the safety off the .45 automatic on his knee.

3

"You'll have to lie quiet. You've been very ill." The woman in the nurse's uniform adjusted the bed lamp so that she sat in the shadow.

Spud moved his head wearily on the pillow, fighting a nausea that clutched at his stomach threateningly. His senses were numb and dull, yet beating against his brain with the rhythmic blows of a woodsman's ax was the thought that somewhere in the not so distant past he had rushed headlong into a trap with all the rash precipitation of an arrant fool.

He opened his eyes and gazed achingly at a wall. The room he was in was windowless and quiet except for the woman's breathing and the monotonous hum of a ventilating fan heard through a grille in one corner. Rough cloth was against his skin. He glanced down at his chest. It took him several seconds to realize that he was in a single bed clad only in a hospital nightgown.

Memory began to trickle back slowly. Cappo, Fifty-seventh Street, the girl with the perfume bottle, and the House of Bonnée. Then the tiny stream of thoughts rose and grew until he felt himself drowning in bitterness as he remembered Maclain.

The Captain trusted him as he trusted no other living man. He had given him a job to do, a simple job, and Spud Savage had bungled it by showing no more foresight than a ten-year-old boy. The mechanism of the Ediphone seemed to be grinding against his nerves, mockingly repeating the message from Duncan Maclain: —

"Be cautious, because it's dangerous as hell! . . . I've become the quarry now. If you find anything suspicious, get in touch with Colonel Gray. Tell him to keep an eye on me."

No one knew the Captain's methods better than Spud Savage. The Captain was about to walk deliberately into a situation where a single slip meant death. He was pinning his faith on Spud and Colonel Gray, and Spud had failed.

He tried to move his arm and found that the sheets were tucked in tightly about him. Then a stab of hope cut into the pressure of his self-recrimination, bringing the painful relief of a surgeon's lance.

He had thought of Cappo. Cappo knew where he had gone, and Cappo was free. Spud relaxed with a lethargy even more foreboding than before. An organization which struck with such surety and finesse in a game played for nations would not have overlooked Cappo.

One single chance remained—a chance that he had not been unconscious too long, and could find some desperate means of getting away. Even if he failed to escape alive, he must get the Captain's message to G-2.

He lay quiescent, certain that the woman's eyes were looking at him all the time. Moving the fingers of his right hand as unobtrusively as possible, he began to work the covers free. The sheet was nearly untucked at the side of the bed when a key turned in the door. Spud drew a long breath, held it a few seconds, and released it cautiously.

A powerful, thick-set man in interne's white came into the room. He wore an operating mask which almost entirely hid his face. Spud watched him from under lowered lids as he carefully locked the door and pocketed the key.

"He's restless," said the woman in the nurse's uniform.

"I was afraid of that." The doctor spoke throatily. "I'd better give him an injection which will help him sleep until dawn."

Spud felt a constriction around his heart when he learned it was not yet day. There might still be time to save Maclain if he acted immediately.

The doctor came forward, stood beside the bed for some minutes looking down at Spud, then lowered the sheets a trifle and bared Spud's arm. The nurse left her chair to stand on the other side of the bed. Spud drew up his knees, forming a tent of the bedclothes. At the same instant, the table lamp gleamed on a hypodermic in the doctor's hand.

Once Spud Savage was aroused, few men living could move with such unexpected agility. The doctor took a pinch of Spud's flesh between the thumb and forefinger of his left hand and leaned over to drive the hypodermic home. As he did so, Spud's arms snaked from under the covers, reached up with simian strength to grasp the doctor's head, and smashed the masked face down with crushing force against an upraised knee.

Blood stained the surgeon's face, and the hypodermic clattered to the floor. The whipcord fingers of Spud's right hand fastened on the doctor's throat with a strangler's grip, searching for the carotid artery. With his left hand, Spud jerked the covers free and threw them over the doctor's head. He left the bed like a dementia praecox case fighting for freedom and landed on top of the physician on the floor.

The doctor cried out hoarsely from beneath the muzzling covers, circled Spud's arm with muscular hands made doubly strong by fear, and vainly tried to tear the throttling fingers free.

Lights went up in the room. Spud's yellow eyes glared up at the nurse standing above them with an automatic in her hand. His lips curled back in a grin which held a tinge of insanity.

The woman fired just as Spud whirled underneath the doctor,

lifting the hundred and ninety pounds two feet clear of the floor. He heard the shot as the bullet plowed up splinters three inches from his ear. He hoisted his feet with a wrestler's trick, planted them in the doctor's stomach, and heaved the struggling man free. The hurtling body smashed into the nurse, slamming her against the wall.

Spud came to his feet like a rubber ball. Before the woman could raise the gun again, he hooked a left to her jaw. She sagged down unconscious to the floor. Spud snatched the automatic from her limp fingers and cracked the butt down twice on the doctor's head. He ripped the covers from the helpless form, undid the belt, and jerked the interne's trousers free, slipping them on over his own bare legs and tucking in the hospital gown. The doctor's white coat followed. He took the key from the coat pocket and unlocked the door.

He pushed the switch, turning off the ceiling lights. Again the room was dim, lit only by the table lamp. Spud turned the knob and opened the door cautiously. He stuck out his head, reconnoitering the dimness of a narrow uncarpeted hall.

From the ventilator up in the corner of the room a gun popped with no more noise than a champagne cork being drawn. With a bullet in his back Spud sank slowly to his knees just as he stepped through the door.

CHAPTER XXII

1

Officers Sheridan and Dietz of the Connecticut State Police had just turned their patrol car halfway between Bridgeport and the New York State line on the Merritt Parkway and headed north again when they got the call: —

"Watch out for black convertible coupé," the radio announcer droned into the darkness of their car. "New York license N-0002. Better block the tollhouse if necessary to stop this car. Driver must be drunk. Outran patrol car at entrance to Parkway doing better than ninety-two."

"Holy mackerel!" said Trooper Dietz. "Maybe if we step on it and head her toward New York City, we'll be in time to see him go by. He'd outrun this crate of ours if he's doing seventy-two. The last time I got her up to sixty-eight, she nearly threw a wheel."

"What are you grousing about?" asked Sheridan. "We can always fire our guns at him and toot the siren."

"Yes—if we see him," said Dietz. "If he got up to ninety-two at the entrance to the Parkway, by the time he gets here he'll be running a temperature of a hundred and four."

He whirled the patrol car skillfully through a cutoff and backed it into a siding to wait for the prey.

"Maybe it's Barney Oldfield trying out a new set of tires he wants to give his kids for Christmas," Sheridan asserted with a sigh. "You remember last week when that guy—"

He broke off. Far up the road they heard a roar.

"Step on it," he told Dietz. "You wouldn't want New York State to pick up such a fine."

"Hell," said Dietz, "if I have to run him across the state line, he'll be so far ahead the New York cops'll never see him, and they'll probably pinch me."

He shot the patrol car out onto the Parkway with the siren pulled wide. The band of light that flashed before his eyes followed by a streak of black gave him the impression that somebody had suddenly drawn a paintbrush along the sky. Dietz coughed uneasily and jammed the accelerator to the floor.

"Don't try to pass him," Sheridan advised facetiously. "It'd be dangerous at this speed, particularly if he's drunk."

"I don't think he's drunk. I think he's had a shot and he's trying to fly."

"Look out," Sheridan warned. A sedan was pulled up at the side of the road.

"He missed her," said Dietz as they flashed by. A distraught lady leaned from the automobile window waving her hands hysterically.

Warning signs reading "Slow" popped up and were gone. Ahead, the yellow lights of the tollhouse rushed to meet them. Dietz heaved a sigh of relief. Parked in wedge formation beyond the tollhouse, four other state cars were blocking the road efficiently.

Sheridan wiped sweat from his forehead and climbed out as

Dietz braked down beside the New York coupé. A man in a felt slouch hat and a camel-hair coat was sitting behind the wheel.

He looked at Sheridan as though the officer were a bad oyster and said, "Good God! I paid my toll—why are you fellows bothering me?"

"There's a fifty-mile speed limit on this parkway," Sheridan began.

"Yes," the man exclaimed impatiently, "and it's too damn slow." He reached down for the pocket of his car and Sheridan, ready to suspect anything, went after his gun.

"Don't shoot," said the man. "I'm Santa Claus, and I'm heading for a Christmas party for motherless orphans."

"You're heading for the cooler," said Sheridan.

"That's what you think." The man opened his fist and laid his hand palm up on the side of the door.

"Nuts!" said Sheridan. "I wish you fellows would shoot off rockets."

He turned around and called to the blockading cars. "It's a Sewer Inspector, boys, from the WPA. Get out of his way and let him go by."

The man at the wheel looked up into the rear-view mirror and with one hand went carefully to work on the shoulder of his camel-hair coat, brushing off imaginary snow.

2

The clerk behind the desk in the apartment hotel at Seventy-second and Riverside Drive looked up from working on his transcript just in time to see the man with slightly graying hair disappear behind the elevator door. The clerk sat idly chewing his pen, watching the elevator indicator ascend to the top floor.

"Who was that?" he asked when the boy came down again.

"Somebody calling on Captain Maclain."

"In a pig's ear it is! Why don't you send people over to the desk when they come in? Captain Maclain's away."

"So's my father, most of the time," the elevator boy said disgustedly, "but my mother's almost always there."

"I can figure out without using mathematics," said the clerk, "just what days your father was gone. Mr. Savage is out, too, and there's nobody up there. Now go up and get that man and bring him down again."

"I don't have to take such talk," the elevator boy muttered as he slammed the door.

Five minutes later he was back down again.

"Where is he?" asked the night clerk.

"How do I know?" The boy stared back defiantly. "He's not up there."

"Not up where?"

"Where I took him," the boy explained impatiently. "On the twenty-fourth floor."

"Oh, is that so?" The clerk turned to the switchboard, plugged in Maclain's apartment, and rang the bell.

After a couple of minutes of continuous ringing on the clerk's part, the elevator boy inquired with a jocular air, "Well, what did he say?"

"I'll show him," the clerk said nastily between his teeth. "He can't come into this hotel and just disappear."

He walked out from behind the desk and went to the lobby door.

"Mike," he told the doorman, "get a cop. A burglar just came in here."

"Sure," said Mike. "Where is he?"

"How the hell do I know?" the night clerk demanded. "That sap Thomas took him upstairs and let him off at the twenty-fourth floor. He's probably started up there and is working down. Don't let any vans back up here, load, and drive away."

The doorman put a whistle to his lips and whistled shrilly. A taxicab swept up to the curb and stopped.

"Beat it!" said Mike. "I'm trying to get a cop."

"I'll send you one." The cab driver gave a loud Bronx cheer, and pulled away.

"You could phone," the elevator boy reminded the clerk when he returned to his desk.

"That's why you're an elevator operator instead of a night manager." The clerk dipped his pen in the ink and threw a blob on the floor. "Well-run hotels don't have police cars screaming up to the doors."

"No," said the elevator boy. "They whistle for taxis to carry their burglars away."

"You go to hell!"

An officer, wheezing slightly, lumbered in through the front door.

"I'm sorry," the clerk told him, "I didn't mean you."

"Where's the burglar?" the cop demanded.

"Ask the elevator boy." The clerk turned back to his transcript. "He took him up to the twenty-fourth floor."

"Come on," said the cop efficiently. "I'll have him in the wink of an eye."

3

Arnold C. Cameron waited on the twenty-fourth floor until the elevator had dropped from sight before he stepped into the private lift close by and pushed the button which took him up two flights more. There he rang the bell on Maclain's penthouse door. There was no answer, and after a short wait he took a leather key holder from his pocket, selected a key, and opened the door. A night light burned dimly in the small reception room. Cameron went into Maclain's office, turned on soft indirect lights concealed in the molding, and stood still for a while appraising the furniture and equipment. His gray eyes opened a shade wider at sight of the Ediphone.

He took a few soft-footed strides and sat down in Maclain's chair. There he adjusted the transmitter by moving the needle back to zero, let it down on the record, and turned it on.

He sat immobile until Maclain's voice said: "*If you find anything suspicious, get in touch with Colonel Gray. Tell him that I'm more important than anything for the moment, and to keep an eye on me.*"

He clicked off the record and put his elbows on the desk. Resting his chin in cupped hands, he stared at the telephone. The number on the dial was Susquehanna 7-0039, Ext. 2.

Cameron puckered his lips, pushed back the chair, and swiftly began to go through the desk drawers. In the top one on the left-hand side he found another phone. He dialed a number with automatic precision and leaned back in the chair.

After a few rings someone answered and Cameron said, "Jack, it's me. The barge is loaded with women and children and it's about to go down. They moved too fast for us. Sometime between nine and ten o'clock they snatched Maclain and a girl."

The listener's voice broke in, crackling insistently over the phone.

Cameron said, "Sign off for once, will you, and listen to me. The girl's name is Cheli Scott, a visitor at The Crags. She was driving Maclain in to the Hartford Post Office. They must have been held up on the road. Police found her deserted car."

"Where are you now?" the voice demanded peremptorily.

"I'm in Maclain's office," said Cameron with a patient sigh. "I highballed it down here to see if I could find something that would give me a lead. Maclain sent a message down to New York by his chauffeur several hours ago. It's on a record. Hold tight, and I'll play it to you over the phone."

He picked up the recording mouthpiece from the combination Ediphone and after a couple of tries succeeded in shutting off the Capehart and making the mouthpiece talk into the phone.

When Cameron put the telephone receiver to his ear again, the voice said excitedly, "That's a pretty kettle of stew. Where does this Bonnée come into the picture?"

"I don't know, do you?"

"No." The voice became icy and authoritative, snapping out orders over the phone. "Everything's set for a round-up from here to the coast tomorrow night—Christmas Eve. Any tip-off now and a whole year's work is undone. Maclain's been let down cold. He thinks he's being protected, and he isn't. Get back up to Hartford as fast as you can haul it, and see what you can do."

"And what about the House of Bonnée? I might dig up something there."

"They'll have to wait until tomorrow night. I'll include them in the show."

"But Maclain's been kidnaped," Cameron protested. "He's

carrying around a lot of information. God knows what they'll do."

"I don't care if they snatch Jim Farley and nine Cabinet members," the voice barked back. "You let that House of Bonnée alone!"

"All right," said Cameron, "but it strikes me that the House of Bonnée is my only chance of ever finding out where they've taken him."

"I'm giving you orders," said the voice. "Let the House of Bonnée alone."

"You're murdering the Captain and an innocent girl," Cameron declared metallically, and hung up the phone.

He swung around in the chair to look straight down the long dark tube of Patrolman Heeney's Police Positive. The officer's round moon face hung like a crimson pie over the sight as he lumbered through the office door.

"Put up your hands," he commanded thunderously.

"Don't shoot," said Cameron pleadingly. "If you miss me, the bullet will hit the desk and there's a baby in the drawer."

"Git up," ordered Heeney, "and tell me how you got in here."

"Skeleton key," said Cameron. "How did you?"

"With a passkey," the policeman explained, slightly confused. "What are you doing with a baby in that drawer?"

"It's my little boy," said Cameron. "I brought him in under my coat—I thought his mother was here."

The officer's guileless blue eyes narrowed disapprovingly.

"You're a crook," he said with dawning comprehension. "I've seen your face someplace before."

"It's posted from coast to coast," Cameron told him. "Do you ever go into the post office?"

"Yes," said Heeney, "to mail letters. What else would I be going in there for?"

"I think you're impersonating an officer," Cameron said. "Sit down in that chair."

"Is it you that's givin' orders," Heeney demanded, "or is it me?"

"It's me," said Cameron. "What do you mean by breaking into my apartment? I'm Duncan Maclain."

"He's blind," said Heeney.

"So'm I," said Cameron. "Only you can't tell it without my glasses on. Sit down in that chair!"

The policeman felt that his head was whirling giddily. "I know you now. Why aren't you in jail? You're a murderer."

"I am not," Cameron denied. "The fellow that accused me of killing him appeared in court and they set me free. Sit down in that chair. You have a gun, and I'm very busy."

The power of suggestion became too much for the over-wrought officer, and he sat down gingerly on the edge of the red leather chair.

"Now lean back," said Cameron. "You can keep me covered with your gun; but there's something I want to show you before we go."

"Don't try anything," Heeney advised.

"Look." Cameron held both his hands out in front of him and wiggled them. "All I want to do is push a button and get the time. If the time doesn't come, you can shoot me."

He pressed the button marked "Time Connection" on the desk at his side.

Beside Officer Heeney, from a loud-speaker in the wall, a woman's voice said, "When you hear the signal, the time will be exactly three twenty-three."

Heeney fidgeted uncomfortably, but kept his eyes on Cameron. "'Tis quite a trick," he mumbled, "but you'll not be after trickin' me!"

"Now listen," said Cameron. "You know that Duncan Maclain's blind. He's a private detective, and he has to have means of protecting himself. Did you ever hear of an electric eye?"

"Yes," said Heeney. "And what's that to do with me?"

"Nothing," said Cameron, "except it's going to keep you sitting in that chair. When I pushed that time-connection button, I turned another one on."

The officer tensed.

"Don't move," Cameron warned. "There's a gun set in the upholstery in the back of that chair. If you try to get up you'll break the ray of an electric eye which goes from arm to arm. In other words, officer, you'll be shot in the back."

"I'll get you first," said Heeney.

"You'd better keep your hands down, too," Cameron told him. "You'll shoot yourself in the back if you try to raise your gun."

He got up and picked his soft felt hat from off the desk.

"If you don't believe me, you can try it," he said, "and the blood won't be on me. Clever chap, that Duncan Maclain."

He started toward the door. "I wouldn't try to wipe the sweat off my forehead either," he warned Heeney commiseratingly. "I'll write a letter to the Commissioner about you. I'm tired of having you fellows stop me at every street corner to try to put me back in jail. *Hasta la vista*—or, as the Swedes say, *au revoir.*"

He walked from the room and closed the door, descended rapidly down a service stairway to the basement, and let himself out into an alley by way of the delivery entrance. At the corner of Seventy-second and Broadway, he located an all-night restaurant with a phone booth where he dialed Spring 7-3100, and finally got Inspector Davis on the phone.

"This is the Shadow," he told Davis. "I just wanted to let you know that one of your minions named Heeney wants to see you up in Duncan Maclain's office without delay."

"What's he doing up there?" the Inspector sputtered furiously.

"He's sitting in a chair," said Cameron, "and he thinks he's being kept there by the Seeing Eye."

Five minutes later, he was smashing every speed limit on his way back to Hartford in the convertible coupé.

CHAPTER XXIII

1

Duncan Maclain manipulated his hands vigorously together in an attempt to restore circulation. Spasmodic cramps had seized his shoulder muscles and were traveling downward. He could feel small excruciating knots bunching up along each arm. He spread his elbows outward, twisting and writhing to get his manacled wrists up farther behind him. There was one position where the tightly locked handcuffs seemed looser, where the hampered blood could flow in his veins a little more freely.

The air about him was damp, penetratingly cold. Its smell, with an overlying trace of metal and oil, was reminiscent of fungus and mush-rooms. The Captain breathed it cautiously, keeping his lips tightly closed against the nauseating taste of adhesive tape which gagged him formidably.

Time had drifted by in a dark overpowering wave. He judged it better than most people. Years of sightlessness had instilled in his mind a faultless chronometer which ticked off pulse and heartbeats, dividing them into seconds, minutes, and hours with an almost fatalistic regularity.

His feet and legs were tightly bound. He lay face down, disdaining muscular struggle against obvious impossibility. Limp and inert as though anesthetized, he husbanded his strength, waiting for a moment when someone would come and set him free. Somewhere his carefully laid plans must have slipped.

He pressed his cheek down against the roughness of an unplaned board. Unhampered by any extraneous distraction, he reviewed the events of the past few days, checking each item from the time the man who he thought was Madoc brought him the instructions in Braille to the moment when Cheli Scott's car was blocked by a truck on a deserted stretch of highway. He analyzed each move he had made, ruthlessly scrutinizing each weakness in the chain.

Duncan Maclain had been guilty of an unpardonable sin: carelessness. The price might be the life of Duncan Maclain. The enemy had moved too fast, had gone to work without wasting an hour. Never had he expected them to act with such precipitancy. Their move gave Spud no time whatever to receive his message, investigate the House of Bonnée, and get in touch with Colonel Gray.

The Captain had predicated his plans on the belief that he would be forcibly abducted some time during the following day. He intended to give his adversaries every chance, to put himself up as a bait. *Saboteurs* must have a base. Maclain's taped mouth twisted into a grin. He had found the base, gotten himself unerringly into the headquarters of an airtight, organized band, only he had arrived there about twenty-four hours too soon to be of any use to the competent workers of the F. B. I.

"—And this one may end your career," he thought bitterly, recalling the words of Colonel Gray.

He wormed himself sideways with maximum caution, trying

to find a wall. His exploring feet encountered nothing. After a time, he decided he must be lying on a packing case a foot or two high. Inaction began to pall. He held his breath and listened. A water pipe dripped steadily. Not far away, some mechanism which might be a tiny motor ran with an almost inaudible purr. Maclain judged that he was close to an electric meter and that the noise he heard was the spinning of the recording wheel. Lights were on somewhere in his prison, although he felt sure that outside it was day. His entire body ached dolefully and he knew that he must have spent much time sleeping fitfully.

Taking a chance of injury, he swung his feet violently to one side and rolled off onto the floor. The drop was higher than he expected and it stunned him momentarily.

He eased his weight from off his hands and listened again. Small feet pattered flutteringly as a rodent scuttled away. Maclain was satisfied that no one had been in to look at him for some time. Otherwise a timorous rat would not have been so near.

He planned a tour of exploration. His only means of moving would be to bend his legs and shove himself along the floor. There were always identifying marks that his sagacious fingers might see, and if he ever escaped he wanted to know that place again.

By aiding himself with his elbows against the side of the packing box which had served him as a couch, he managed to sit erect. Awkwardly he rocked himself around to one end of the box. Sitting up as straight as possible, he went over the wood with his fingers, starting at the bottom each time and moving his hands upward from the floor.

The packing case was large. Nailed-down metal tape bound it at each end. The Captain had covered almost the entire surface when his fingers touched a series of small indentations. He went over them once, then sat unbelievingly with sweat staining his forehead as he traced them again more carefully. Underneath them, punched into the wood, was a tiny arrowhead.

The Captain left the box and began to inch across the floor. It was cluttered with debris. Pieces of old iron, several camshafts from automobile motors, and assorted junk of all description put hazards in his way.

He backed into a wall. It was damp and felt as though it had been whitewashed in the past. He moved along it until stopped by another packing case. It, too, was punched with the letters and the arrowhead. A trip around it brought him in contact with several more. He was certain then that, whoever his captors might be, they never intended him to leave the place alive.

The name punched into the end of the boxes was that of the great Eagle Munitions Works. The arrowhead was the stamp of the British Government. He was imprisoned in a storehouse filled with looted British supplies of war.

Behind him a bolt slid back in the door.

2

There were several people in the room. The Captain sat in a straight-back armchair with wooden arms and an upholstered seat. Adhesive tape held him motionless, binding his wrists to the arms of the chair. One man standing close beside him was breathing wheezily.

The Captain fought to divorce his mind from the asthmatic inhalations of the man beside him so that he might better judge how many men were in the room. He segregated them after a while and gave them numbers.

Number 1 was sitting down. Maclain placed him as being in charge and pictured him sitting behind a table. He had spoken once or twice in a velvety whisper which had sounded at a height approximately on a level with the Captain's face.

Number 2 seemed to be a confrere. He was also seated, more to the right. Maclain had followed his footsteps across the room and acoustically watched him take a chair.

Number 3 had adenoids and was standing with his back to a door. Now and again he shuffled his feet uneasily, either touching the doorknob with his buttocks or moving it with his hand.

Asthma was Number 4.

Papers rustled. The Captain decided that Number 1 was reading, hence the silence. He followed the unmistakable crackle of fingered paper and the swish as each sheet was finished and laid face down on the table. Once the man with the velvet voice smothered an exclamation of annoyance.

A chair creaked slightly under shifted weight. Once again the Captain pieced together a sequence of sounds and divined that a single sheet of the paper had fallen to the floor, to be retrieved by Number 2, who handed it back to the reader.

The man with the velvet voice suddenly spoke aloud. "It's to be infinitely regretted that a brave man and an officer should be put to such inconvenience, Captain Maclain."

The words were spaced. They rolled out dispassionately, without rancor or any noticeable mark of emotion. Unctious with an olive-oil texture, they managed to be detached, and terribly impersonal. There was no patriotism behind them, no warmth. Neither was there any coldness or inhumanity.

The Captain was seized with hopelessness at their sound.

Trained to estimate others by voice and cadence instead of appearance, it was brought home to him crushingly that he was face to face with a living body whose mind possessed no attribute subject to human appeal. He felt himself in the grip of the ultimate, as though cast by fate into some strange universe. He stood before Mars himself, the god of war and destruction. It would be futile to argue with a being whose voice had only beauty; as futile as to try to check a headlong rush of nations into ruin by casting himself bodily into the maw of their lancinating machine.

A hand materialized, seized the end of the adhesive tape which muzzled his lips, and tore it loose with a single pull.

"Your solicitude overwhelms me," said Duncan Maclain. "I judge that I'm supposed to talk now that my lips are free."

"Assuredly," the Number 1 voice agreed in a single word of unaltered pleasantness. "We find ourselves in an age-old situation, Captain Maclain. I possess something which in your peculiar scale of values is rated most highly—the life of a fellow being. A woman. You possess something which in my peculiar scale of values is rated equally high—the knowledge of plans to defend five salient points in New York City. I'm offering you an exchange, Captain Maclain—one which is more than fair. I want the name and location of those five salient points, and I want to know what measures have been taken to make them safe. I'm offering you the life of a woman in exchange. I say the exchange is more than fair, because whether you decide to tell me or not, a little more work on the part of the organization I represent will inevitably make those points known to me. The defense plans might take longer to obtain. Nevertheless, I'd learn them eventually."

Duncan Maclain lived in a world of sound. He knew each

note in the scale of speech; how to make it ring deep with compassion and equally well how to make it pump blood to the face of a listener under the coruscating stab of jibe and irony.

He threw back his head, opened his mouth, and suddenly began to laugh. It came from his heart, mirthful and unfeigned, and struck against the confining walls with rolling peals of jollity. Immoderately and long he continued, shaking his pinioned body in the chair.

The hand which had torn the adhesive loose flashed out and struck him cruelly. Blood stained his lips and a single drop slid quietly down his chin.

"What are you laughing about, you fool?" asked the voice of Number 1.

"I'm laughing about nothing," said Duncan Maclain. "I'm laughing at you. In my peculiar scale of values, I possess two things which you know nothing about. They go by the names of perspicacity and integrity. The perspicacity tells me that neither I nor the woman you're holding will ever leave here alive no matter what I say; the integrity would silence me more effectively than a hundred yards of adhesive no matter how the woman or I might die. Add them both together, my friend, and you have the cause for my laughter. I'm blind and helpless, but I'm an American officer who lost his sight on active service and you're a renegade plotting the downfall of the country you're living in. It amuses me to know that you're the fool and not I."

"A blind man's ears are sensitive, Captain Maclain. Certain steps have been taken to prevent this country you speak about so staunchly from manufacturing war supplies to sell to enemies of mine. Those steps will be felt from coast to coast, joining the bells on Christmas Day. Nothing you can do, or anyone else, can interfere. You can, however, save yourself the maddened screams of a tortured woman pounding against your receptive ears. Hours of them, Captain Maclain. Hours of pleading and entreaty from a woman unwittingly involved in this by you. When you meet death in the end, the thought of those screams will be your torture. Do you know of any more difficult way to die?"

"One," said Duncan Maclain. "Giving satisfaction to a fool."

The chair behind the table moved back and the pleasant voice said, "Perhaps we'd better give you a few hours to think it over, Captain Maclain."

CHAPTER XXIV

1

Louis Madoc, his long neck drawn turtle-like through the collar of his cardigan jacket, stood against the sheltering wall of the new addition and watched the men file by. It was Christmas Eve and occasionally one man more friendly than the rest would wave or call a greeting; but for the most part they passed him silently or deliberately turned away. The surliness of his fellow workers was lost on Louis entirely. He resented the noisy groups which formed to pass on ribald pleasantries and give advice about not eating too much dinner on the following day.

He was glad when they trickled on into the parking space, found their cars, and drove off. Only a handful of men was left when Louis forsook the shelter of the wall. He started toward the gate. A short distance up the road toward Glastonbury he had sighted the truck he wanted so much to see.

The watchman on duty hailed it. Louis quickened his steps and was just in time to prevent an altercation between the watchman and the driver.

He broke it up by showing his long teeth and saying, "That's plumbing equipment. What are you stopping for? I've been waiting for it all day."

"This is a hell of a time to be bringing it in." The watchman glared from Louis to the driver and back to Louis again. "This shebang's supposed to be shut down. Tomorrow's Christmas Day."

"And we go to work again the day after." Louis hopped on the running board beside the driver and said, "Take it through."

The watchman looked after them until the truck stopped by the new addition and disgorged the driver and helper. The watchman shrugged and went back into the warmth of his little house. It was cold outside, anyway.

Louis waited while the two men unloaded a short squat box, handling it gingerly.

"Bring it in here," he ordered, and clicked on a flashlight to dispel inside shadows grown long with the fading of the day.

The two men followed him through skeleton walls down the length of an uncompleted hall.

"Here." Louis pointed to a spot with his flashlight. "This'll do. Any more?"

"This is plenty," said the driver.

Louis guided them out and stood in the doorway until he heard the motor roar. When the truck had gone, he made his way back to the building without using the light. Near the box, he stood silently, turning his head from left to right and back again. Not quite satisfied, he knelt on the floor, put his ear against one end, and gave a wolfish grin.

It was dark when he reached the other side of the parking lot and opened the door to turn on the lights of his car.

A hand reached out and fastened itself firmly to the throat of his cardigan jacket.

"I'll help you in," said a voice.

The arm went back into the sedan with Madoc attached to one end of it. He had a sensation of falling through space as his shins scraped along the running board, and his feet kicked vainly in protest. Not more than five seconds elapsed before Louis found himself tucked neatly behind the driver's wheel.

"You drive, Hawkface," said the voice.

The dashlight went on and shed rays on the camel-hair coat.

"That uncomfortable lump in your side is a Luger 7.65. I'd hate to have to shoot it because this coat set me back sixty-nine fifty and at a hundred feet this Luger will penetrate eighteen inches of pine. Now drive on like a good lad because some friends of mine will be here in a few minutes to take your little box away."

Louis stepped on the starter with a foot that seemed suddenly affected with frostbite. "Who the devil are you?"

"I'm the Spirit of '76," said Arnold Cameron, "but you can just call me Toots and I'll call you Hawkface, and we won't get in each other's way. When you get outside the gate, turn toward Hartford—and don't dillydally."

"This is kidnaping." Madoc's bony frame began to shake with a chill of sheer fury. "You can't get away with it. I'll signal the first policeman I see."

"All you need to do," said Cameron, "is raise your right hand and wiggle your fingers in the rear-view mirror. There's a state trooper named King riding in the back of your car."

"You can't arrest me without a warrant."

"Who said I was arresting you?" Cameron demanded bitingly. "I wouldn't waste my time."

"What do you think you're going to do?" Madoc's voice wasn't quite so brave as before.

"I'm going to torture you," said Cameron. Something terribly sincere in his tone caused Madoc to swerve the car.

"Keep on the right side of the white line," Cameron told him, "or the Sergeant will run you in. I said I was going to torture you and I mean it, too."

"You can't scare me," Madoc told him, but the force of the words was lost on a quavering note which crept in on the end.

"Scare you?" Cameron repeated, surprised. "I'm not going to scare you, Hawkface, I just don't like you. I'm going to feed you to rats and throw what's left of you away."

2

It was cold and extremely dreary in the top-floor room of the closed-up, deserted hotel. Wallpaper which had long ago served its purpose was beginning to scale in tiny curls from the wall. Louis Madoc, stripped down to shirt, socks, and shorts, lay on the pancake mattress and stared at the flinty, clean-lined face of Sergeant King. Arnold Cameron had just finished a neat job of trussing with sash cord cut from the long closed windows. Madoc had taken it unresistingly, gazing with feverish, birdlike eyes into the steady muzzle of the Sergeant's gun.

Cameron took off his camel-hair coat and hunted for a dust-free place to hang it up. Failing to find one, he went over the top of the bureau with a handkerchief and deposited his treasured garment there. That done, he sat down and began to rock himself slowly back and forth in a squeaky rocking chair.

"It would be quicker," said Sergeant King, "to shoot him and be done with it. I hate these stinkin' foreigners. He chopped off the head of a girl."

"I never killed anybody in my life," Madoc whimpered protestingly.

"Shut up," said Cameron, "or I'll stick my finger in your eye."

He rocked back and forth a dozen times more, each separate squeak stabbing into Madoc's nerves with the pain of a dentist's drill.

"I'd match you," said Cameron, still rocking, "to see who'd shoot him first. In that way one of us could start and we could riddle him with bullets. Maybe we'll do that after he tells us what they've done with Duncan Maclain."

Madoc's wrinkled lids slid down as though the light of the single bulb in the room had become too strong. He raised them quickly as Cameron left the chair.

A suitcase carried upstairs by the Sergeant sat just inside the door. Cameron picked it up and held it in his hand for a moment, weighing it appraisingly.

"It's funny as hell about you fellows," he stated flatly, looking down at Madoc. "You figure everything out on earth except that two can play at a game. You and your gang of *saboteurs* have kidnaped a blind man who'll never talk if you cut him to pieces. I'm interested to see if our side isn't better than yours. I'm giving you a chance to tell me right now what they've done with Duncan Maclain."

"I've never heard of him." Madoc was drooling slightly on the mattress.

"Now that you've got that lie out of your system," said Cameron, "I can get on with my work without having to start all over again."

He lifted the suitcase suddenly and set it down on the bed close to Madoc's ear.

"Listen." The glint of merriment usually present had left his eyes, leaving them poisonously gray and clear. Leaning over, he rapped with his knuckles on the side of the suitcase, to be answered with scurrying and a tiny squeak sharp as the slice of a machete against the silence of the room.

Madoc's lips worked convulsively and his beak-nosed face grew ugly with pallor.

"Those rats in there are hungry." Cameron took the suitcase from the bed and put it on the floor. "The Sergeant kindly got them for me from the hospital laboratory where they're used for experimental purposes."

He turned toward King. "It's a very pleasant custom, Sergeant, handed down from the last world war. I've heard that the Sikhs and Gurkas, who were noted for their fortitude, could stand as many as three, only to become raving maniacs at number four."

He swung back unexpectedly on Madoc and said, "Weak men talk and so will you."

Reaching down, he picked the trussed-up man from the bed as though he weighed nothing at all, strode across the room to the closet, opened the door, and dumped Madoc's struggling form down on the floor.

"We'll see how long you can stand it, Hawkface. One at a time I'm taking those rats from the suitcase and tossing them in there with you."

He slammed the closet door. Sergeant King mopped his forehead and said, "Holy Saint Cecilia! If this is police work, I think I'll go back to farming."

"This isn't police work," Cameron told him. "It's a bloody war."

He unstrapped the lid of the suitcase, clicked the latch, and walked to the closet door; then came back and seated himself in the squeaky chair.

The Sergeant looked at his watch and said, "It's quarter past seven on Christmas Eve."

A sudden scream, prolonged and terrifying, started a tingling at the roots of the Sergeant's hair. It rose again and died away.

"Hark!" said Cameron. "The herald angels sing."

He got up and walked to the closet door. "Where is Duncan Maclain?"

"He's in the basement of a deserted house on Sunset Hill in Glastonbury," Madoc poured out sobbingly from behind the closet door.

"Who's there with him?" asked Cameron.

"Four men. Oh God, they'll murder me!"

The scream rose up again and died off lingeringly.

"Damn it all," said Cameron. "He's fainted."

He opened the closet door, lifted Madoc's unconscious body, and laid it on the bed with the head hung over the edge. He returned to the closet, groped around for a minute, and picked up the tiny furry animal from one corner. Holding it in his hand, he came back into the room and said: —

"If you'd had the time to get rats, he probably would have given us a certified list of every spy in the United States. It's funny what a bit of talk, a lot of darkness, and a guinea pig can do."

3

Heavy-footed men had been coming and going for a long time, moving crates out of the cellar. Duncan Maclain played a game by following their approaching footsteps and guessing which box they would take out next. The men worked silently, indicating the effort of their labors by occasional grunts and groans.

Lying in a corner on the damp floor, the Captain traced their burden-laden steps and reached the conclusion that the boxes were being taken outside through a cellar door. Big plans were apparently in the process of completion. Several times he heard the start of a powerful motor and the rumble of wheels as heavy trucks came to life and moved off. It was doubtful that such dangerous contraband would be assembled in a place of safety and summarily whisked away unless a culmination was near.

His hands had been loosened long enough for him to eat. Afterward the handcuffs were restored, but his lips were left untaped. He read that courtesy as a preliminary step to letting him talk with the girl.

He was not surprised when they brought her in and laid her down beside him after the last of the boxes was taken away.

Her whisper was tremulous and startlingly close to his ear when she asked, "Captain Maclain, can you hear?"

"Perfectly, Cheli," he answered gently. "This unforgivable situation we're in is entirely due to me."

After he spoke she breathed erratically as though finding it difficult to know just what to say. At last she asked him, "Have you any idea where we are?"

"No," said Maclain, "except that we're in a house near the top of some small hill."

"Hill?" she repeated leadenly. "They've kept me blindfolded. I haven't been able to see."

"Nor have I, Cheli, but I have heard trucks approaching in second gear, and the ease with which, once loaded, they roll away."

Twice she began to speak and faltered. The Captain knew

what was in her mind. It was better to refrain from prompting her, preferable to let her face the task alone, find the difficult words she must inevitably choose to tell him of cool-voiced threats made against her. He could only wait and listen when finally she sobbed out her story of carefully calculated torment and coercion. Cheli Scott had become part of their plans, and Duncan Maclain was powerless to do anything but remain inert and receive like dripping acid on his delicate eardrums every soul-scarifying word she had to say.

"Captain—"

"Yes, Cheli." His voice held rich, full assurance, never betraying the fact that for the moment he had almost ceased to live inside of himself, that his blood had almost ceased to flow under heartbeats, so tense had become his concentration. It was one of those moments when Spud would have told him, "Dunc, you've ceased to be a man and become an unemotional machine."

"—Those men in there, they're going to—"

"Listen, my dear," said Duncan Maclain. "There are some things in life greater than the human body; some things even greater than the working of imagination, which is the acme of all fear. Love of humanity is one, and another is faith in an ideal. You've been placed on a pedestal which the gods might envy. The lives and happiness of a nation and the preservation of its ideals are in your hands, dependent on your courage and you."

She suddenly began to cry. "They're going to put a band around my head and tighten it until I die. I haven't your strength, Captain Maclain. They said that you're a man without feeling, told me that I could never break you down."

"So you'd have me talk?" asked Duncan Maclain, and the glass-edged question silenced the sobbing girl. "You value yourself too highly, Cheli; yourself and me. To save you I'd have to sack a city, throw eight million people at a stroke into a pit of pestilence."

He stopped, and with him the noise in the basement window to which he had been listening so intently stopped too.

"I'm afraid, Captain." Her words were scarcely coherent. "They murdered Bella so brutally. I can't forget it. They said if torturing me didn't make you talk, they'd start on you."

The Captain felt that she was stifling an imminent scream.

"They murdered her," she went on, with hysteria taking command. "They'll have no pity on a girl. They'll torture me until I'm dead, and then they'll start on you!"

"They won't," said Duncan Maclain.

Across the cellar the bolt slid back in the door and the Captain heard the methodical tramp of three pairs of feet coming for him and the girl.

A Luger 7.65 coiled back and spat four times with the speed of a striking rattler. Somewhere upstairs the Captain's ears heard the crash of glass and the splintered fall of a door.

Above his head from the cellar window a voice said, "One miss, one in the middle of the forehead, and two in the eye."

"You're a good shot, Mr. Cameron," said Duncan Maclain.

CHAPTER XXV

1

THE POLICE car with Sergeant King at the wheel worked its way rapidly through streets festooned with Christmas lights overhead and sped out toward West Hartford up Asylum Street hill. In the back, wrapped up warmly, sat Cheli Scott and Duncan Maclain. Sticking close to the rear, nosing occasional late merrymakers out of the way with a quick imperative blast of the klaxon, came Arnold Cameron's speedy convertible coupé.

It was after midnight when the center of the city dropped behind. The streets grew darker, broken only now and then by the light of some late-closing store. A watery moon battled ineffectively against smoky clouds and finally sank down behind them defeated. As Sergeant King sighted the single yellow square marking The Crags and turned up the hill, it began to snow. They waited some time before Maclain heard footsteps answer the Sergeant's peremptory ringing and Pierce opened the door.

"Captain Maclain!" the butler exclaimed, taking in the Captain's disheveled appearance with a trained servant's eye. "You've been hurt, sir—and Miss Scott, is she with you?"

"Yes, Pierce." Maclain stepped inside. "You might give the Sergeant a hand and help her in out of the car."

He leaned wearily against the wall, concentrating on the abnormally loud tick of a grandfather's clock.

Pierce came back in and Cheli's voice said, "I'm quite all right now, Captain. Pierce has just been saying that the Tredwills are all away."

"You've had a terrible shock," Maclain told her commandingly. "I'm going to call Dr. Trotter. Get to bed immediately."

Pierce said, "Mr. Tredwill had a call from Boston. They found Miss Barbara."

"I thought they might," put in Arnold Cameron. "That means they've washed up the show. I have to get to a telephone right away."

"There's one here," said Pierce.

Maclain heard Cameron go into the closet booth and close the door. He took two steps, opened it, and said, "I wish you'd get Dr. Trotter for Miss Scott before you make another call."

Cameron's gray eyes flashed with a quick admiring glint as he said, "Okay."

"Dominick was to drive Mr. Tredwill and Mr. Gilbert to Boston in the car," Pierce went on when Maclain had shut Cameron in behind the door. "The ladies insisted they be allowed to go so they took Mr. Stacy along. The cook and parlormaid have gone into Hartford for the night with their people, but they'll return in the morning. For the moment I'm the only one here."

"It's quite all right, Pierce." Maclain pulled himself together with an effort. He heard Cheli go upstairs and added, "I wonder if you'd see me to my room, Sergeant," and followed her up, leaning on Sergeant King's arm.

Pierce came close behind them. "Your dog's waiting for you

in your room, Captain. The police found her when they located Miss Scott's car. Apparently it was left exactly where you were stopped last night and never moved at all."

The Captain said nothing. He needed no one to tell him that Schnucke was waiting on the other side of the bedroom door. She had already acknowledged his arrival with a welcoming scratch and a whine. When she broke her rigorous training long enough to put both feet on his chest and caress his nose with a warm soft tongue, it was a moment before he could find the voice to order her down.

Pierce clicked on the lights. "You'll find everything just where you left it, sir. Your other dog's in the basement. I brought him over here because Dominick's away and the heat's turned off in the garage. I was afraid he might be cold. Is there anything more I can do?"

"Nothing, but accept my thanks," said Maclain.

"I'll turn down the bed before I leave," the butler told him, "and lay out your things. If you need me for anything more, my telephone button is Number Seven, the top one in the left-hand row." He went off with a quick "Good night."

Sergeant King said, "He's a damned efficient man."

As the Captain started to undress, King told him, "Lie down on the bed. I know you're butt-headed and independent, but you've been through hell-and-gone, and tonight, for once in your life, a policeman's playing nurse to you."

"I'm afraid it'll be a pleasure." The Captain stretched out on the bed with a smile and added, "How in the name of heaven did you locate me?"

"I didn't," said Sergeant King, tugging at a shoe. "You'll have to thank that madman in the camel-hair coat. He picked up a fellow named Louis Madoc, shut him up in a closet, and turned rats loose on him. I'm afraid when the Commissioner hears what I've been mixed up in tonight I'll have some real explaining to do."

Maclain started to sit up, but the Sergeant pushed him back again.

"Then he must have been in touch with Spud, my partner in New York." The Captain paused and added, "Did you know Cameron was a member of the F. B. I.?"

"I learned it tonight," said King, "but how did you?"

"It was fairly obvious, if you had all the details as I had," said Maclain. "He confessed to a murder he hadn't committed and pointedly dragged in an innocent girl. She was promptly thrown into jail and held there under a prohibitive bond. I tested her with a trick, a friendly suggestion written in violet ink. She reacted to it and proved herself a member of the sabotage gang by jumping at the idea that she back up Mr. Cameron's fake confession and make a stab at sending him to the chair. While everyone in this very smart spy organization thinks Mr. Cameron is in jail too, he's most annoyingly running around free."

"You said it," Sergeant King remarked, breathing heavily. "He's certainly been plenty of annoyance to me."

Schnucke stood up beside the bed as Cameron came in the door. The F. B. I. man closed it swiftly behind him, walked over, and sat down on the bed beside Maclain. "Captain," he said, "I have bad news for you."

Two thin lines appeared at the sides of the Captain's nose and smoothed themselves out again.

"They found your partner, Spud Savage, in a room in the Tanner Building when they raided it tonight. He was shot in the back. He's in New York Hospital and the doctors say his chances are good, but it was touch and go. Your chauffeur was there too, knocked out with a hypo of scopolamine. He isn't seriously hurt."

Cameron slid an arm under the Captain's shoulders and raised him up while the Sergeant slipped his pajama jacket on.

Maclain asked, "When did Spud talk to you?"

"I didn't see him," said Cameron. "I'm afraid I burgled your apartment last night and played the record containing your message. The F. B. I. has in its possession twenty-three names of ringleaders in an organization which planned wholesale sabotage in the United States tomorrow. Eleven of them they knew. Twelve more they found, thanks to you, in the House of Bonnée. The President of the United States has sent you a word of thanks, Captain Maclain, conveyed by Colonel Gray."

The Sergeant said, "Gentlemen, if you'll excuse me, I'd better be traveling. I have a report to make. Are you coming, Mr. Cameron?"

"No," said Cameron. "I have some things to talk over with the Captain. I think I'd better stay."

The Sergeant paused at the door. "If you turn up anything that will throw a light on the murder in this house, for God's sake let me know."

"I will," said Duncan Maclain.

Pierce's footsteps sounded in the hall. When the butler rapped, Sergeant King opened the door and said, "I'm just leaving, Pierce. Mr. Cameron's staying. If you don't mind, you can go down and lock up after me."

"Yes," said Pierce. He hesitated a moment, looking about the room. "I'm afraid I'm getting a bit nervous, gentlemen, but something peculiar happened after the Tredwills left. I thought I'd better report it, although I imagine it's nothing more than a petty theft."

"What's that?" Maclain asked quickly.

"It's so silly that I almost hate to bring it up at such a time," Pierce went on. "I heard a noise downstairs about an hour before you arrived. I went out on the side porch to investigate and found that somebody had stolen the untrimmed Christmas tree."

"A Christmas tree!" Cameron exclaimed. "Now what the hell—"

The Sergeant's face was a study. He adjusted his uniform jacket to a closer fit and looked at Maclain. The Captain lay motionless, staring unblinkingly with hypnotic intensity at a bright bulb in the table lamp. It made the Sergeant's eyes water. He shifted his gaze to Cameron, then back to Pierce again.

"It wasn't exactly stolen," Pierce corrected in the steady manner he had of getting everything right to a T. "Somebody took it from the porch and dragged it down the hill at the end of the house to the edge of the driveway. I found it there and brought it back again."

"Probably some kid who lost his nerve," said Sergeant King. "I really must go."

The butler told Cameron, "There's an empty room across the hall. I can supply you with everything you need if you decide to stay."

"Thanks," said Cameron. He stood in the doorway watching Sergeant King and the butler until they disappeared downstairs. When they were out of sight he closed the door.

"There's whiskey in my bag," said the Captain. "Will you join me?"

Cameron lifted the lid of the suitcase and said, "Will the angels sing?" He poured two stiff drinks, handed one to Maclain, and tossed his own down.

"There's something queer going on, Captain Maclain," he remarked as he took the empty glass from the Captain's hand. "I phoned the Boston police as well as Colonel Gray. They have no record of Thad's daughter being found at all."

"I was afraid of that," said Maclain. "I thought that something important had made you decide to stay."

2

Dr. Trotter came, left sedatives for Cheli and Maclain, and went away.

Cameron sat on the foot of Maclain's bed and said, "It's heartless not to let you sleep, but the lives and property of a lot of people are in terrible danger, and time is slipping away. We've broken the back of a spy organization which has wormed itself even into the army and navy. It was through you that we turned up their headquarters."

The Captain heard a match strike and smelled tobacco.

"The F. B. I. wants to know, Captain Maclain, how you got wind of this House of Bonnée."

"There's a stencil and a copy of a letter in a false compartment in the top of my Gladstone bag, Mr. Cameron. You'll find a brass stud in each corner of the bag in the inside. If you pull them, the lining will come free."

He lay quiet while Cameron secured the stencil and the copy of the letter made by Bunny's secretary. He pressed his fingers to his eyebrows and listened as the F. B. I. man read the letter aloud.

"It sounds like an ad," said Cameron.

"It's intended to sound like an ad." The Captain was thinking of Spud and fighting an apprehension which threatened to dull his every faculty. "Actually, Mr. Cameron, that's a code hiding a message which says that I have information much more important than Gilbert Tredwill's plans, and telling the agents here in Hartford to concentrate on me."

"You found the code?"

The Captain felt the movement of the bed as Cameron leaned forward. His snapped-out question indicated his tenseness. He went on speaking, holding himself still: —

"Let me tell you what that means, Captain Maclain. We don't know how many tons of high explosives set with time bombs have been planted throughout this country today. We've found some, it's true, but enough others exist to cause a holocaust tomorrow if they're not uncovered. The prisoners we've taken either don't know where these bombs have been planted or they refuse to say. If you've found a code, Captain Maclain, for God's sake give it to me. Colonel Gray believes that the information we're seeking is buried somewhere in a lot of dummy contracts taken from the files of the House of Bonnée."

"The code is based on the odor of violets," said Duncan Maclain, and swung his feet to the floor. "The key to it is the abbreviation for the name Violet, the word *Vi*. Lay the letter you're holding down on the writing table, and make a perpendicular fold down the middle. See that the edges meet all the way around."

The Captain heard the rustle of paper, and Cameron said, "Okay."

"Now take a ruler—you'll find one in the drawer. From the upper left-hand corner of the letter draw a line to the middle of the page at the bottom. It must be exact. From the bottom draw another line upward to the right-hand corner. You should have a V covering the entire page bisected by an I. Now read down on

THE HOUSE OF BONNÉE
TANNER BUILDING
EAST 57TH STREET
NEW YORK CITY

Dear Madam,

The problem of the well-groomed woman is to obtain, in the city's turmoil and grime, a complexion superior to, and more vital than, that of her country cousin.

Unfortunately most modern cosmetics have failed on many points. Nothing is more detrimental than force when cleansing and purifying the delicate skin. Once use caustics and the entire defensive membrane is injured. The sight of rough pitted skin more often than not indicates some balm of injurious content. It's important to demand far more than economy when purchasing. Don't forget this pertinent fact—the integrity of the makers is an essential ingredient. In purchasing face cream look for these assuring words—

By THE HOUSE OF BONNÉE

the left only those words touched by the left-hand line of the V, and up on the right, the same."

Cameron read down, "City's vital points and defensive more important," and up on the right-hand side, "than balm sight use force to obtain."

Almost unbelievingly, he grouped them together and read it aloud once more. "City's vital points and defensive more important than balm sight. Use force to obtain."

"You see," said Maclain, "it's right before you in plain English. I possessed, locked in my head, the knowledge of the city's vital points and defensive. This was the tip-off to get that information by force. If it hadn't been for your swift, clever work, I'm afraid—"

"Skip it," Cameron hastened to say. He wrinkled his forehead and muttered, "Balm sight!"

"For bomb sight," said Duncan Maclain.

"I'll let you sleep in peace," Cameron told him. "I have to get to the phone."

3

The Captain turned over and grimly resettled himself, trying to rid his mind of the fiendishly obsessing rhyme: —

> 'Twas the night before Christmas
> And all through the house,
> Not a creature was stirring,
> Not even a mouse.

The jingle proved just as bad on his left side as on his right. Persistently it dug rabbit warrens in his brain and circulated through it, turning his night into day. Mixed in with it to form a disturbing phantasmagoria worthy of a hashish smoker was Pierce's story about the Christmas tree.

At ten minutes to two, somnolence was put to flight by a pair of facts that struck into his consciousness, carrying with them an internal clarity of vision bright as the light of a magnesium flare. Duncan Maclain was even more sensitive to silence than he was to sound. Like Nature, his well-trained ears abhorred a vacuum. Unlike most people who found themselves wakeful, his insomnia was not being caused by chafing noises, but by lack of a subconsciously expected sound. That was fact number one. He had not heard Arnold Cameron return from his downstairs trip to the telephone.

Fact number two had come more laboriously, built up piece-meal by selection and rejection of various reasons why anyone should want to make off with such a prosaic object as an un-trimmed Christmas tree.

Pierce had said the tree was dragged down to the highway at the end of the house. At the end of the house was Thad's intimate theater, and at the back of the stage in the theater was a door. Maclain's methodical mind had tabulated that information and weighed it with care. The result was a log-ical conclusion that dragging the Christmas tree around the house to take it down to the road formed a clumsy piece of work unworthy of a sneak thief. Straight down in front of the side porch where the tree had stood was another hill, a much smaller one, and certainly a much easier one on which to drag a tree down to the state highway.

> Not a creature was stirring,
> Not even a mouse.

And he knew what they'd done with Thaddeus Tredwill's girl.

As though he had fitted two pieces of some great puzzle together, the Captain visualized a new niche of irregular design. Its edges were drawn with wavering lines of blood in the darkness. Into it, far too late for his own personal safety, he thought morosely, he fitted fact number three: Gerente's assassin and Bella's killer were the same, and should have been apparent from the time he entered the Tredwill home. Yet not until this moment had he known. No careless person could ever have built the House of Bonnée, no one with any loophole in life's record which could be unearthed by Maclain or the F. B. I.

He clenched his hands despairingly, blaming himself entirely for the dangerous delay, refusing to condone his own remissness with the fact that the State Police had also been off trail.

Norma Tredwill was attacked and nearly killed when she returned to Hartford after discovering the body of Paul Gerente. There was no way anyone could have gotten in or out of The Crags—he had checked that himself, and the State Police agreed. Therein lay the vital flaw. He and the police had concentrated on the Tredwills and their servants; the Tredwills because they were in New York when Gerente was killed, the servants because he and the police were hunting for a spy. Colonel Gray had checked everyone in the Tredwill home; he was getting information from Bella, his operator, who lost her life posing as a servant—murdered because she was the only one who knew that Paul Gerente's killer had been driven into New York in Bunny Carter's car with the tracings of Gilbert's plans.

The puzzle line changed again and driving himself malevolently, Duncan Maclain fitted in piece number four: the reason the police had found no other tire tracks leading up to The Crags. Bunny's car had brought Mrs. Tredwill home from the station. It had brought Barbara home from New York just a short time before, accompanied by the cleverest slayer it had ever been Maclain's misfortune to know. The police and Maclain had overlooked one vital fact. Bunny's car made two trips to The Crags that night, not one.

Coldly and carefully, staking everything on the assumption that he was right, Maclain began to forge a chain of events which would satisfy him as true. Gilbert's plans had been traced by a master spy. The tracings were bulky, and risky to entrust to the mail. One thing that spy did not know: that Bella was a counterespionage agent who had wormed her way into the Bonnée crowd while working for G-2. It was unfortunate for the spy, because Bella had brought a man into the House of Bonnée ring—an actor named Paul Gerente. Not until the spy arrived in New York did it come to light that Paul Gerente was working for the F. B. I. A column seen in the morning paper had aroused the spy's suspicion of Gerente. Gerente, posing as a member of the House of Bonnée, had unquestionably expected to receive the tracings and make an arrest. Instead, he had been tricked and murdered by the master spy.

The Captain lay awhile, listening for Cameron's footsteps in the hall.

Babs must have encountered the killer in Paul Gerente's room. The killer must have persuaded her to drive back to Hartford in Bunny's car.

Maclain tensed suddenly.

If arrangements had been made to intercept Bunny's car and abduct Babs Tredwill, the fake kidnaping might leave the killer in the clear in the event anything went wrong.

The Captain sat up in bed more than satisfied. It fitted all the way through. Babs would be left alive. Gil was working on the final steps of his bombing sight, and, alive, his sister might be used in extorting information from him.

Maclain left his bed with the smoothness of a materializing apparition, found trousers, heavy shirt, and soft-soled shoes, and put them on. Schnucke came up beside him to receive her brace and harness, which the Captain took from a chair. His flat automatic in the shoulder rig was still in the drawer. He strapped it on, covered it with a dark overcoat, and with a slowness which would have been impossible for an ordinary man opened the bedroom door.

Something which had puzzled him badly was finally clear: how his own abductors had known exactly the time and place to stop Cheli's car.

4

The granite of resolution and the marble of anger had driven out every lovable quality in Duncan Maclain. As he stepped into the hall he was as impersonal as a piece of metal come under a powerful magnet's sway, and forced by the immutable laws of physics to answer its imperious command. He had no eyes, but he could shoot with the devastating accuracy of lightning at the most infinitesimal sound. He was blind, but it was the implacable blindness of Justice. Duncan Maclain and his dog, pitted against a world full of fools; no more a man, but a killer out to destroy the God of War's machine.

He found the stair top and went on down. Not a tick of the grandfather's clock was lost in the sound of any movement he made. As though the keen mind of the dog beside him felt his need, Schnucke became part of his stealthiness.

At the bottom of the stairs, his thumb found the light switch, felt the smoothness of the pearl knob sticking out and the roughness of the black knob, in. He knew from that that the lights were out in the downstairs hall. He crossed it with counted steps, opened the phone-booth door, and touched Arnold Cameron's shoulder. His hand moved on to the knife hilt in Cameron's back. The F. B. I. man was still breathing, but he'd never had a chance to phone.

Duncan Maclain had no time now to help him. Indeed, he had no time at all, yet he went back up the front stairs slowly, and slowly walked to the other end of the hall. There, in the servant's wing, another flight led down. He took it, and, knowing that avoiding squeaks meant life, he kept his feet pressed close on each step to the angle of tread and wall.

At the bottom he stopped again and the grandfather's clock ticked off six hundred seconds as he opened another door. His hand went through before him to find another switch and tell him that the lights were out in the armory hall. He crossed it in the darkness, found the other door he was seeking, and descended the basement stairs.

A chain clanked in a corner. Maclain spat out a single word, and Dreist was silent without a warning growl.

When he came back up the stairs again, he was on his own, for Dreist, wearing Schnucke's brace, was beside him; and Dreist could not guide him. In his other hand, the Captain held a ball of heavy twine. Step by step he ascended, paying out cord behind him. He had attached the other end of the cord to the handle of the main light switch at the foot of the stairs, so that every light in The Crags could be put out with a single pull.

At the top, with Dreist leading, he stepped into the hall. With the basement door almost closed behind him, he reached through with one arm, pulled the slack cord tight, and deftly tied it around the knob on the basement side of the door. He put the remainder of the ball down on the floor so that it held the door ajar.

Cold air struck against his face as he stepped inside Thad's theater. He stood at the back with Dreist's powerful body shivering beside him. He had intended to go outside through the back of the stage and put Dreist on that trail wiped out of the snow by the dragging Christmas tree—the trail of Thaddeus Tredwill's girl; but someone had been in the theater before him and opened that backstage door. Someone was in there now.

"Steady, Dreist," the Captain whispered, but his words were lost, for Dreist had gone, obeying the training so carefully instilled in him, to attack without warning when an adversary of Duncan Maclain showed a gun.

The Captain heard the rush of feet down the aisle, followed by Dreist's snarl, and saved his life by dropping to the floor. The sound of the report which would normally have served him as a target proved confusing, for caught up in the acoustics of the theater it echoed hollowly.

Thinking with split-second speed, the Captain judged that whoever had fired the shot must be standing in the center aisle. Lying full length behind the last row of seats, he reached around and shot upward down the center aisle three times, resting his gun on the floor. Someone fell with a groan.

Maclain said, "The dog will tear you to pieces if you try to shoot again. You'd better stay where you are. Guard!" he ordered Dreist, and, standing up, felt his way toward the stage by the seat backs until his foot encountered clothing.

Bending over, he touched closed eyes, a straight nose, and a close-clipped mustache.

"Al Rutgers," he muttered. "At least you feel that way from the description I've had of you. Come, Dreist," he said aloud, "that's one more out of the way, thanks to you."

He slipped the gun into his overcoat pocket, and holding tight to the police dog's brace turned to the rear of the theater and stepped through the door into the armory hall.

Upstairs he could hear someone pounding vigorously on a door.

"Pierce!" Maclain called.

An almost muffled voice answered him some distance down the armory hall. "He's locked in, Captain Maclain. There isn't much use in calling."

The Captain went after his gun and swung himself aside, saving his life by inches for the second time within ten minutes. The ancient battleax hurtling toward him, instead of crushing his chest, struck a glancing blow on his arm. He staggered back under the impact and his gun dropped to the floor, irretrievably gone. The light ax swished on by to crash behind him against the wall.

Near him, Dreist whimpered. The dog had the bravest heart in the canine world, but something was approaching which he had never met before, something inhuman; a faceless being, neither man nor woman—a terrible machine.

"Get it, Dreist!"

The Captain's words had the sting of a whiplash, and their heat fused anger into the dog's quick fear. Dreist seldom barked, but when he did his bark spelled murder. With a three-foot leap he left his place beside Maclain and drove in sideways for the kill.

"I can't control him," the Captain said quietly, "if you don't lie down and stay still."

A laugh, metallic and hollow, was followed by the clank of teeth on metal and the scrape of Dreist's claws. The Captain realized that the lights had been turned on while he was in the theater; no ax hurled at him in the dark could have come so near. At the same time, he recognized that he must have darkness to defeat the death approaching him down the hall. To reach the switch meant walking into the swing of a halberd or a broadax similar to the one which had beheaded Bella. He was facing a new kind of foe; one who had watched him come up from the cellar with Dreist and refrained from shooting him then because of the knowledge that Dreist would attack without warning at the sight of a gun; a clever foe who had taken steps that would insure safety against the vicious police dog's skill. The Captain had stepped from the theater to meet an enemy who had cunningly figured that without Schnucke to guide him Maclain could not run; an enemy prepared in a most unorthodox fashion to murder not only the Captain, but Dreist too, in a good old medieval way.

"Schnucke!" the Captain called loudly. "Come here. Schnucke!"

He heard the curdling scrape of Dreist's claws on burnished steel as the big dog leaped again. Then Dreist whimpered and his powerful body thudded to the floor.

"If you've killed my dog," said Duncan Maclain, "you'll never live to reach the electric chair."

"You'll never live to put me there," the reverberating voice declared. The terrible clumping started again, drawing very near.

The patter of Schnucke's running feet sounded on the basement stairs. The Captain gave an agonized call when he heard her stop at the partly open basement door. She hesitated only a second before she thrust her muzzle in the crack and forced her body through, darkening The Crags as she pulled the light switch off at the foot of the basement stairs.

The muffled voice gave a gasp.

Maclain said, "I think the honors are even, now that there's darkness."

He dropped to the floor and began to roll. Metal swished down above him as a madly swung halberd buried its blade in the floor. His powerful arms circled chain-clad knees, and tackled. The dull clang of a fall echoed through the vaulted hall.

Maclain found a steel-clad arm, twisted it into a hammer lock, and said in a voice that dripped like water on stone, "A suit of mail armor has one great disadvantage. It slips on like pants and sweater, but it's clumsy. You're under arrest for treason and murder, Cheli Scott, or should I call you Madame Bonnée!"

CHAPTER XXVI

I DISLIKE ax-killers. It's a method of murder accompanied by a certain amount of unavoidable messiness which I find deplorable," announced Duncan Maclain.

"In other words, you want your murders clean." Spud Savage gave the nurse who was arranging his pillows an approving smile and waved her away. "If you'll just run along, sweetheart, and eat yourself some Christmas dinner, I promise I won't die."

"Also shooters from the rear, and stabbers in the back," the Captain continued when the nurse had shut the door behind her.

"And I dislike friends and relatives who sit around my hospital room and swill highballs without mixing me a second one on Christmas Day," Spud declared.

"They'll move you to the alcoholic ward." Rena smiled and filled his glass. "You've already lost count."

"It's a trick I learned in the army." Spud turned his head and winked at Colonel Gray.

"—And kidnapers and spies," Maclain went on. "They lack the primary traits of humanity."

"It's a pity you haven't a notebook, Rena," Spud broke in.

"Dunc's about to hold forth on the Joan of Arc who put Dreist into the dog infirmary. Properly deleted, his remarks might be collected for the benefit of posterity. Tell the Colonel how you tackled her, Dunc, and threw her for a ten-yard loss on her cuirass."

"Spud!" exclaimed Rena. "I'm going to take your drink away!"

"It's French, and my pronunciation is flawless," Spud protested with indignant scorn.

"Perhaps," Maclain suggested, "you'd like me to go into details about blondes and their methods of purveying perfume."

"That's right, strike me in an open wound." Spud found a cigarette, lit it, and held his empty glass out to Rena with an appealing smile.

She tried to look grim.

"I hear the plaintive tinkle of ice in an empty glass," said Maclain. "Instinct tells me that the glass is in Spud's outstretched hand. Give him another, Rena. I've never known a man who could bleed Haig and Haig from an open wound. The idea interests me." He turned toward Colonel Gray. "Have you had further news of Cameron today?"

"I talked with Hartford Hospital an hour ago. They've operated and collapsed one of his lungs. He'll be on the sick list for many a day."

"He's a brave man—and a good one," said Maclain.

"And so are you." The Colonel took a rose from a vase by the bed and absently smelled it. "That code you phoned me last night enabled us to locate every time bomb in the country today. We dug them out of a mailing list of customers in the House of Bonnée. We also found another flock of *agents provocateurs* scattered from California east to New London."

"I've encountered my share of fanatics." The Captain was

thoughtful. "Frankly, I've never been so close to failure as I was with that Scott girl, or whatever her name may be."

Colonel Gray replaced the rose he was holding in the vase, and asked: "What about her using Bunny Carter's car?"

"He's innocent as you are, Colonel. Just as Cheli fooled the Tredwills, Bunny was taken in by his chauffeur. The Crags was filled with false leads, too—Gilbert Tredwill's monetary difficulties, and his foreign-born wife, didn't make things any easier for me. Here's the information we got from Babs Tredwill today."

The Colonel sighed. "I'm glad that they spared that girl."

"Only because they thought they might use her." Resentment marked the Captain's tone. "Babs admitted herself to Gerente's apartment with a key. He was already dead. Babs turned around to leave and faced Cheli Scott standing in the door. Cheli said: 'My God, you've killed him, Babs!' and the distraught girl broke down and began to cry. It never entered her head that Cheli could have been there before her and murdered Paul."

"It never entered mine," said Colonel Gray.

"Babs said this morning that she thought Norma had put Cheli up to following her into New York to persuade her from seeing Gerente."

"You'd have thought Babs would have insisted on giving an alarm," Rena ventured.

Maclain nodded. "That she didn't was one of many circumstances I put together last night to form the answer: Cheli. I've said before that this Scott lady is infernally quick-witted. She told Babs: 'It doesn't matter who killed this man. Nobody must know you've been here. Get your things from the Ritters', and I'll be waiting for you to come out. Walk a few blocks up Park

Avenue and I'll pick you up and drive you back to Hartford in Bunny's car.'"

"The use of that car still has me puzzled," the Colonel admitted.

"I'm coming to it," said Maclain. "I reasoned things out this way. Norma Tredwill thought there was someone in Gerente's apartment. Babs must have encountered that person, too."

"Was there anyone there when Norma was there?" Spud inquired.

"Certainly," said Maclain. "Cheli. She was in a quandary, too. If Norma hadn't left as she did, there would have been another job of killing to do. She'd taken care of Babs through fear. Norma might not prove so easy; but Norma left in a panic, leaving Cheli to ransack the place at her leisure, find the Braille instructions in Gerente's drawer, scent them with violet—"

"Why?" Spud broke in again.

The Captain answered by questioning Colonel Gray. "Did you by any chance, Colonel, round up a blind man in this ring?"

"A Russian Communist cobbler," the Colonel supplied, "with a place on Third Avenue."

"I thought so!" Maclain displayed his pleasure by a triumphant smile. "Cheli gave those instructions to Madoc, who had driven to New York with her and Al Rutgers in Bunny's car. Bunny was away—and using his car was far safer than using her own. She had a happy faculty of shifting blame onto others. Even communications sent her from headquarters were addressed to Norma, as you know."

"And the blind man?"

"Translated the Braille, Colonel Gray. Cheli scented the instructions so the blind man would know they came from the House of Bonnée. When he heard the translation, Madoc realized he had important information, if he could trick the defense plans of New York's vulnerable points out of me. Cheli had already left for Hartford with Rutgers and Babs. Madoc took a long chance and impersonated Gerente—"

"A chance that proved too long," muttered Colonel Gray. "If you hadn't recognized that fellow's speech at International, I hate to think what we might have faced today."

"But I did," said Duncan Maclain. "Now let's follow Cheli. She picked up Babs and drove her back to Hartford. She had made previous arrangements by telephone—as she did with my abduction night before last—to have the car intercepted on the way. I wondered at the time I was abducted how that truck knew exactly the time and place to stop Cheli's car.

"Babs's abductors drove her around while Rutgers took Cheli back to The Crags and rejoined them. Babs was put in a vacant room over Bunny's garage—set far apart from the house on the side of the hill. They left her there, doped, and paralyzed with fear. At The Crags, Cheli decided to do a little more investigating while the family was away."

"And nearly added Mrs. Tredwill to her victims," put in Colonel Gray.

"She was cornered in the workshop." The Captain snapped his fingers irritably. "She was the only one in the house besides Norma and the servants. It was infernally dense of me not to suspect her right away."

"I like it when you're dense," said Spud, grinning. "It bolsters my failing ego tremendously."

Maclain began to tick off points with his fingers. "Don't forget that the previous afternoon Cheli had sent all the servants away except Bella, who she thought was working with her. She knew that Norma had been in Paul's apartment, for she saw her there. She took a look at the parcel Norma had brought home, and knew that Mrs. Tredwill had rescued Babs's galoshes from Gerente's hall. That suited her fine, for Norma must have thought, as everyone else would think, that Babs had run away."

Colonel Gray said thoughtfully: "She must have been on to Bella. Why did she pick such a brutal way?"

"On to her?" Maclain repeated. "What did this clever lady think of a co-worker who had vouched for a member of the F. B. I.? Bella knew her peril and was watching Cheli closely. The day I got to The Crags we were down in Gil's workshop. I wanted to see if there were lingering traces of perfume on Gil's plans, indicating that they'd been traced. I'd just put it over by pretending that I was smelling the plans for gasoline—"

"Gasoline?" asked Rena.

"I'd wiped my hands with it," explained Maclain. "It was lucky I did so, for Cheli was with us. If she'd suspected that I was tracing down an odor of violets I'd have gone out with Bella in some similar pleasant way."

Rena shuddered.

"I heard Bella on the stairs," Maclain continued, "and thought she was spying on me. I know differently now. She was watching Cheli, who got her that same afternoon. Cheli had a zipper house coat on—and deliberately picked a sanguinary method of killing the girl. Cheli stripped the house coat off and left it in the hall, killed Bella, ran down to her room, where she took a shower, and a few minutes later was downstairs with her house coat back on. Remembering that house coat was a final point which made me certain I had to get Cheli."

"God above!" breathed the Colonel. "I'd have taken an oath that murder was committed by a man."

"She did everything possible to make you think just that, Colonel Gray, although I don't believe she intended to behead the girl. The executioner's ax she used was heavier than she knew—and sharp as a scalpel, too."

The Colonel stood up and said, "Before I go, I'd like to know how you located Barbara Tredwill so suddenly."

"By asking myself why anyone would drag away an untrimmed Christmas tree, unless it was to obliterate footsteps in the snow. Babs escaped, Colonel Gray. She recognized where she was as soon as she got outside of Bunny's garage. She dashed down the hill, across the road, and up the other hill toward her home; but she was weak from her ordeal, and Rutgers caught her. He took her back to the garage, hurried over to the Tredwill house, and effaced his and Babs's footsteps with the Christmas tree.

"Those footprints must have been desperately incriminating for one reason: because they led to a hiding place which was very near. The nearest place was certainly not Bunny's house—so it must have been in the quarters of Bunny's chauffeur. He came to talk with Cheli late last night after Babs escaped. Cheli had admitted him through the theater stage door. He was leaving when he encountered Dreist and me. I'd already placed him as one of the band."

"How?"

"By the odor of violets, Colonel—left from Cheli's trip to New York with scented tracings in Bunny's car."

"And how the devil did an odor of violets mean anything to you?" asked Colonel Gray.

"My head is filled with bits of extraneous information accumulated through the years," said Duncan Maclain. "It's vital to me because I have no eyes—because I cannot see. I'm always interested in the foibles of a potential enemy. Somewhere in Europe is a little man with a black mustache and plastered-down hair. I've learned all I can about him against the time when civilization may find it necessary to put him out of the way. Where I heard it, or where I got it, I can't tell you, Colonel, but the odor of violets is that madman's favorite perfume!"

THE END

DISCUSSION QUESTIONS

- Did any aspects of the plot date the story? If so, which?

- Would the story be different if it were set in the present day? If so, how?

- Did the social context of the time play a role in the narrative? If so, how?

- If you were one of the main characters, would you have acted differently at any point in the story?

- Did you identify with any of the characters? If so, which?

- What skills or qualities make Duncan Maclain such an effective sleuth?

- In his foreword, Baynard Kendrick talks about wanting to create a realistic character with Maclain. Do you think he succeeded?

- Discuss other disabled detectives you have encountered in mystery fiction. How does Duncan Maclain compare?

- Did this book remind you of any present day authors? If so, which?

AMERICAN MYSTERY CLASSICS

from

PENZLER PUBLISHERS

*Available now
in hardcover and paperback:*

AMERICAN MYSTERY CLASSICS

from